Dwight, my friend,

Wishing you a comfy beach chair as you enjoy this adventure!

[signature]
5/25/18

Chincoteague Calm

Other Emerson Moore Adventures by Bob Adamov

- *Rainbow's End* – released October 2002
- *Pierce the Veil* – released May 2004
- *When Rainbows Walk* – released June 2005
- *Promised Land* – released July 2006
- *The Other Side of Hell* – released June 2008
- *Tan Lines* – released June 2010
- *Sandustee* – released March 2013
- *Zenobia* – released May 2014
- *Missing* – released April 2015
- *Golden Torpedo* – released July 2017

The Next Emerson Moore Adventure:
- *Flight*

Chincoteague Calm

Bob Adamov

PACKARD ISLAND PUBLISHING
Wooster ❀ Ohio
2018
www.packardislandpublishing.com

Copyright 2018 by Bob Adamov

All rights reserved.

No part of this book may be used or reproduced in any manner whatsoever without written permission from the author except in the case of brief quotations embodied in critical articles or reviews.

www.BobAdamov.com

This book is a work of fiction. Names, characters, places and incidents are either products of the author's imagination or are used fictitiously. Any resemblance to actual events, locales or persons, living or dead, is entirely coincidental.

First Edition • April 2018

ISBN: 978-0-9786184-7-6

(ISBN 10: 0-9786184-7-5)

Library of Congress number: 2018931564

Printed and bound in the United States of America.

Cover art by: Denis Lange
Lange Design
890 Williamsburg Court
Ashland, OH 44805
www.langedesign.biz

Printed by:
BookMasters, Inc.
PO Box 388
Ashland, Ohio 44805
www.Bookmasters.com

Layout design by: David Wiesenberg
The Wooster Book Company
205 West Liberty Street
Wooster, OH 44691
www.woosterbook.com

Published by:
Packard Island Publishing
3025 Evergreen Drive
Wooster, Ohio
www.packardislandpublishing.com

Dedication

This book is dedicated to the VOLUNTEER FIRE DEPARTMENT OF CHINCOTEAGUE ISLAND. It is also dedicated to KAREN HOGLE HUMMEL, DAN GENET and JIM RIISE who passed away last year as well as the Norton High School Class of 1967.

A portion of the proceeds from the sale of this book will be donated to the Volunteer Fire Department of Chincoteague.

*They that wait upon the Lord shall renew their strength;
they shall mount up with wings as eagles;
they shall run, and not be weary;
and they shall walk, and not faint.*

—Isaiah 40:31

Acknowledgements

For technical assistance, I'd like to express my appreciation to my Chincoteague Island friends: Donna Roeske at Captain Bob's Marina; Denise Bowden, the Vice Mayor, Chincoteague Volunteer Fire Department spokesperson, and owner of Teaguer's Tump Tours; Evelyn Shotwell at the Chamber of Commerce; Holt Shotwell at NASA Wallops Island; Chincoteague police chief James Mills; and master duck carver and local legend, Roe "Duc-Man" Terry; as well as to Keith Koehler in the Office of Communications at Wallops Island Flight Facility for the tour of the launch pads and flight operations! A special thank you to my friend, Detective Clay Cozart of the Akron Police Department.

I'd like to thank my team of editors: Cathy Adamov, John Wisse, Peggy Parker, Julia Wiesenberg of The Wooster Book Company, and Andrea Goss Knaub.

For more information, check these sites:
www.BobAdamov.com
www.VisitPut-in-Bay.com
www.MillerFerry.com
www.chincoteaguechamber.com
www.nasa.gov/centers/wallops/home

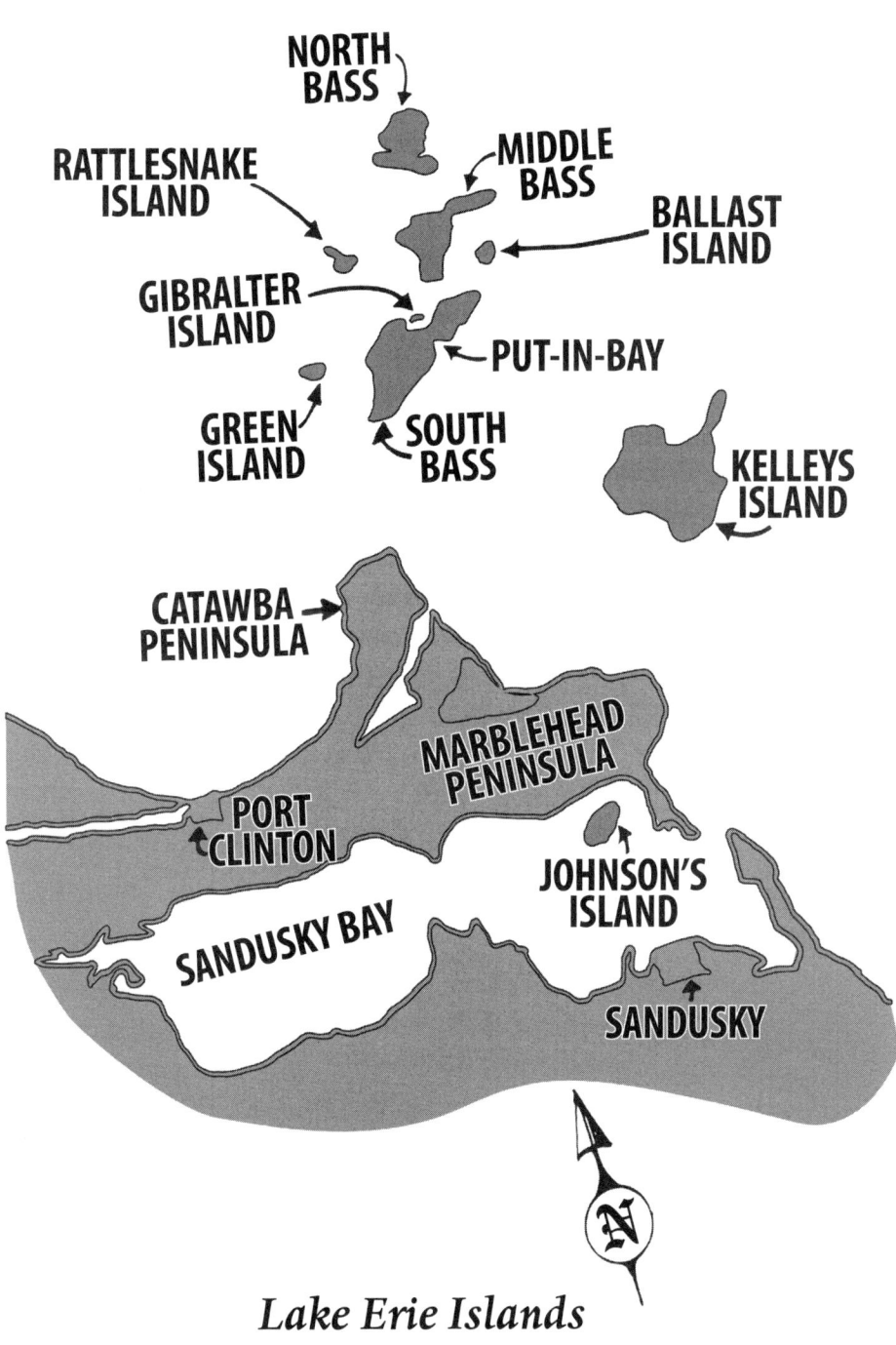

Lake Erie Islands

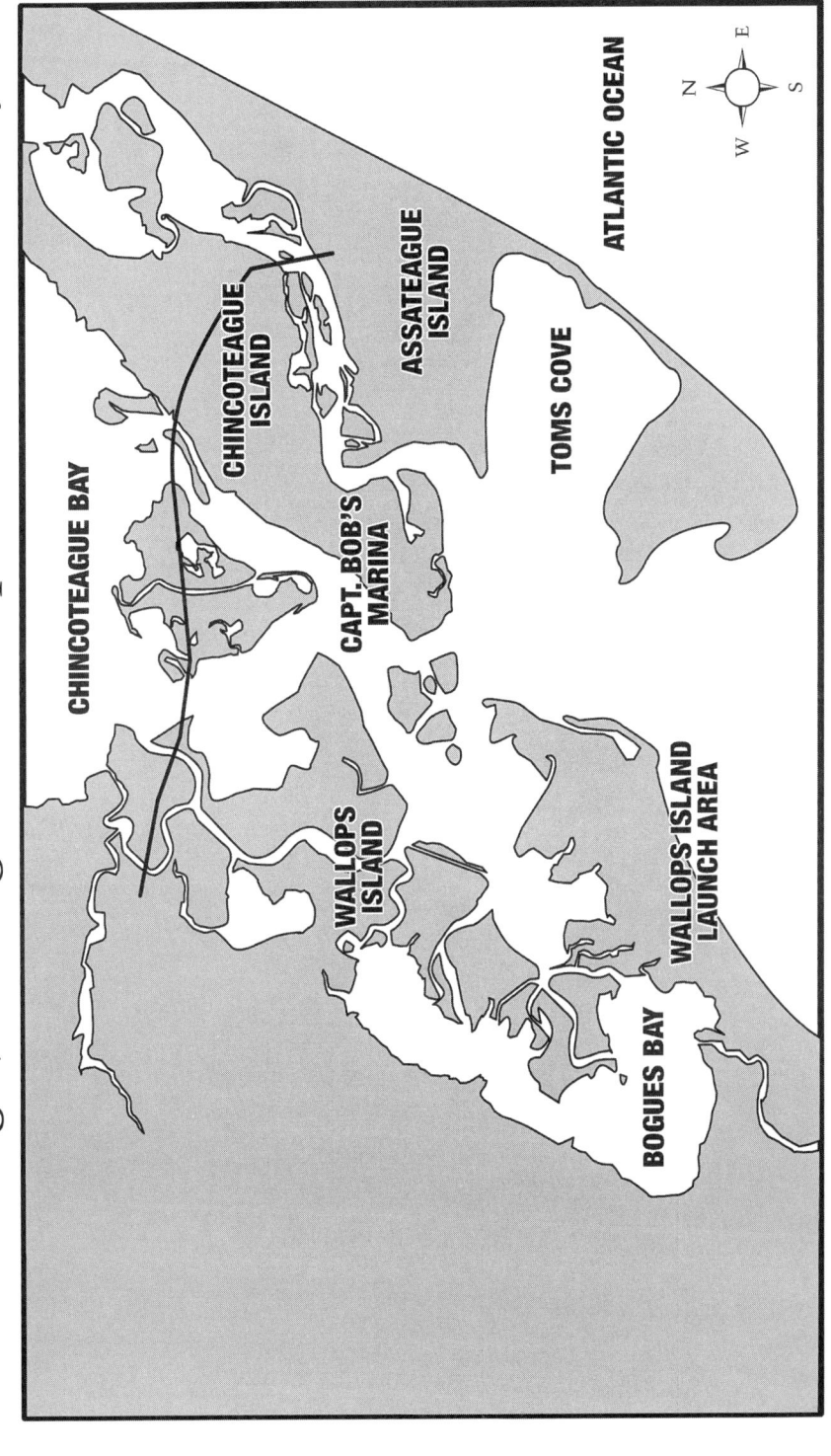

Chincoteague, Assateague and Wallops Islands with Causeway

Chincoteague Calm

CHAPTER 1

Police Department
Chincoteague Island, Virginia

"That's him! That's the man who assaulted me!" the blonde woman shrieked hysterically as she pointed to her alleged perpetrator. "Arrest him! He was wearing that brown cat's-eye ring when he grabbed me from behind. I saw it when his hand went around my waist and he assaulted me!" she screamed.

The police detective, who had been taking the woman's report inside the Chincoteague Island police station, stood and walked over to the counter. "Mind if I borrow your ring?" she firmly asked the man.

"It's not my ring. I found it on the roof of my car this morning. It looks valuable so I thought I should bring it over here for your safekeeping," the man said as he handed the detective the ring.

Taking the ring, the detective walked over to the woman and showed it to her. "Ma'am, are you absolutely certain that this is the ring?"

The woman, who by then had just barely calmed down, examined the ring and answered without hesitation. "Yes, it is."

"Interesting. Only one person on this island had a ring like this," the detective said as she turned back to the man. "Her name is Maya Simon."

"I know her," the man declared. "I'll give it back to her."

"Not quite," the detective responded. "Miss Simon's torched body was found in a dumpster on the island this morning. We're waiting for positive identification through her dental records. Whoever did that to her was sloppy. Her purse was found on the ground behind the dumpster," the detective said as she carefully eyed the man who appeared to be shocked by the revelation.

Recovering slightly, the man stuttered, "It can't be Maya. I was with her last night at the Clam Shells Pub and drove her home. She was fine and quite alive when I left her."

"She's not fine now," the detective confirmed as she stared suspiciously at the man.

"I didn't have anything to do with her murder," the man pleaded nervously.

"You better follow me back to one of the interview rooms," the detective firmly directed.

"Am I being charged?" the man asked.

"Not unless we have a reason. Are you saying you don't want to be interviewed?" the detective asked as she raised an eyebrow in distrust.

"No. I don't have anything to hide."

"Good," the detective said as she started walking toward the interview room. "What did you say your name was?"

"I didn't, but it's Emerson Moore," the man replied softly. His island vacation getaway was taking an ugly turn.

CHAPTER 2

Eight Days Earlier
Port Clinton, Ohio

Opening his umbrella, the tanned, dark-haired man in his early forties exited his bright red Mustang convertible and ran through the downpour, across the sidewalk and into the relative dry safety of the Northern Exposure Gallery and Candle Company on Madison Street.

"Got drenched, didn't you?" co-owner Billy Rigoni observed as a clap of thunder boomed overhead.

"Oh yeah, Billy. No ferry service tonight. Lake's too rough," the man replied. His name was Emerson Moore.

Moore was an award-winning investigative reporter for *The Washington Post* who resided with his aged Aunt Anne on nearby South Bass Island in the western basin of Lake Erie. His aunt had a two-story waterfront home on East Point with a view of the popular island resort village of Put-in-Bay.

"Emerson, do you have a place to stay?" Rigoni's pretty-eyed wife asked as she walked into the front of the store.

"Yeah. I was able to get a room at Our Sunset Place." Moore's head turned as lightning flashed outside the front window. "This is like a monsoon."

"If this nor'easter keeps up like this, we could have water overflowing the Portage River and flooding the streets. I'll need to bring up my life raft from the back," Rigoni said somewhat seriously.

Moore chuckled as he recalled a Facebook picture of Billy rafting down the flooded street during a storm that spring. He liked the Rigonis, who were two of the most creative and funny people he knew.

"How can we help you?" Kelly asked.

Moore looked around the shop filled with Kelly's lake photography, candles, resort wear, and nautical gifts and signs. His eyes spotted the candles.

"Sure, I need three candles."

"Which ones?" Kelly asked.

"Freighter Fudge," Moore said as he picked up one and twisted off the top of the small metal canister. Lifting it to his nose, he inhaled the rich chocolate scent. "Mmmm. Smells good."

"You buying that for yourself?" Billy asked.

Putting the lid back on and picking up two more, Moore replied, "No. My Aunt Anne loves these. I'll give them to her in the morning when I catch the ferry back over." He walked to the counter and withdrew cash from his pocket.

"You have time for dinner?" Billy asked.

"I already have plans," Moore said. "Meeting friends at the Mon Ami."

"They've got great food," Kelly said as she rang up the sale.

"And great wine," Billy said as his eyes cheerfully bulged at the thought.

Moore grinned as he walked to the door and paused before opening it.

"This keeps up, I'm going to start building an ark," Billy quipped as the relentless downpour showed no sign of stopping.

Moore walked out the doorway, reopened his umbrella and ran through the drenching rain to his car. Starting it, he wistfully smiled to himself, then drove over to the historic Mon Ami Restaurant and Winery, one of his favorite dining spots.

He was looking forward to ordering walleye bites as an appetizer and a yellow perch dinner. He was also anticipating listening to his friends' music and watching their antics on stage.

As he pulled onto East Wine Cellar Road, Moore was pleased to see the sign announcing the evening's entertainment—THE RAT PACK AND MORE. The three entertainers who resembled Frank Sinatra, Dean Martin and Sammy Davis, Jr. put on an amazing show and had become friends with Moore. He couldn't wait to catch up with Damion Fontaine, Scott Brotherton and Stan Davis to hear the latest news about their adventures.

Moore was greeted inside the restaurant's entrance by a dark-haired hostess. He glanced at her name badge and saw that her name was Linda Hall.

"How many for dinner tonight?" Hall asked.

"Just me, Linda, and I'd like to sit in the chalet," Moore answered. "There's something magical about tonight's entertainment," Moore added as he walked with Hall toward the chalet.

"They're magicians, that's for sure," Hall agreed. "I've got a friend. His name is Bobby Warren. He's a magician."

"Is he good?"

"I'm not sure."

"What do you mean?"

"He was doing a trick and he disappeared. No one has seen him in a week," she teased.

"Hope he reappears," Moore joked back.

"Not sure if he will. He disappeared quite often at his regular job. No one could ever find him," Hall grinned as she escorted him to a table near the stage.

Seeing Moore enter the chalet, Damion Fontaine called out from the stage, "Emerson, how you doing?"

Walking over to the stage, Moore responded to the Frank Sinatra look-alike, "I'm still waiting for you to change the name of your group to the Rat Pack and Moore," he teased.

"We'll do that when you start singing with us," Fontaine replied before turning to Brotherton. "Scott, we have an extra mic, don't we?"

The Dean Martin look-alike grinned at Moore. "We sure do."

"I don't think so," Moore said as he laughed and shook his head. "I'm just going to enjoy your show."

"Come on, Emerson, live a little," Fontaine urged. "You got to love livin' baby, because dying is such a pain in the ass," he quoted the real Sinatra.

Moore shook his head and headed to a nearby table where he placed his dinner order. He then turned his attention to the stage as the show started.

The three entertainers were focusing their attention on an attractive blonde seated close to the stage.

"Lady, you sure are puzzling to me," Brotherton sullenly said as he stared at her.

Fontaine leered at the lady and smiled as he spoke, "She may be a puzzle, but I sure do like the way the parts fit!"

"Be careful there, Frank," Brotherton cautioned Fontaine.

"Why?"

"Her husband looks mean. You might end up with six of your friends carrying you by the handle," Brotherton added.

"Sammy, did you know that Frank got religion?" Brotherton asked.

"No, I didn't know that." Davis turned to Fontaine, "Is that true?"

"Yes. I just read the Bible the other day."

"No!" Davis and Brotherton responded simultaneously.

"I found one passage that stuck with me."

"Which one?" the two asked together.

"It was the one talking about alcohol being man's worst enemy."

"Ooooh!" the two chorused.

"Yes, but it goes on to say to love your enemy and I'm loving this drink," Fontaine quipped as he took a sip from his cocktail.

"Sammy, I had a scary incident the other day," Brotherton commented.

"What was that, Dean?" Davis asked.

"I shook hands with Pat Boone and my entire right side sobered up," Brotherton said as he sipped his martini.

"Dean, do you know which holiday is my favorite?" Davis asked.

"No, Sammy. Which holiday is your favorite?"

"The day after Thanksgiving?" Davis answered.

"Sammy, that's not a holiday," Brotherton retorted before sipping his drink.

"Yes, it is. It's my favorite. Black Friday!" Davis replied as Brotherton moaned.

"Oh," Fontaine groaned. "Sammy, I noticed that you got here late."

"I did. The hotel clerk forgot to wake me up, daddy-o," Davis answered.

Looking at Brotherton, Fontaine joked, "I hear Sammy does his best work undercover."

Brotherton and Davis moaned in unison, but Davis wasn't going to let up.

"You name it; I did it. I'd like to say that I did it my way, but that line belongs to someone else."

"That's right, baby," Fontaine responded as the music started and he began singing the Sinatra classic "My Way."

After finishing his meal and enjoying the group's songs and comedic repartee for an hour, Moore slipped away out of the restaurant. He drove the short distance to Our Sunset Place. The cedar-sided, one-story structure with walk-out waterfront rooms was perched on the edge of a limestone cliff overlooking Lake Erie and offered spectacular sunset views.

Seeing that the front door was being held open by the affable owner, Bart Erwin, Moore parked and quickly exited his car holding a small kit of shaving gear and a change of clothes that he kept for emergency stays.

"Come on in and join the party," Erwin greeted Moore as he walked in.

"Thanks for letting me spend the night," Moore said as he followed Erwin to the registration area. Moore signed in and paid for his room.

As Erwin produced his receipt, Moore looked around the room which offered magnificent views of the lake through its wall of windows. Two couples were seated at the bar as they chatted over several bottles of wine. The fireplace to the left of the bar had a small fire going to take the chill out of the evening air. Next to the fireplace, another couple was seated at the grand piano and was playing a song.

"Busy night," Moore observed.

"You're lucky. You have the last room," Erwin commented.

"Which one did I get?" Moore asked. He had stayed there several times and loved the uniqueness of each of the rooms.

"Guess. Birding, Nautical, Beachfront or Vineyard?"

"Nautical?"

"Nope, you've got Beachfront," Erwin smiled.

"Perfect. I love all of your rooms," Moore said.

"That's a good thing," Erwin commented.

"Looks like the rain is letting up," Moore said as he glanced outside.

"Should be blowing over shortly. Might get to use the deck outside this evening."

"I'm hoping to use the hot tub," Moore said wistfully as he thought about its placement on the cliff's edge overlooking Lake Erie. "Is Sandy around?"

"She's closing up the Dairy Dock and should be here shortly," Erwin replied.

"You have the nicest wife," Moore said.

"I know and I appreciate her. That woman works circles around me," Erwin grinned.

"Come on over and I'll introduce you to our guests. I bet they'll love meeting a Pulitzer Prize-winning reporter," Erwin said as he ushered Moore over to the piano.

Moore spent twenty minutes speaking with the couples. After noticing the rain had stopped falling, he politely excused himself and, with wine glass in hand, made his way directly to his room. In a few minutes, he had changed and walked out of his room to the cliffside hot tub. He gently lowered himself into the hot water and relaxed.

In a few minutes, the two couples from the bar joined Moore in the hot tub and together they all watched the sunset. Its rays of light glimmered over western Lake Erie, then faded as night crept in and the pale moon peeked out amidst the stars.

CHAPTER 3

The Next Morning
Catawba Point, Ohio

Moore arose early at the B&B and jogged shirtless to Port Clinton's beach. When he returned, he grabbed a quick breakfast and checked out. He then drove over to the Great Lakes Popcorn Company on Madison Street where he visited with owner Bill Shepherd and purchased root beer-flavored popcorn for his aunt before heading to the Miller Ferry at Catawba Point.

Sitting in line to drive aboard the ferry, Moore relaxed and thought about his morning run. His daily regime of exercises and running were instilled a couple of years ago when he trained with an ex-Special Forces vet in Cedar Key, Florida. Moore liked how his body had been sculpted by the training and vowed to maintain his condition.

He had also learned hand-to-hand combat skills and how to kill a man if in various extreme scenarios. That knowledge, Moore promised to himself, he wanted to keep on the back burner as much as possible. Killing someone, even justifiably, wasn't in his line of work, but the unique skill set had come in handy several times before by saving his life.

As the procession of cars moved toward the ferry, Moore rolled down his window, handed his ticket to the crew member and drove aboard. Following a crew member's instructions, he eased his car within inches of the car parked in front of him and set his parking brake.

"Full load," Moore thought to himself as he stepped out of his car and saw that there were four lanes of vehicles parked on deck. When he noticed that the horde of walk-on passengers was about to board, Moore raced up the stairs to the top deck. He was going to grab a seat in front of the pilothouse so that he had a good view of South Bass Island as they approached it from the mainland.

As he walked by the pilothouse, a little voice yelled, "Welcome aboard."

Moore turned and a large grin appeared on his face as he recognized the twenty-six-month-old Liam Market at the wheel of the ferry. His father, Billy, who co-owned the Miller Boat Company with his siblings, was holding Liam while instructing him on how to drive a big boat.

"Starting him young, Billy?"

"Never too young for a Market," Billy cheerfully replied. "It's in his blood."

"That's certainly a given," Moore agreed as he noticed passengers heading in his direction. "Better grab my seat," Moore said as he looked at Liam. "You take us safely across, okay Bub?"

Liam nodded his head vigorously and waved. It reminded Moore how much the lad enjoyed waving at passengers when they disembarked the ferry at the island's Lime Kiln dock. He could be seen sitting with his dad on their ATV that they rode together all over the island.

Moore chuckled at how the young boy's smile and frown resembled his father's. He also furrowed his brow like Billy. Moore chuckled again as he remembered a comment that Billy's wife, Allie, had once made. She said that they each, father and son, had cute bellies and tiny butts.

"When you hear the blast from the horn, that will be Liam. He loves that part of the job," Billy commented.

"They grow up too fast," Moore said wistfully as he thought back to his own son. With his son's death years earlier, he didn't get to know the enjoyment of raising a son like Billy was now enjoying. Moore quickly turned and found a seat below the pilothouse, while nonchalantly placing his finger near the lower corner of his right eye to remove a growing teardrop.

Within minutes, Moore saw the deck ramp being raised and heard the horn blast to signal the ferry's departure. Her powerful engines roared as she backed out of her berth and turned about to head outbound to South Bass Island, a short twenty-minute ride across the lake.

Moore chilled out in Lake Erie's fresh morning breeze as the ferry made its way across the South Passage on a relatively smooth lake surface. Several fishing boats were out off nearby Mouse Island and two sailboats were taking advantage of the prevailing light wind.

Put-in-Bay and the surrounding western basin Lake Erie islands were known for being a tourist "hotspot" and a great getaway weekend to swim, sail, boat, fish, jet ski, dine and party at the various attractions and venues.

As they neared the island shore, Moore made his way down to the main deck and his car. After the ferry docked, Moore drove off and headed home to his aunt's house on East Point.

He knew that she'd be pleased with the candles and popcorn he brought for her. He had a number of things to wrap up around the island before he returned to the mainland the next day and began his drive to Alexandria, Virginia. He also planned to stop in the newspaper office to see his boss, *Washington Post* editor John Sedler. Moore then would be off to join Sam Duncan, his good friend and a former Navy SEAL, for a fishing adventure on Chincoteague Island in Virginia's Eastern Shore region.

Moore drove past Perry's Monument and parked in his aunt's driveway. He grabbed the candles and popcorn and carried them into the kitchen where his energetic aunt was wrapping up a phone conversation.

"There you are, Emerson. Have a good evening on the mainland?" she asked as her eyes widened at seeing the popcorn in his hand.

"Aunt Anne, if I didn't know better, I'd say that you manipulated the weather so I'd have to stay there overnight and bring you some goodies today," Moore quipped good-naturedly as he handed her the popcorn.

"Mmm," she moaned as she munched on the fresh popcorn. "I hope you gave that darling Bill Shepherd a big hug for me."

Moore chuckled. "I couldn't. There were ten women in line ahead of me."

"That Bill is such a chick magnet," Aunt Anne grinned as she looked at the bag in Moore's other hand. "Is that for me, too?"

"Yep. Stopped at Northern Exposure and picked up some candles for you. I know how much you like them."

Twisting off the lid of one of the candle containers, she held it up to her nose. She sniffed its fragrance and pronounced, "That fudge smells so good, I could almost eat it."

"I don't think candle wax and popcorn go well together," Moore chided her.

"You still leaving in the morning?" she asked.

"Yes. I've got a few things to do here and the first is to call Sam to make sure our fishing trip is still on."

"I remember you telling me that boy will cancel at the last minute."

"Yep. Like he did on the U-boat hunt in Key West, although it worked out nicely for me because I got to be his replacement," Moore said as he walked out of the kitchen and through the house to the enclosed waterfront porch. After exiting through a screened door, he walked out to the dock and took a seat facing the bay, a view that he always enjoyed.

Moore reached into his pocket and pulled out his cell phone. He called Sam Duncan while his eyes took in the recreational boat traffic entering and exiting the nearby harbor.

"Hi, E!" Duncan answered.

"Hello, Sam. We still on for the Chincoteague R and R?"

"Oh yeah."

"You're not going to cancel on me, right?" Moore asked.

"I'm all in. Got the charter boat all lined up and we're good to go."

"Great!"

"You driving straight through from Ohio?"

"No. I'm leaving tomorrow and I'll spend a couple days in Alexandria. Need to do a few things to the houseboat and see my boss."

"I love that houseboat, E. Man, but you're living the life. Island paradise on Lake Erie. Houseboat on the Potomac. Go on adventures around the world."

"I don't think my adventures compare to anything you do, my friend." Moore knew that Duncan lived life on the edge being involved with various government agencies and their black ops missions.

"But your adventures aren't as dangerous as mine. Wait a second, I guess I better take that back."

"Yes, you should," Moore agreed with his rascally buddy. "Anyway, I just wanted to be sure that we are set for Chincoteague."

"Roger that. I'll email you the address for Captain Bob's Marina on Chincoteague. We'll meet there and head out fishing as soon as you arrive."

"Good. See you then, Sam."

They ended their call and Moore walked around to the rear of the house. He drove his Mustang over to Delaware Avenue and found a parking space in front of T & J's Smokehouse. He was ready for a barbecue pork sandwich.

The former Crescent Tavern, which Josh and Tim Niese, Jr. recently purchased, was remodeled into a western-themed BBQ joint with outdoor seating, a mechanical bull and live country music. Several of the inside barstools had a saddle strapped to them, offering customers authentic cowboy-style seating.

Moore noticed a familiar face at the bar—entertainer Mike "Mad Dog" Adams, who was finishing up the remains of his smoked brisket sandwich. He was alternating bites of the brisket while flirting with the two attractive female servers.

"Some things just don't change, Mike," Moore said as he slid onto a barstool next to Adams.

"Hey, Emerson. What have you been up to?" the burly entertainer asked.

Glancing at the two ladies and back to Adams, Moore quipped, "Nothing compared to the mischief you get into."

"That's me. The King of Mischief!" Adams teased.

"You've got that right!" one of the women said as she turned around.

Adams watched her walk away. "I'd like to get that right!" he murmured before adding, "I like the *'mis-'* family."

"What?" Moore asked, not understanding where the conversation was headed.

"Yeah. You know words like mischief, misbehave, misfit, misdeed, misfire and my favorite—mistress!" Adams rattled them off with glee.

Moore reacted quickly. "I expected that your favorite would be missile!"

With a twinkle in his eye, Adams cracked, "You getting up close and personal, Emerson? Talking about my missile like that?"

"That's one thing I like about you, Mike."

"What's that?"

"You're always so consistent."

"Consistent?"

"Yeah. Consistently up to no good," Moore joked.

"Comes with the turf, my friend," Adams grinned as he took the last bite of his sandwich.

Moore ordered a sweet tea and a pulled pork sandwich. He turned back to Adams. "Anything new with you?"

"I'm expanding my counseling practice."

"I didn't know you were a counselor."

"Yeah. Yeah. I counsel a lot of people when I sit at a bar. Buddy of mine had a real problem."

"What was that?" Moore asked.

"He was hitting on this attractive blonde at a bar. They seemed to be connecting and he asked her what she did for a living. She said she was a female impersonator."

Moore laughed as he pictured the exchange. "What did your friend do?"

"Panicked. He got up and left. When he told me about it, I told him it was a good practice not to date outside of his species," Adams teased as he reached into his pocket to pay his bill. "I've got a show today. You have time to stop by?"

Moore loved seeing his show at The Round House Bar. The place was usually packed to hear Adams' songs and humor. It was especially fun to watch Adams call unsuspecting victims from the audience on stage where he'd embarrass them.

"I can't today, Mike. Need to run a few more errands before I leave tomorrow for Alexandria on my way to Chincoteague Island."

"Where?"

"Chincoteague. It starts out like the word *shin*. Shin-co-teague," Moore explained.

"Where's that?"

"Off the Virginia coast, the Eastern Shore. You remember Sam Duncan?"

"Like I could forget him? We former SEALs never forget each other," Adams added.

"That's right. Sam invited me on a fishing trip on Chincoteague. Just relaxation. Peace and quiet. Calm. No drama. No adventure. Just fishing and clamming."

"Sounds a bit boring to me. You think you can ever sit back and relax and do nothing, Emerson?"

"I do, but I have to work at it. I'm so high energy."

The server returned with Adams' change and then he eased his frame off the barstool. "You have a good time, Emerson."

"Will do. Have a great show," Moore replied as Adams walked out. He turned back to his sandwich, thinking of the relaxing vacation ahead.

CHAPTER 4

Washington Sailing Marina
Alexandria, Virginia

After driving six hours to Alexandria, Moore turned left off George Washington Parkway and drove down the peninsula's tree-lined Marina Drive, which ended at one of his favorite restaurants, Indigo Landing. As his car followed the lane on Daingerfield Island, Moore gazed at the rows of sailboats, powerboats and houseboats rocking in the breeze at the docks.

Moore found a parking spot near "A" dock and pulled in. Grabbing his gear, he headed for the dock as he took in deep breaths of the fresh late afternoon air. Moore glanced at the Potomac River and smiled as he saw dozens of sailboats taking advantage of the breeze. He headed down to the *Serenity* and stepped aboard his 1987 Adam cruising houseboat that was fitted with twin 170-horsepower Detroit diesels. She was sixty feet long with a breadth of twenty feet.

The accommodations included the stateroom with a queen-sized bed, a crew's quarters with two side-by-side single beds, and a sofa bed in the lounge. The boat also had a head with full bathroom facilities. The modern galley was located aft of the living room. The interior was trimmed in a highly glossed teak wood and contained Horner green carpet.

After stowing his gear and checking over the houseboat, Moore walked the short distance to Indigo Landing. The low green structure on the banks of the Potomac provided an island-like atmosphere with its overhead paddle fans and teak wood decor. From its large windows, Moore could view the Washington Monument and the Capitol. He could also view the party deck where a local singer was providing island music to the crowd of young Washingtonian office and government workers.

Moore was seated on the first tier and ordered a Captain Morgan and Coke. When the waitress returned with his rum and Coke, Moore decided to eat light and ordered a small salad and cheeseburger. He sipped his drink and watched the boat traffic on the river until his meal was served. He then quickly devoured his food and returned to the houseboat to handle his chore list, which filled the rest of his evening.

The next morning, he had a brief meeting at *The Washington Post* with his boss before returning to his work onboard the *Serenity*. Soon, Moore would be embarking upon his three-hour drive to Chincoteague Island. He was really looking forward to a relaxing vacation.

CHAPTER 5

The Causeway
Chincoteague Island, Virginia

Passing the NASA Visitor Center on Wallops Island, Moore drove his Mustang across the causeway as he followed Route 175 through the marsh and across the Blacks Narrows and Chincoteague Channel onto Chincoteague Island. This is a nine-square-mile barrier island situated off the northeast Virginia coast with approximately 3,000 year-round residents. The island's highest point is three feet above sea level and tourists are drawn to its sub-tropical climate.

It was Moore's first trip to the island. He turned right at the traffic light onto Main Street and drove south through the downtown filled with charming antique shops, art galleries, souvenir shops and restaurants. In contrast to Put-in-Bay, Moore noticed there were few bars on the main drag. He was getting a sense that Chincoteague was like Put-in-Bay on valium. The island seemed so calm compared to the more raucous Put-in-Bay.

On the right, he saw a number of chain hotels and independent boutique hotels dotting the waterfront as well as many fishing piers. As he drove, Moore remembered the children's novel, and subsequent 1961 film, *Misty of Chincoteague* that highlighted the island's annual July mega-event—the annual Pony Penning, the swimming of the ponies to auction.

Saltwater cowboys herd the wild ponies each summer from nearby Assateague Island into the channel between the two islands. The ponies then swim to Chincoteague Island where they are herded through the street to the carnival grounds for the pony auction. It's a huge fundraiser for the Chincoteague Volunteer Fire Department and it attracts thousands of tourists every year. It also allows the number of wild ponies to be properly managed as Assateague Island can only support so many.

Continuing south, Moore drove past the carnival grounds which were quiet in the late morning sun. Within another five minutes, he turned right into Captain Bob's Marina, the largest marina on the island, and parked his Mustang.

"E! You made it!" the cheery voice of Sam Duncan greeted Moore as he stepped out of his car.

Moore looked toward the open door to the marina office and saw Duncan. A large grin covered his face.

"Did you have an easy drive?" Duncan asked as Moore walked over and followed Duncan into the office.

"I did," Moore replied. "I like the feel of this island. There's just something really inviting about it."

"I told you. I told you," Duncan repeated himself as he beamed. "I knew you'd like this place, E."

"What was with that NASA site on Wallops Island that I drove by? I saw a visitor center on the right and huge hangars on the left," Moore curiously inquired.

"You didn't see anything. On the south side are the rocket launch sites," a voice spoke from behind Moore.

Not seeing who walked up behind him, Moore turned toward the man who had answered. He pegged the stranger as in his mid-forties, and he had long graying hair that was tied back into a ponytail and he wore a headband, torn t-shirt and cutoff jean shorts. He looked like a cross between a hippie and someone out of *Duck Dynasty*.

"E, this is the Duc-Man, Roe Terry," Duncan said as he introduced the pair. "He's going to be fishing with us today."

Moore couldn't help himself when he heard Terry's nickname. "Have you been on *Duck Dynasty*?"

"No, but I've been on *Swamp People*. I just got back from alligator hunting in Louisiana," Terry smiled. "Shot some big ones too," Terry said with a twinkle in his eye.

Moore could tell that Terry was a bit of a rogue, just the type of person that Duncan would surround himself with. Moore looked at Duncan and muttered, "Nothing unusual here; you seem to have the most colorful characters around you."

"As always," Duncan retorted with a smile. "Me and my buds. Makes for an interesting life, E," Duncan said before continuing. "You need to visit Roe's studio while you're on the island. He's an award-winning duck decoy carver. Right Roe?" Duncan glanced at Terry.

"I've done some carving," he replied in an unassuming manner.

"I'd love to see them," Moore said.

"I'm easy to find. Just on the north end of the island on this street," Terry smiled as he pointed out the door. "You'll see the sign in front of the house."

Before Duncan could introduce another man, Terry asked, "Tell me, Emerson. Did I hear you say something about this island being calm?"

"Yeah. Strange feeling I had when I drove onto the island.

Seems real peaceful here."

"You're going to fit right in. We call it 'Chincoteague calm.' Nothing like it anywhere," Terry explained.

"That's right, Roe. It gets hectic during pony swim time, but otherwise it's real quiet here," another man said. He had a medium build, brown hair and appeared to be in his early fifties.

"Got one more guy to introduce you to," Duncan said as he motioned to the man in a light blue polo shirt and khaki shorts. "This is Ebe Deere, our local police chief. He's our fourth fisherman."

Deere seemed more reserved and the most serious of the group as he shook hands with Moore. "Welcome to Chincoteague," he said as he leaned against the counter.

"And the person who has put this all together for us is Donna Roeske. She owns Captain Bob's Marina," Duncan said as the attractive blonde nodded her head at Moore.

"You boys better be getting on the water if you want to catch some fish," she said. "You're wasting time with all of your yakking!"

Moore guessed she was in her late forties. "Thank you for everything you've done," he said appreciatively.

"I didn't do anything but take your reservation and deposit. You staying on the island?" she asked.

Moore smiled. "Yes. There's something magnetic about this island that seems to be attracting me."

"Be careful, Donna. I think my reporter friend has an alternative reason for staying here. The magnetic attraction for Emerson is *you*," Duncan flirted good-naturedly with Roeske.

"Go on now," Roeske replied as she gently pushed back at Duncan's comment before turning to Moore. "If you are going to write anything about our island, Emerson, you can give me a call," she said as she wrote a number on the back of her business card. "That's my cell number in case I'm not here."

Moore looked at the number which ended in 1010. "This should be easy to remember. Bo Derek was a '10.'"

"Very astute, Emerson. I tease my friends that my figure makes me two '10's," she joked good-naturedly.

Moore chuckled softly as he noticed her shapely figure. "And Donna, you look like one very nice '10' to me!"

"Flattery will get you nowhere, Emerson. Come on now boys, your charter awaits," she said as she glanced at her watch and shooed the men out of the marina office. "And so does Captain Oz, your charter captain."

"I hope he's the Wizard of Oz when it comes to catching fish," Moore said as the group walked out the rear door to the boat slips.

"I guarantee you that Oz Morgan knows his business. I've lived here all of my life and he's the real deal," Terry assured Moore as the men walked to the slip where Morgan awaited them.

"Come aboard," the tall, silver-haired captain greeted them as the men boarded the 35-foot center console Boston Whaler with twin 250-horsepower Mercury outboard engines. "It's going to be a great day for fishing."

"What day isn't?" Terry laughed.

The men stowed their gear as the boat headed down Chincoteague Bay to the Atlantic Ocean where they would spend the rest of the day pulling in tuna, dolphin and maybe a couple of marlin.

As they motored down the bay, Moore saw the gantries for the rocket launch sites on Wallops Island. "Is that where they launch rockets?" Moore asked as he eyed the structures. They were on the other side of the sand dunes lining the beach on the Atlantic Ocean side.

"Yes, when they don't blow up," Chief Deere answered.

"There's been a problem?" Moore asked sniffing out a potential story.

Terry shot Deere a warning look and Moore clearly saw it.

"Roe's a bit sensitive to rockets blowing up. He worked there for a long time," the chief explained.

"I take a lot of pride in what we accomplished there. It's just unfortunate that the last three Antares rockets exploded," Terry explained.

"Sabotage if you ask me," the chief added.

Moore turned and looked directly at Deere. "Have you been investigating the explosions?"

"They have their own security there. They're handling it with the Feds."

"I'm sure they'll get to the bottom of it," Terry said firmly.

Moore's interest was piqued. "Roe, can you tell me about Wallops?"

"Oh no!" Deere moaned. "Get ready to drink from a fire hose. He's like a walking encyclopedia on Wallops. Roe was their public affairs officer."

"I'm a good listener, Roe. Fire away," Moore encouraged as the fishing vessel turned eastward and headed out into the Atlantic.

"One of my favorite topics. Today, Wallops has 84 major facilities on 6,200 acres. It has an airport, hangars, research labs, payload and rocket assembly buildings, machine shops, operations and instrumentation control facilities and launch complexes stretching from one end of the island to the other. But let me take you back a few years. Wild ponies inhabited Wallops ..."

"Where did the ponies come from, Roe?" Moore interrupted.

"There's all kinds of stories—from being washed ashore from shipwrecks to owners freeing them so they didn't have to pay a tax on them. The ponies were moved to Assateague Island in 1946, shortly after NASA bought Wallops from a group of Pennsylvania sportsmen. They used it for hunting and fishing. Wallops Island isn't that far from Washington, as you experienced in your drive here today."

Moore nodded his head in agreement as the boat struck some larger waves in the bay as they neared the open ocean.

"NASA wanted to expand their missile research and establish a rocket launch facility on Wallops. It just grew and grew. NASA started out with launching Tiamat missiles on June 27, 1945. They were primarily an air-to-air missile. They launched an Explorer X payload on a Scout rocket in February 1961. They also launched and recovered live monkeys in 1960. They were testing high stress reactions to the effects of being in outer space. NASA ran more than two dozen tests of the Mercury space capsule.

"For years, it was a top-secret site that tested and fired various missiles including surface-to-air missiles designed to intercept other missiles, including long-range intercontinental weapons. And the Aegis weapon system was developed there."

The chief interrupted Terry, "Roe, tell him about the window-breaking incident in Chincoteague."

Moore furrowed his eyebrows. "What?"

Terry chuckled. "Back in the day, they had a pilot fly an F-101 Voodoo supersonic jet fighter at 25,000 feet over Chincoteague and he broke the sound barrier."

"And a bunch of store windows in town!" the chief added.

Moore shook his head as he listened intently. He found the information interesting as he previously hadn't known anything about Wallops Island's existence.

Terry smiled. "Sometimes things like that happen. Speaking of planes, Wallops was a backup landing site for the space shuttle and its runways are long enough so that Air Force One can land there if needed."

"Roe, tell Emerson about the Chinese and Russians invading Wallops," Deere suggested.

"Really?" Moore asked. A number of ideas began formulating in his mind about the explosions and international intrigue. His mind was anything but calm.

"What the chief is talking about is that there are joint projects with the Russians and Chinese and others like the Brits and French. They've launched satellites for the Brits there," Terry explained.

"Interesting," Moore commented. "Do they stay in Chincoteague?"

"No. There's housing at the main facility that you drove by before you hit the causeway," Terry answered. "In fact, they recently added housing and administrative offices by the gate to the launch area. A lot of the foreign visitors stay there."

"It sure makes me curious why they've had three of the Antares rockets explode. That gets expensive, let alone the impact it has on supporting the International Space Station," Deere added.

"They support the space station from Wallops?" Moore asked.

"Yes. That's why they've got Russians on the base, now. They're working more closely with them on the resupply rockets to the space station."

Moore nodded his head in understanding. He looked over the stern as the fishing boat continued out into the Atlantic. "I'm amazed that the launch pads are so close to the ocean."

"That's a real problem," Terry admitted. "Erosion. They've taken shoreline stabilization measures with a seawall and dunes. They're trying to protect the island from tropical storms and hurricanes. And there's always the danger of coastal flooding when a nor'easter hits. It seems like it's a constant battle to fight shore erosion."

"Any chance I can get a tour of the facilities?" Moore asked as his interest was piqued.

"Doubtful," Terry replied. "Their security team clamped down on visitors."

"You should get Emerson introduced to their head of security. Hal Horner is a piece of work, if you're looking for someone to interview," the chief suggested.

"Not a good idea," Terry replied as Moore's curiosity grew.

From the console, Captain Oz turned his head, "Not too much longer and we should be ready to fish. You might want to check your gear."

"Great idea," Duncan said. "I'm tired of these guys feeding E information about Wallops. He'll forget about fishing and want to write a story!"

"Hey Sam, that's not true. I'm all in. Let's get some big ones today!" Moore retorted.

Terry and Deere echoed Moore's enthusiasm and the men turned from storytelling to readying their gear. Within minutes they were fishing and soon pulling in tuna.

Three hours later, the boat filled with happy fishermen and their tuna catch made its way back up Chincoteague Bay to its slip at Captain Bob's Marina. As the men unloaded their catch, Moore walked up to the marina store and entered.

"How did you boys do?" Roeske asked as she looked up from her desk.

"Not bad," he smiled.

"I knew Captain Oz would treat you well," she said proudly. "Did you all have a good time?"

"Yes. It was great to be out with those guys. They're funny guys, especially that Roe Terry."

"I'll say," she agreed. "They don't make people like Roe anymore. He's one of a kind."

"And he knows so much about Wallops Island."

"He should after working there all those years. If you get a chance, you need to get down to his shop and see the ducks he carves. He's won all kinds of awards for his craftsmanship."

"I'll make a point of it," Moore said as he caught a movement out of the corner of his eye and turned his head. He saw a muscular black man with a graying beard walk by the window. Moore had noticed the fifty-something man tinkering on a boat engine when he arrived earlier in the day.

"Who's that?" Moore asked.

"Who?" Roeske asked in return.

"That guy. The one with the tools."

When she saw where Moore was looking, she turned in her chair and looked out the window. "That's Bo White."

"Does he work for you?"

"He does. He's pretty talented. Can fix just about anything you throw his way."

"I guess you need to be self-sufficient when you live on an island."

"Pretty much so," she agreed.

White walked by again.

"Was he born on the island?" Moore asked as he watched White. Instinctively, Moore felt there was something intriguing about the man. Moore couldn't put his finger on exactly what it was, but he knew there was something to learn.

"No. He showed up one day a few months ago and asked if I had any odd jobs he could do. He's done a terrific job for me. Saved me a lot of money."

"Does he live on the island?"

"He lives here."

"In the marina?" Moore asked.

"He used to sleep in his truck and clean up at my outdoor

restrooms. I let him do it because he provided security for the marina at night. Then he surprised me one day."

"How's that?"

"I guess he got comfortable enough with me that he decided to make this his permanent home. I came back from lunch one day and I saw a 20-foot long shipping container sitting on the other side of the restrooms. I drove over to see what was going on and there was Bo. He had a sheepish look on his face."

"What happened?"

"I asked him if he knew where that container came from and he told me that he had it delivered there. He planned on using it for housing and hoped I wouldn't mind."

"So, it was okay with you?"

"What are you going to do? I'm a kind person and he did so much for me. I told him it was all right even though I didn't like it. You need to go see how he fixed that thing up. Cut in a door and window. Painted it white and calls it the White House." She chuckled at her last comment.

"He sounds like a real character."

"He is. Just like that Roe Terry you went fishing with. We got a lot of characters on this island."

"Reminds me of the characters back home on South Bass Island," Moore added with a smile. "I think I'll go over and talk to him."

"Don't expect much."

"Why?"

"That man is not a talker. Scarcely says anything. He likes to keep to himself. Doesn't really hang out with anyone. He usually goes to bed when the sun sets and is up at the crack of dawn, although I don't know how he does that."

"What do you mean, Donna?"

A conspiratorial look filled her face as she lowered her voice. "I think he drinks a lot at night."

"How do you know that?"

"You'll see a bunch of beer cans outside his door most mornings. And sometimes he smells like beer when he walks by."

Moore nodded. "I think I'll head over and visit with him sometime."

"Come back at sunset. You get the best views on the island here and then you can say hello to him. If he's drinking, he'd be more likely to open up to you."

"E! You done flirting with Donna?" Duncan yelled from the open back door to the marina office as he interrupted the conversation.

Moore looked at Donna and grinned. "You know how I am when I get around a pretty lady."

Roeske's face turned crimson red.

"Yes, I do, and you can't hold a candle to what I'm like around them," Duncan teased. "We're ready to go."

Moore thanked Roeske for the conversation and joined Duncan outside where he waited next to Terry's Toyota Highlander.

"Follow us and we'll show you where you'll be staying."

Moore walked over to his Mustang, giving a quick look toward the big shipping container where Bo White lived. He was looking forward to meeting White, he thought as he settled into the Mustang and followed the other two men.

They drove a half-mile north on Main Street when Terry stopped his SUV in front of a bed and breakfast. A sign hung from a post in front of the two-story house to display the name of the popular B&B. It read, THE BARE NECESSITIES.

Terry stepped out of the vehicle and called to Moore. "That's where you'll be staying. You can park there." He pointed to a parking lot behind the house. "Just go ahead and check in. We'll call you later and catch up for dinner."

"Okay," Moore said as he pulled onto the drive and parked. "Talk to you all in a bit."

Moore didn't notice the mischievous grin on Terry's face as he climbed back into his SUV or hear the ensuing laughter between Terry and Duncan as they drove away.

Moore walked around to the rear of the Mustang and retrieved his duffel bag and briefcase from the trunk before walking upstairs to the wide front porch and entering the early Victorian-decorated house. He walked over to the front desk and rang the bell on the counter, and then set his belongings on the floor.

When Moore straightened up, he found a shirtless man in his late sixties standing behind the counter. He quickly then noticed, too, that the man was more than shirtless; he was naked.

"Checking in?" the man asked the stunned reporter.

"Yes," Moore stammered.

The man turned his head and called into the small office. "Got a fresh one, honey. You want to check him in?"

"Be right there," a feminine voice responded as a puzzled look crossed Moore's face.

An equally naked woman in her late sixties with short blonde hair joined the man behind the counter.

"What name is the reservation under?" she asked as her blue eyes looked up at Moore.

"Moore. Emerson Moore," he answered a bit reservedly as he felt his face turning red.

While the naked woman checked the reservations, a nude couple in their late seventies descended the stairs, openly displaying their physical features. They each were carrying beach towels over their arms and proudly wearing a smile.

"Off to the pool?" the naked man behind the counter asked.

"Yes," the couple responded in unison as they disappeared down the hallway to the rear of the house.

Seeing the perplexed look on Moore's face, the man from behind the counter asked, "You ever stay at a clothing optional B&B for seniors?"

"No. I think there's been a mistake."

"I think so, too," the woman agreed. "I don't have a reservation for you, Mr. Moore. We do, however, have one vacancy available if you'd like to stay with us," she said warmly as she eyed Moore up and down. "We don't often get young, muscular men like you staying here."

Bending over to pick up his gear, Moore sputtered, "No. That's quite okay. I do believe my friends pointed me in the wrong direction."

As he walked through the front door, the woman called out, "If you change your mind, I'm sure we can accommodate you."

"Thank you, but I think I'd be more comfortable elsewhere."

When Moore walked out onto the porch, he saw Terry's SUV had returned and was parked in front of the house. Terry and Duncan were bent over laughing.

"I hope you two got a kick out of that," Moore fumed good-naturedly at being the butt of their practical joke.

"We could only imagine the look on your face!" Duncan guffawed.

"The owner's wife had to be real excited about getting a young buck like you to stay there!" Terry laughed.

"Yeah, young buck-naked!" Duncan chortled.

"Ha ha! Real funny," Moore replied sarcastically.

"But Emerson, they're not naked all of the time. They wear clothes when they fry bacon and weed the poison ivy," Terry chimed in as he continued snickering.

Moore walked down the steps and stood in front of the two jokesters. "Okay. Now where do you really have me staying?"

Still laughing, Terry answered, "You're at the Day's Inn. Go back through town to the light and turn right on Maddox Boulevard. Follow it out past the roundabout and you'll see it on your right."

"Are you staying there, Sam?" Moore asked.

"I'm hanging out at Roe's place," Duncan answered. "I love going through his collection of weaponry," he added.

"We'll meet you in an hour for dinner. Sound okay to you?" Terry asked.

"Sure. Where are we going?"

"The Village. You'll see it on Maddox before you get to the roundabout."

Moore glanced at his watch. "Sounds good. See you there."

Moore turned and walked to his car while the other two drove off. He drove back through town to Maddox Boulevard and followed it eastward. He noticed some of the local bike rentals and ice cream stands like Mr. Whippy's and The Island Creamery. He drove by Steamers and Maria's restaurants before spotting The Village, where he'd soon meet the guys for dinner. On his way he also passed AJ's on the Creek and Woody's Beach BBQ, an outdoor restaurant with an interesting collection of beach and hippie memorabilia and an old flower power VW minibus.

Driving through the roundabout, Moore spotted his hotel on the eastern side of the island and pulled in. After parking, he grabbed his gear and walked into the lobby where he leaned against the counter.

"Can I help you?" a fully-clothed, brown-haired lady asked Moore.

Noticing her name badge, Moore answered, "Yes, Paula. I have a reservation for Emerson Moore."

Paula looked through her computer and spotted Moore's reservation. "There you are, Mr. Moore," she said as she handed him a registration form to fill out. "First time here?"

"Yes," Moore responded as he began to complete the form.

"You should like it. Calm, peaceful and family-oriented, too. You been to the beach yet?"

"No, just got in from fishing."

"You'll love the beach. You just keep going east across that causeway and you'll be there."

"It's not on Chincoteague Island?" Moore asked as he slid the completed form across the counter to her.

"No, it's on Assateague Island and it sure is beautiful. No buildings. Just a wide strip of sand to enjoy. As you drive over to it, you'll see some of our wild ponies grazing and the lighthouse. It's just so pristine over there."

"I'm looking forward to going over," Moore said as he took the key handed to him and walked to his room.

CHAPTER 6

The Village Restaurant
Chincoteague Island

Parking in the white limestone parking lot, Moore exited his car and walked up the steps into the long, one-story restaurant that was set on the edge of the marsh. As he entered, he was greeted by Terry and Duncan.

"Found it with no problem?" Terry asked.

"Hard to miss," Moore grinned as he looked around the beach-themed facility.

"Hope you're hungry E, I am," Duncan said as the three men followed their hostess Christina Lyberg down the hallway and into one of the dining rooms that provided a view of the marsh.

"Famished!" Moore replied as he settled into a chair facing the window.

"I'd recommend the flounder if you like fish," Terry suggested.

"I love flounder," Moore said.

The men took a few minutes to review the menu and placed their drink and meal orders when the server appeared.

"What do we have there? A mini-United Nations meeting?" Duncan asked as he looked at a nearby table where several foreign-looking people were seated and speaking English with heavy accents.

"You've got Russian, Chinese and Syrian," Terry explained.

"How do you know, Roe?" Moore asked.

"They've been around for awhile. They're working on Wallops and representing their respective governments."

"I bet the woman wearing the veil is the Syrian," Duncan smiled as his eyes roamed over the beautiful woman.

"That's a hijab and it's not a veil. It's a headscarf," Terry corrected him.

"Same thing, Roe. I prefer veil, like in the veils a belly dancer would wear. I wonder if she can belly dance," Duncan mused playfully.

Ignoring Duncan's comment, Moore asked, "Roe, what do they do at Wallops?"

"Sure. I'll start with the Syrian woman since Sam seems to be so intrigued by her," Terry suggested.

"Good choice, Roe," Duncan commented with rapt attention as he stared at the stunningly beautiful woman in her mid-thirties. The hijab didn't hide her olive skin, wide brown eyes, full lips and jet-black hair. She reminded Duncan of someone with exotic beauty like Angelina Jolie.

"Her name is Hala Yazbek…."

Interrupting Terry, Duncan murmured quietly, "Hello, Halaaaaaa."

"Easy there, Sam," Moore tried to cool Duncan's jets.

"That approach will get you nowhere, Sam," Terry added.

"Why, Roe?" Duncan said as a look of consternation crossed his face.

"Hala is on the quiet side. Very cool and aloof," Terry cautioned.

"I can fix that," Duncan grinned.

"What does she do?" Moore asked as the server returned with their drinks and placed a loaf of fresh bread on the table.

"She's involved with the payload and launch operations," Terry responded as he sliced the bread and offered it to his tablemates.

"I bet the guys line up to work with her!" Duncan said as he continued to gaze at the attractive woman.

"She's from Syria?" Moore asked Terry as he continued to ignore Duncan.

"From what I've heard, she was born there, but educated here in the States. She moved to France and works for the European Space Agency."

"Never heard of it," Moore said with a perplexed look on his face.

"It's been around since 1975. It's headquartered in Paris where she worked and it has around twenty-two member countries. You get to know bits and pieces about folks around here. The community is so small."

"I bet the guy with the white hair is the Russian," Duncan guessed.

"Right. That's General Grigori Orlov. Goes by Greg. He's the lead for Russia's interests on the rocket launch to the space station," Terry explained as they looked at the burly patriarchal figure with a mane of thick hair, a bushy white beard and piercing blue eyes.

"Intimidating," Moore suggested as he looked at the powerfully-built man who he guessed was in his early fifties.

"Physically, yes. The guy's real smart, too. He's developed a lot of the space programs for the Russians and is an expert in launching large payloads into space."

"Probably pretty astute in stealing ideas, too," Duncan suggested. He warily eyed the man leaning uncomfortably close to Yazbek who reacted by pushing him away with her hand.

"I'd venture that's a good guess," Terry agreed. "Probably the same goes for the Chinese guy."

The three men looked at the slightly built Chinese man with dark-rimmed glasses and black hair as Terry continued.

"His name is Wu Tang. A brainiac! He's in his thirties and knows rocketry inside and out from what I've heard. Sort of like a rocket whiz kid growing up in China. Wu works closely with operations and the launch team."

"Roe, it sounds to me like any one of those people would have access to the rocket or payload and could be responsible for the explosions," Duncan surmised.

"They could, but why would they do that?" Terry asked.

"Embarrass the United States?" Duncan guessed.

"Maybe," Terry replied.

"Who are the other two at the table?" Moore asked

"The guy is Hal Horner, Director of NASA Security and oversees all security on Wallops. He's had his hands full with the last three consecutive Antares rocket explosions. One exploded before clearing the pad and two exploded in midair shortly after their launch."

Horner was drinking brandy. He was tall and lean with a stern-looking face. He had a thin, waxy nose, bar-straight black eyebrows, a black mustache and graying hair parted on the side. He looked tough and unquestionably cynical.

"I don't like the vibes I'm getting from that one," Duncan offered as Horner's eyes locked on Duncan's eyes, giving him a cold stare.

"Good hunch, Sam," Terry said as Duncan looked away from Horner. "The guy is a know-it-all. He thinks he's never wrong, never makes mistakes."

"So he must be real frustrated about the rockets blowing up," Moore interjected.

"It's got to be killing him. I hear he's on a short fuse. No one likes being around him," Terry said.

"I'd guess that no one likes being around him when things are good, either," Moore added. "He reminds me of that cartoon character Snidely Whiplash—a stereotypical villain and maligned character."

"He does," Duncan agreed and with a grin on his face added, "So we have astronauts from the U.S., cosmonauts from Russia and taikonauts from China. All that we're missing is Mexicans. I bet they'd call them taconauts."

Terry and Moore groaned at Duncan's feeble joke.

Roe then said, "Actually guys, astronaut comes from the Greek word meaning 'star sailor.'"

"I didn't know that," Moore said.

Suddenly, the woman seated with her back to the men pushed her chair away and stood while placing the strap from her gaudy handbag over her shoulder. As she turned, her face lit up when she saw Terry.

"Roe, how are you?" she asked as her eyes locked on Terry and she walked over to him. "Give me a peck on the cheek like the dear man you are," she said as she leaned forward and offered her right cheek to Terry, who obediently complied. When she spoke, she had a syrupy voice like molasses and she seemed full of herself.

Staring at Moore and Duncan as she straightened, she pushed her tangled dark hair back from a pale face framed by high cheekbones. She was tall and attractive, but overbearing.

"And who are these two good-looking gentlemen?" she asked, the words dripping out of her mouth.

"Two fishing buddies of mine. Emerson Moore and Sam Duncan."

The forty-something woman blinked her blue eyes unabashedly at the two men. "Catch any fish, boys?"

Duncan responded to the shapely woman before Moore could react. "Tuna. Made a good haul today."

"Guys, this is Maya Simon. She's in charge of the Wallops Operations while the director recovers from a heart attack," Terry said. "It happened right after the third rocket blew up."

"I can understand why he'd have a heart attack," Duncan offered.

"My official title is Interim Director of the NASA Goddard Space Flight Center at Wallops Flight Facility," she explained pompously and without any show of compassion for her ailing predecessor.

"I bet you have your hands full, Maya," Moore said as he greeted her.

"Honey, you have no idea. I'm doing two jobs now. I still do my old job, too. But that's why they depend on me the way they do. I'm just the person who can handle anything they throw at me," she boasted as she waved her hands while speaking.

Simon allowed a small smile to cross her face. "I better excuse myself. I need to run to the little girls' room," she said capriciously as she bent down again and presented her cheek to Terry for another peck. She then walked out of the dining room and down the hallway.

"That woman is a piece of work," Moore observed.

"Understatement, E. Did you see that expensive crossbody messenger bag she had? It was a Louis Vuitton," Duncan added.

"Yep. Those cost a bundle. I also noticed the expensive rings she had on her fingers," Moore commented.

"She's well off and likes to flaunt it," Terry added. "Did you notice how she waved her hands around while she talked?"

"She Italian?" Duncan chuckled.

"No, but she likes to show off the expensive rings on her fingers," Terry explained.

"I did see them now that you mention it," Duncan said.

"I'd be a bit wary of her," Terry warned.

"Why?" Moore asked.

"She goes through men like a sinus infection goes through tissues."

"My kind of woman," Duncan said as he watched her walk away.

"They all live on Chincoteague?" Moore asked.

"Maya does, but the others live in the base housing on Wallops inside the island gate. Horner lives in Salisbury on the mainland, about 45 miles from here," Terry responded.

Moore nodded as he recalled driving through Salisbury on his way to Chincoteague. "I'm curious," Moore said. "Did the explosions happen before or after the three foreigners got here?"

Terry thought for a minute. "It was after," he replied.

"Interesting," Moore said.

"What's more interesting is this seafood platter," Duncan said as the server placed his meal on the table. "Look at the serving size!" Duncan exclaimed as his eyes devoured the large helpings of crab, shrimp, oysters and clams as well as the lobster tail and flounder.

"And look at this serving of flounder. It's hanging over the plate," Moore added with glee as his eyes relished his meal.

"They have great food here. You'll enjoy it. Bon appétit!" Terry said as he attacked his crabmeat baked in a butter and garlic cream sauce.

The men set aside their babble about the Wallops Island people, who finished their meal and departed, and instead focused on savoring their hearty and succulent dishes. Afterwards, the men passed on dessert and agreed to meet with Moore the next morning at his hotel. They'd rent bikes to ride over to Assateague Island for an early morning tour.

After they parted, Moore drove down Maddox Boulevard and turned left on Main Street. He was headed to Captain Bob's Marina to watch the sunset that Roeske had mentioned earlier. When he pulled in the parking lot, he noticed several cars parked and their occupants standing or sitting next to the bay to watch the sunset. Moore walked over to one of the outbuildings to the right of the parking lot and leaned casually against it.

By the time the sun was setting, the sky was painted an array of pink, orange and yellow, while the pale glow of the rising moon was beginning to show. The wispy clouds held the promise of a calm, peaceful night.

The crunching of a wheel on the limestone parking lot disrupted Moore's quiet solitude. He turned and saw Bo White approaching as he pushed a wheelbarrow holding an outboard motor.

"Need a hand?" Moore offered.

"Nope, but thank you," the black man responded politely as he kept moving.

Moore straightened and started walking next to the man. "My name is Emerson Moore."

White didn't respond. He continued moving toward his container home which was set on the far right side of the property. There were several buckets overflowing with empty beer bottles outside of the unique dwelling.

Moore wasn't about to be deterred in his quest to open a dialogue with White. "I was here this morning with my friends.

Donna fixed up a charter fishing trip for us with Captain Oz."

Still no reaction from White. He was a man on a mission and plodded forward.

Tagging along, Moore continued. "I saw you this morning and Donna said your name is Bo White."

White dutifully carried on with his progress without making a comment.

Moore decided to push to get a reaction. "Kind of funny with a black man having a last name of White," Moore said.

White stopped and set down the wheelbarrow, not because he was going to engage, but because he had reached his destination. He decided to respond to Moore. "I don't see anything funny about that," White glared at Moore.

Moore decided to take another approach. "Good thing that your last name isn't Peep."

"Why's that?" White asked with a sullen look.

"Then you would be little Bo Peep," Moore said as he tried to be funny.

"Is that supposed to be funny?" White asked.

"Yes."

"It isn't." White said stonily. He was quiet for a moment as he looked over the water. "I don't have time for your foolishness. I've got work to do."

"Sorry. I didn't mean to get off on the wrong foot with you," Moore said.

White turned and looked squarely into Moore's eyes. "What do you want from me? I just mind my own business and prefer other people mind their own business too."

Moore saw that this was going nowhere. "Listen, I am sorry. I was just interested in your home and what you have here."

"You work for the zoning commission?" White asked suspiciously.

"No. I'm an investigative reporter from Washington," Moore explained.

"That's the last thing I need. I don't need nobody writing anything about me or my living arrangement!" White stepped closer to Moore and loomed over him in an intimidating fashion. "You get what I'm saying, newspaper man?"

Despite the ugly turn this confrontation was taking, Moore was still drawn in by this mysterious man.

"Honest," Moore began. "I won't write anything, especially if you give me a tour to satisfy my intellectual curiosity."

"Intellectual curiosity, huh? From a reporter out of that intellectual ghetto they call Washington, D.C.?"

Moore realized that forging a friendly discussion with White was going to be nearly impossible, but Moore wasn't one to easily give up. It wasn't part of his DNA, so he tried a different track.

"I agree with you," Moore offered. "There's a lot wrong over there and I report on it."

That comment seemed to resonate with White who let out a long sigh. It appeared to Moore that White relaxed a bit as he stepped back and created more space between the two of them.

"There's nothing more that I enjoy or find challenging than exposing corruption or people who have wronged others," Moore declared.

"You being straight with me?" White asked as an idea began to formulate in the back of his mind, but instead he quickly filed it away for another day.

"I'm known for that," Moore assured White.

"I don't like people messing with me," White warned as he suddenly produced a sharp knife from the sheath on his belt. "I can gut them as easily as I gut fish."

Moore could tell from White's tone that he meant business. Moore took a deep breath as he watched White put his knife away.

"I have no doubt in your capabilities."

"You shouldn't," White spoke confidently.

Transitioning to a discussion about White's living quarters, Moore asked, "What's the size of this? Eight-by-twenty?"

"That's it," White replied.

"Did you paint it white?" Moore asked as his eyes ran over the metal exterior.

"Yes. And I made the sign over the door."

"'The White House?"

"Yes," White said as a chuckle slipped out between his lips.

There's hope, Moore thought to himself when he heard the chuckle. "I like it."

"The difference is that we do things right here, not wrong like the other White House."

"Must have been a job to cut in the door and window," Moore surmised as he continued with his examination of the structure's exterior.

"Not a big deal. I found the door and window in the trash."

"Can I peek inside?"

"Go ahead. Not much to see," White said as he opened the door and stepped back to allow Moore to enter.

In the fading light from the open door and only window, Moore saw a solitary and worn single-size mattress on the floor. Various cardboard boxes turned on their sides served as shelving for clothing and cans of food. Some clothes hung from hooks affixed to the metal wall. There was a propane stove on the floor and two lamps which had seen better days. One was missing the shade.

"No TV?" Moore asked.

"What do I need a TV for? I got my radio and iPad."

Moore saw the radio and iPad sitting on top of a board across two upended crab traps. A crate served as a chair.

"IPad to stay in touch with your Facebook friends?" Moore asked with a touch of levity.

"I don't have any friends," White replied.

"Why do you have it then?"

White hesitated before answering the nosy reporter. "Research."

"What kind of research?" Moore's curiosity was piqued.

"That's my biz."

Moore looked around. "Do you have Wi-Fi?"

"I use the marina's."

Moore saw an electrical extension cord. "You have electricity here?"

"I run that cord over to that outlet."

Moore looked toward the doorway and realized that White was pointing to a building next to the one that housed the outdoor restrooms. Seeing the restroom, Moore remembered that he didn't see a bathroom in the dwelling. "You use that restroom?"

"Yeah. It has a shower, too. You finished now?" White asked, tiring of the invasion on his privacy.

Moore smiled as he stepped outside, almost knocking over a rusty charcoal grill that was covered by a small metal roof. "Thank you for making an exception for me and letting me see your place," Moore said. "You've done a great job here, Bo."

"Don't be thinking that this is your second home," White cautioned in a slow drawl. "I like to be left alone."

"Why's that?"

"You know you're really starting to wear out your welcome with all of the questions you've been asking me tonight."

Taking the hint, Moore said, "I apologize. I'll hit the road." Moore started walking toward his Mustang. "I hope to see you again soon."

"And I hope not to see you soon," White said as he disappeared into his bay-front home, pulling the door closed behind him.

Strange bird, Moore thought to himself as he entered his car and drove back to his hotel.

CHAPTER 7

The Next Morning
Moore's Hotel

Sitting on the hotel's back steps, Moore saw Terry pull into the rear parking lot. He glanced at his watch and saw that it was eight A.M. Terry was right on time. On the back of his SUV was a bike rack that held two beach bikes. Terry stepped out of the vehicle and walked around to where he saw Moore approaching him.

"Ready for an early morning ride?"

"I am. Where's Sam?" Moore asked as he noted that only one person exited the vehicle.

Terry spoke as he unstrapped the first bike. "He sends his regrets. He got a call last night and went back to Washington. Something urgent came up."

Moore shook his head from side to side. "That boy!" he exclaimed. "Something is always coming up and he runs off." Moore was miffed at his friend's disappearance.

"He does this to me all the time. We get started on something and poof, he's gone!" Moore said slightly irritated. "We're supposed to go fishing."

"Well, I've got some good news and some bad news for you," Terry said as he lifted the first bike off the rack.

"What's the good news?"

"I'm also a fishing guide. So, we'll get some fishing in."

"What's the bad news?"

"You can move into Sam's room at my place for the balance of your stay."

"What's so bad about that?" Moore asked with a puzzled look on his face.

"If he left any cooties or bed bugs, you've got to deal with them," Terry chuckled as he lifted the second bike off the rack.

"Right," Moore remarked.

Pointing to one of the bikes, Terry said, "That one is yours. Ready to ride?"

"Yes."

Terry hopped on the other bike and began to pedal and Moore followed behind him.

"Ride 'em like we stole them!" Terry shouted as he cycled down the limestone drive and turned right onto Maddox. "Because I did!" he teased over his shoulder as he biked toward the causeway.

"If you get a chance, you'll want to pay a visit to our museum," Terry yelled as they rode past the Chincoteague Museum. "Besides a lot of historical stuff, you'll find the real Misty there. They stuffed her and she's on display," he said, referring to the pony featured in *Misty of Chincoteague*.

They crossed the causeway onto Assateague Island. As they peddled onward, Terry gave a quick wave to the ranger manning the entrance booth. They followed Beach Road with Terry pointing at the wild ponies on their right and the massive Assateague red-and-white-striped lighthouse. They biked past Little Toms Cove and turned right into the beach parking lot, following it to the end where they dismounted and secured the bikes to a post.

"The beach is on the other side of these dunes," Terry explained as the two men walked through the deep sand.

"What a beautiful island," Moore said. "I didn't see any homes here."

"It's pretty natural now. It's more of a daytripper's site. No one lives on this island, though the National Park Service does permit some overnight camping."

When they crested the path on the small dune, they stopped. Moore took in the wide expanse of pristine beach. "This is amazingly beautiful. No condos or hotels overlooking the beach."

"Natural, like I told you. Great for fishing or swimming. You can walk for miles in the morning without seeing anyone."

"Or run," Moore added. "I haven't had my morning run. Want to join me?"

"Run? I don't run for anybody. My running days are behind me. You go ahead if you want. I'll just sit there on the edge of the beach and enjoy the waves breaking," Terry said.

"I won't be long," Moore said as he began to run along the water's edge toward Toms Cove Hook on the horizon to the south.

Forty minutes later, Moore returned. He was carrying his t-shirt in his hand as beads of perspiration showed on his face and chiseled chest.

"How'd it go, Emerson?" Terry asked as he stood.

"Fantastic. I didn't see anyone, Roe. It was just me and the seagulls," he recounted as the two men walked back to the bikes and mounted them.

"You don't find many beaches like this anymore. No commercialization here," Terry commented as he started to peddle.

"Beautiful. Absolutely beautiful and peaceful."

Chincoteague Calm

"That it is!" Terry agreed.

When the two men arrived back at Moore's hotel, Terry said, "I'll take care of the bikes if you want to grab a quick shower and check out. We've got a lunch date in about thirty minutes with the Vice Mayor of the island. She owns the island tour company, works on the volunteer fire department and runs a lawn care company."

"Sounds like a busy lady."

"That's an understatement. She does so much for this island to make it successful. She'll give you a tour when we're done with lunch. Now you get going. You're burning daylight," Terry urged.

"I won't take long," Moore said as he turned and headed for the building's entrance.

Within twenty minutes, a fresh Moore in a clean aqua t-shirt and khaki shorts reappeared with his duffel bag and backpack. "I told you I wouldn't take long," he said as he walked to his Mustang and threw his gear into the trunk.

"Right you are," Terry said. "Why don't you follow me to the restaurant? Then when you're done with your tour, you can drive over to my place."

"Sure. Where are we going?"

"The Ropewalk. Nice place next to the Fairfield Inn. Looks over the Chincoteague Channel," Terry said as he began walking around his vehicle.

Before getting in, he shouted, "When we go on the roundabout, you'll see a building in the center. That's the Chamber of Commerce office in case you need anything. Evelyn Shotwell is the executive director and one of the nicest ladies you'll ever meet. Her husband, Holt, works on Wallops Island, too."

"Thanks," Moore said as he sat in the driver's seat and lowered his convertible's top. It was a cloudless day and he wanted to enjoy the fresh sea air.

Within fifteen minutes, the two men parked their vehicles at the Ropewalk and walked past the outdoor patio area with its tropical decor of beach chairs, tables with brightly-colored umbrellas, palm trees and sand. They walked up a flight of stairs and entered the second story which overlooked the channel.

"Denise!" Terry greeted a short, muscular woman with dark brown hair and sunglasses perched on top of her head. He gave her a quick hug and turned to Moore. "This is Denise Bowden, the lady I mentioned."

"I'm Emerson Moore," Moore said as he shook hands with her.

"You're the newspaper reporter," Bowden said, confirming what Terry had said over the phone.

"Right."

"You doing a story about the island?" she asked.

"Hadn't planned on it. I was focused on fishing and relaxing until I heard about the rocket explosions," Moore answered.

"We've had a few," she confirmed.

Moore could tell that she was a very serious person. "I met some of the Wallops people last night."

Terry interjected and mentioned who they recently had seen during dinner at The Village.

"You met Maya Simon, huh?" Bowden asked.

"Yes."

"She's an alpha female. So full of herself!" Bowden observed.

"I've met her kind before," Moore said before adding, "I noticed that she got a kiss on the cheek from Roe." Moore grinned.

"I always thought that she was sweet on you, Roe," Bowden teased, looking directly into Terry's eyes.

"Whoa! Whoa! Not my kind. I'm glad that I don't work over there anymore," Terry grimaced at the remembrance.

"I hear that from several people," Bowden said as she turned back to Moore. "Did you see all of those expensive rings she wears?"

"Couldn't miss them the way she was flapping her hands around like a seagull's wings," Moore beamed.

"Like I said, she's self-absorbed."

The three were interrupted by the server who took their lunch order. Bowden ordered the mahi tacos while the men each got burgers. All requested sweet tea.

When the server walked away, Bowden asked, "Are you taking a tour of Wallops?"

"I'd like to," Moore replied.

"Roe should be able to set that up with his sweetie Maya. Right, Roe?"

"Not my sweetie, but I guess I could get that set up for you, Emerson."

"I'd appreciate it," Moore said.

"You been to Roe's place yet?" Bowden asked.

"Not yet. But I'm going to be staying there for the next few nights," Moore answered.

"He has a wonderful place. Wait until you see his workshop. That boy has so many hand-carved ducks."

"I'm looking forward to seeing it," Moore said.

"You'll enjoy spending time with Roe, our Duc-Man. Not only does he carve ducks, but he also has the personality of a duck."

"How's that?" Moore asked Bowden.

"Calm above water, feet going like crazy below water."

Moore laughed and Terry groaned at the crack.

Bowden was on a roll. "Roe likes carving those ducks. He takes out that carving blade and does it little by little—or should I say whittle by whittle. Right, Roe?"

Roe didn't comment. He just rolled his eyes in reply.

"Yeppers. If he really likes you, he might carve you a duck to put in your bath water, Emerson."

"I can think of some other things I'd rather have in my bathtub with me," Moore suggested in reply. Moore then changed the topic. "You've lived here all of your life, Denise?"

"Yes, up through today."

Relieved to see the subject change, Roe interjected, "There's a long history here with the Bowden family. Goes back to the early days."

Moore looked back at Bowden.

"That's true. The family was one of the first to settle here." Bowden then went into a brief history of her family on the island. Her overview was interrupted when the server returned with their food and refilled their drinks. Between bites of her tacos, she continued with her story.

"That's amazing," Moore said when she had finished. "I'm really looking forward to taking the island tour with you."

"I think you'll find it interesting. Not quite as exciting as watching the rocket launches at Wallops, although I can show you some of the best places to watch those here on Chincoteague." Turning to Terry, she asked, "Did they ever decide what day the next launch is?"

"Not yet. I expect to hear shortly. It might be something for you to watch, Emerson," Terry suggested.

"Sounds like fun," Moore said as they finished eating and Moore paid the bill and left a tip.

The three left the restaurant and walked to the parking lot, where Moore saw a white nine-passenger van. The side of the van was lettered and identified the vehicle as TEAGUER'S TUMP TOURS.

"Must be my ride," Moore guessed as he followed Bowden to the van.

"I could tell you were smart," Bowden teased as she walked around and entered the vehicle.

Before Moore joined her, Terry gave Moore directions to his place on the north side of the island, about two miles up the road.

"Tighten your seat belt," Bowden said as Moore sat in the passenger seat. "I drive like we're in the Grand Prix," she warned.

"We're going to get up to speed in this van?"

"Only if you want to get a ticket. The speed limit is twenty-five miles per hour and they love to give tickets here."

"Thanks for the warning. I'll be careful."

"I'd be careful too if I was driving a Mustang."

Moore turned his head and stared at her with a look of surprise. "How did you know that I drove a Mustang?"

"The only car in the parking lot with Ohio plates," she grinned as she replied.

"Very observant!" Moore said as he settled back in his seat.

"Nah. You're too easy, Emerson," she said with a chuckle.

"I've been told that in the past," Moore agreed good-naturedly.

Moore allowed a smile to cross his face. He knew that he was going to enjoy the tour as she drove by the brick firehouse, giving him the history of the town, including the devastating impact that the 1962 Ash Wednesday hurricane had on the area.

They drove past the carnival grounds where the fire department hosted the pony auction fundraiser each July. They made their way past Captain Bob's Marina to the Curtis Merritt Harbor and then over to the east side of the island to see where the ponies swam across Assateague Channel for the auction.

Bowden's tour included the Beebe Ranch site that was the home of the famous pony, Misty, a number of cemeteries, and interesting facts about many of the island homes. Following Chicken City Road, they continued to the north side of the island, driving past the future home of the fire department near Deep Hole Road.

When they drove along Main Street, Bowden pointed to a complex of structures behind a house on Chincoteague Bay. "That's Roe Terry's house and business."

"Thanks. That made it easy to find."

"They're good people. You'll enjoy staying with Roe and his wife," she said as she continued her historical overview of the area.

When the tour finished, Bowden returned Moore to his car in the Ropewalk's parking lot.

"Thanks again, Denise. I really enjoyed the tour and learning more about the island."

"You're welcome. You have my business card in case you have any questions," she said as Moore exited her van.

As she pulled away, Moore jumped into his car and turned left onto Main Street heading north to Roe Terry's place. Within minutes, he spotted several signs at the corner of Main and Winder Lane. The signs announced waterfowl carvings by Roe "Duc-Man" Terry at 5191 North Main.

Turning left, Moore pulled into the driveway of the one-story, yellow vinyl-sided ranch with a large front porch. Behind the house, Moore saw a low building which housed Terry's retail outlet and workshop. In front of the wooden deck was an array of weathered clam shells, carved wooden ducks, floats and buoys. It had a nautical theme. A yellow flag with a rattlesnake and the saying "Don't Tread on Me" flew from the corner of the deck. Another sign proclaimed: "Prayer is the best way to meet the Lord. Trespassing is faster." Moore chuckled.

Another sign read: "Open when I'm here. Closed when I ain't."

Moore chuckled again as he walked up the short flight of steps and entered the retail outlet. He stood in awe as he gazed at the wood-paneled walls which were covered with shelves holding expertly-carved waterfowl, oyster cans, deer antlers, shotguns and traps. A large beige oval rug covered the painted green floor as a ceiling fan turned lazily overhead.

A door from the workshop opened and Terry walked through.

"You found me!" he said as he greeted Moore.

"Denise drove me by, so it was easy."

"How did you enjoy the tour?"

"It was great. She was so informative."

"Yeah. She does a fabulous job," Terry agreed.

"Your sales room is just plain awesome," Moore remarked as he looked around the room again.

"Thanks Emerson. It keeps me busy and out of trouble. At least that's what Monnie tells me."

Moore looked over Terry's shoulder. "Is that your workshop?"

"Yes. Come on in," Terry said as he walked back into the workshop and sat in a vinyl executive swivel chair.

Moore's eyes swept the two walls in the small hallway. They were packed with duck carvings. "Oh my," he said as he walked into the main working area which had the aroma of freshly chipped wood. He glanced at the floor and saw wood chips surrounding a tree stump with a carving hatchet buried in it.

The walls were filled with oyster cans and waterfowl carvings. Several shotguns hung from the walls, as did three calendars of bikini-clad females. Country music was playing quietly in the background. Over the work table were two shelves. The top shelf held unpainted ducks and the second shelf held freshly painted ducks. The work table top was covered with various carving tools, paint cans and containers filled with paintbrushes.

"There's plenty of beer in the fridge. Help yourself," Terry said as he nodded to an old fridge that long ago had seen better days.

"I'm good," Moore said as he settled on a maple stool. "This is quite a set up you have. I can't get over how many ducks you've carved."

"That's how I got the nickname Duc-Man," Terry grinned.

"How did you get started carving ducks?" Moore asked.

"I was a kid when the family moved here from the West Coast. My dad was transferred to the nearby naval air station. As luck would have it, Emerson, one of our neighbors here was a duck carver and we hit it off. His name was Doug Jester, Jr. and he was legendary.

"Jester was a waterman, too. That old boy taught me so much about hunting, fishing and crabbing. He'd take me out on his 34-foot scow and teach me the bay life and how to survive."

"What an opportunity," Moore said with admiration.

"There're a lot of good people on this island. They help you out and I return the favor."

"What was your first boat?"

Terry smiled as he fondly recalled that boat. "It was an old fourteen-foot skiff built by Blink Watson. It had a cannibalized 35-horsepower outboard motor. It wasn't long after I got the boat that I started carving. After I got out of the Navy, I got a job at NOAA on Wallops Island and pretty much stayed there until I retired early. I still worked as a hunting guide and a few of my buddies and I built a hunting shanty. We called it THE RED EYE HUNT CLUB."

"Is it close by?" Moore asked.

"Yeah. It's on the north end of the marsh between Chincoteague and Assateague."

"Donna mentioned that you've won awards for your decoy carving. Is that right?" Moore queried.

"Yeah. I've got over 300 ribbons, but a couple awards are the most important to me. Cigar Daisy was a legendary carver on the island and a good friend. Cigar passed away awhile back. One day he stopped by to check out a big white bird I was carving for one show and told me that it wouldn't have a chance. He had won Best of Show that prior year. You don't know how much it meant to me when my big white bird carving won Best Species, Best Confidence Decoy and Best of Show. I didn't let Cigar live that down!" Terry smiled.

"And you were the spokesman for the fire department here, too?"

"Yeah. For a number of years, but Denise does it now," Terry replied. "Hey, enough of this gabbing. Let's go over to the house and I'll introduce you to Monnie," Terry said as he stood from his chair.

"Sounds good," Moore said as he followed Terry out of the workshop to the house and entered it through the side door.

Moore was stunned when he walked in. "This is so you, Duc-Man."

The family room had a cathedral ceiling with wood paneling. The walls were also wood-paneled and a brick fireplace that featured a large mantel was on the north wall. Wooden shelves lined the walls and displayed carved ducks. More ducks hung from the walls as did several wooden framed pictures of duck hunting scenes. Two mounted deer heads with a large rack of antlers were affixed to the wall on both sides of the fireplace. A large-screen TV was flanked by two steel cabinets that contained Terry's collection of shotguns, rifles and handguns. On the other side of the room were a green plaid sofa and two recliners.

"This is really nice," Moore commented.

"I like being comfortable," Terry said. "This décor reflects who I am."

"I'll say," Moore responded as he spotted the large head of a gator with a row of sharp teeth. "You shoot him?"

"Yep. I was in Louisiana with my swamp buddies. That one was eleven feet long. You should come with me on one of my gator hunting trips."

"No thank you. I've been in those swamps and it's too dangerous for me."

"Don't be a pansy. From what Sam told me, you're no stranger to danger."

"I'm not, but I wouldn't want to push my luck around alligators. I've seen some big ones out there."

"Those are the ones I like the best."

"You go ahead then and go after them. I'm passing," Moore smiled.

Approaching footsteps from the kitchen signaled the arrival of Terry's wife, Monnie.

"Meet Monnie, Emerson," Terry said as the slender brunette in her late forties entered the room. "I married my high school sweetheart," he said proudly.

"So you're Emerson. I've heard a lot about you these last few days," she grinned.

"From my buddy, Sam?" Moore guessed.

"Yes. It sounds like you've had some dangerous escapades."

"He fits right in, doesn't he?" Terry grinned.

Nodding her head in agreement, Monnie asked, "And are you a rascal like Sam and my Roe?"

"I'm a rascal, but nowhere near the level of Roe or Sam," Moore smiled. "How nice that you two were high school sweethearts!"

"I should have known what I was getting myself into with this little polecat. Did he tell you about our wedding day?"

"No."

Monnie threw a mischievous look at Terry and then began. "He came home on leave so we could get married on Christmas Eve. At 5:30 that morning, he was sitting in a hunting blind …"

"But I got to the wedding on time," Terry interrupted.

"He did," she agreed as she rolled her eyes. "He made it to the wedding by one P.M. and afterwards we went on our honeymoon." She turned her head to stare at Roe. "Roe Terry, do you want to tell Emerson how long our honeymoon lasted?"

Terry had a sheepish look on his face as he answered, "Emerson, you've got to understand it was hunting season and I only had a few days to hunt."

"Roe Terry, you tell him," she said with feigned sternness.

"Well, my gosh Emerson, it lasted twelve hours. I had to be back in my hunting blind."

"And that's been my life with Roe ever since. But he's a good man and I'll keep him," she said with a genuine smile.

Moore laughed softly at her explanation. Seeing the sliding patio door, Moore asked, "Is that another room like this, Roe?"

Monnie answered before Terry could. "That's my tropical room. Come on. I'll show you."

Moore followed into the adjoining room, which was walled with windows on three sides and reveled in tropical island décor. "I love the tropical colors and the signs. That's something I'd have in my home," Moore said as he looked around the room at the tropical plants and furnishings. His eyes settled on a world-class sailfish mounted above the sliding patio door.

"Did Roe catch that one?"

"He wishes he did. No, that's one I caught," she said proudly. "His smaller one got away and I'll never let him forget."

"I bet you won't," Moore smiled.

After a few minutes of showing Moore around, Moore walked out of the house and retrieved his gear from the trunk of his Mustang. When he returned, Monnie ushered him down the hallway to his room and left him to settle in.

CHAPTER 8

**Clam Shells Pub
Main Street**

After Roe and his wife left for a duck decoy banquet on the mainland, Moore decided to head back into town. He wanted to try the food at the Clam Shells Pub. It was situated on the south side of the bridge over the channel that connected the causeway to the island. According to Bowden, the Landmark Crab House had stood on the site until a fire had partially destroyed it. A local resident named Captain Barry then bought the place and remodeled it, renaming it the Clam Shells Pub. Barry ran his pontoon boat tours out of the bar's dock.

Moore went through the intersection at Maddox Boulevard and turned right into the Clam Shells' parking lot. It was almost full. Moore eyed the pub as he approached and thought it appeared relaxing, carefree and very addictive. Moore smiled. It was his kind of place—one part beach bar and two parts fun.

The outside patio area overlooked the channel and boat docks. It looked like the perfect place to watch sunsets. A man was helping people onto a pontoon boat that had signage announcing CAPTAIN BARRY'S CHINCOTEAGUE TOURS.

Another man, speaking in a New Jersey accent, brushed by Moore as he headed to the tour boat. He was firing off instructions rat-a-tat style to his crew. Moore noticed that his shirt read CAPTAIN BARRY and assumed he was the owner.

Hearing a crunching sound under his shoes, Moore looked down. The patio was floored with crushed clam shells. It was also filled with a number of picnic tables with colorful beach umbrellas. All of the tables were occupied and servers were scurrying about with food and drink orders.

A solitary singer with his guitar sat under a covered patio near the docks as he entertained the crowd before the sun set.

Moore stepped inside and saw that a once dark and smoke-stained interior had been freshly painted in white and aqua blue. It had a nautical-themed interior with pine chairs and tables throughout. Fish nets hung from the ceiling where large fans worked furiously to cool the interior. The walls also had fish nets and lobster traps hanging on display. It looked more like a touristy beach bar and that was the owner's intent. For the summer, he wanted the tourist dollars and it gave the tourists an opportunity to mingle with the locals.

Moore spotted a vacant barstool and quickly made his way through the crowded pub. As he sat down, the server handed him a menu and took his rum and Coke order. When she returned with his drink, he ordered a flounder sandwich and took a swallow of his drink.

"First time here?" an unshaven local asked.

Moore looked to his right and nodded to the man who obviously had been drinking for some time. "Yes. Looks like this is a real hot spot."

"It is. Best drink prices on the island," the toothless man grinned. "My name's Bullet," he said as an introduction.

Shaking the man's hand, Moore replied, "I'm Emerson Moore."

"Pleased to meet you, Emerson Moore. Want to buy me a drink?" he slurred as he asked boldly.

Moore smiled at the man's forwardness. "Sure. Miss, could you give him another?" Moore asked the server as she neared.

"Mighty nice of you." Bullet noticed that his buddy had returned to the barstool on the other side of him. "Mr. Emerson Moore, meet my fishing partner. His name is Tator Bug."

Moore leaned forward and looked around Bullet. A slightly overweight and likewise unshaven man with a worn baseball cap gave Moore a huge wink. "Nice to meet you."

Before Moore could say anything, Bullet said, "He needs another drink, too," while expectantly looking at Moore.

Chuckling, Moore said, "Sure. I'd be glad to buy him a drink, too." He knew that he was being taken advantage of, but didn't mind. When the server returned with his sandwich and Bullet's drink, Moore ordered the drink for Tator Bug.

"Thank you," Tator Bug called.

Moore nodded as he took a bite of his sandwich, then asked, "Bullet, have you lived here your whole life?"

Bullet sat up on his barstool. He then realized that he had an audience and started into his life story about his island days and fishing adventures. Moore continued eating as he listened. When Moore finished his sandwich, he took a swallow of his rum and Coke.

"You've had an interesting life."

"And I didn't tell you half of it," Bullet declared.

Moore commented, "I noticed that Tator Bug got up a couple of times while you were talking and disappeared out that back door. Is that the smoking area?"

"Yeah, but he goes to see Floyd."

A perplexed look crossed Moore's face. "Why doesn't Floyd come in here?"

"He's not allowed."

"Really? Is he banned?"

"Nope. They just don't want him in here. You probably noticed a bunch of folks going in and out that door. And it's not just to go to the head, ya know?"

"Now that you mention it, I have," Moore said.

"They go to see Floyd, too. A lot of the folks take cigarettes or drinks to Floyd." Bullet sipped his drink, then paused a brief moment, and asked, "You want to meet Floyd? He's a real character. Been an islander all of his life."

"Sure," Moore nodded in response.

"You better take him a drink, especially since this is the first time that you'll meet him."

"Okay. What does he like?"

"A beer. Don't matter what brand. Floyd drinks them all."

Moore turned to the server and ordered a Miller. Within minutes, Bullet pushed his wheeled walker and led Moore through the back door where they ran into five people outdoors smoking and laughing. As the group stepped aside, Moore saw a billy goat tied with an eight-foot chain to a stake in the ground. The goat had a cigarette in its mouth and wobbled on its legs.

"Meet Floyd," Bullet guffawed as Moore stopped dead in his tracks to watch the goat puff away on its cigarette.

"He likes cigarettes, but not cigars," Bullet explained as he sat on the walker. The goat inhaled a final draw and spit the remaining butt onto the ground. "He's thirsty now. Go ahead and feed him the bottle."

Chincoteague Calm

Moore cautiously approached the drunk goat and inserted the mouth of the bottle inside the goat's mouth. Carefully he allowed the liquid to go down the goat's throat. "Will he drink it all at once?"

"Oh yeah, and then want another," Bullet roared.

When the goat finished the beer, Moore stepped back and watched as the goat leaned up against the side of a shed, trying to keep its balance.

"That's too funny," Moore said.

"Bet you ain't seen anything like that," Bullet grinned.

"Can't say as I have." Moore glanced at his watch. "I better settle up and get going."

As Moore spoke, he saw someone watching him from the corner of the building. When the man stepped under an outdoor light, Moore recognized him as Bo White. He was holding a twelve-pack of beer, which Moore guessed White had purchased at the restaurant. White disappeared when he realized that Moore had seen him.

"Thank you for the drink, Emerson Moore."

"Nice visiting with you, Bullet," Moore said as he returned inside. After paying his bill, Moore walked outside to the patio area. It wasn't the beautiful sunset alone that captured his attention. It was a group of three drunks who were taunting three people seated at one of the picnic tables.

Bullet, who had followed Moore, piped up. "This isn't going to be pretty. Those are the Kronsky brothers. They're nothing but trouble. The big one talking is the oldest. That's Joe. The twins are Luke and Louie."

Moore eyed the burly brothers who were targeting their insults at the international triumvirate Moore had seen at the Village Restaurant the previous night—Orlov, Tang and Yazbek. Primarily, it was Yazbek who was being called names because of the hijab she was wearing.

Moore approached closer. He could see that the slightly-built Tang was cowering and Orlov was glaring at the intruders. Yazbek's eyes were throwing darts at the unruly men.

"Take off that head scarf, you Muslim freak," Joe taunted as he began to reach out to grab the scarf and rip it away.

"No!" Yazbek said firmly as she jerked her head away.

That's when Tang decided to go into action to protect her. He stood up and took a karate-like stance. "Back up," he said as bravely as he could.

"You Chinese all know karate, don't you?" Joe yelled as he quickly closed the space between the two of them and began to pummel Tang, who quickly fell to the clam shell-covered floor where he coiled up.

"Faker, just like I guessed," Joe said as he kicked Tang hard in the ribs before turning to face Orlov. "You want to step in, Ruskie?"

Orlov looked over to Joe and said, "She can take care of herself." He was more interested in picking up his glass of vodka and downed its remaining liquid.

Joe and his twin brothers next turned their attention to Yazbek. "Looks like you're on your own, lady," the older Kronsky said as he began to close in on her.

"Not so fast, friend," a voice spoke from the crowd that had gathered around them.

The three brothers turned to face the new arrival.

"Leave her alone," Moore firmly advised as he stepped out from the crowd.

"This isn't your fight," Joe shot back as he eyed the muscularly-built Moore.

"I'm making it my fight," Moore declared.

Joe grinned as he glared at Moore. "Three against one. You sure you know what you're getting yourself into?"

"Three against three," Moore countered confidently.

The man looked behind Moore and didn't see anyone stepping forward. "Who are the other two? Ghosts?" he bellowed as his two brothers laughed with him.

"Nope. Me, myself and I," Moore said stoically as he quickly moved in and connected with a kick to Joe's groin, immediately dropping him to the ground like a sack of cement.

Seeing his older brother groaning in pain, Luke bull-rushed Moore, who adeptly sidestepped the attack, giving Luke a shove headfirst into a nearby picnic table. Moore then turned to face Louie, who now held a knife in his hand. With a deadly look on his face, he began to quickly advance on Moore. His advance was interrupted when a wheeled walker was propelled into his path and he tripped over it, falling to the ground. Moore jumped on top of Louie and disarmed him as he looked into the crowd and saw Bullet with his mischievous smile.

"Thanks, Bullet," Moore said.

"That's for the drinks," Bullet said appreciatively as he watched Moore grab Louie by his shirt and slam him into the walker before shoving it across the patio into the channel.

"Guess I owe you a walker, Bullet," Moore said.

"I was ready for a new one anyways," Bullet laughed.

A movement out of the corner of Moore's eye caught his attention and he ran over to Joe, who was struggling to get to his feet. Moore gave him a hard knee to the chin and the man slumped backward.

"Watch out!" Yazbek screamed.

Moore turned and saw Luke rushing him again. Moore danced

to the side like a matador and the man's momentum carried him over the edge of the patio and into the channel.

As Moore thought how much he appreciated his earlier hand-to-hand combat training in Cedar Key, he walked over to Tang and helped him to his feet. "Are you okay?"

"Fine. I'll be fine," Tang groaned as he gently sat down on the picnic table. "I think I'll be sore in the morning."

As he stood near Tang, Moore noticed that Bo White was standing in the group of onlookers. When White realized that Moore had seen him, he once again disappeared.

Before Moore and Tang could talk further, their conversation was interrupted by the arrival of several police officers and Chief Ebe Deere.

"Hello, Emerson," Deere said when he recognized Moore. "You causing trouble here?" he asked as two officers rescued the two men from the channel and another secured Joe Kronsky. Joe was rubbing his chin and walking gingerly from Moore's groin kick.

Moore, Yazbek, Tang and Orlov gave the chief a brief recap of what had occurred. When asked, Yazbek didn't want to press charges.

"You've been here about forty-eight hours, Emerson. You always stir things up wherever you go?" Deere asked.

"Not usually. I'm quiet and reserved," Moore teased.

"Sure you are," Deere said dubiously as he looked at his officers who had the three trouble-makers in custody. "Take them in." Deere turned to Moore and said, "You're one lucky fella, Emerson. Those are the Kronsky brothers. They're mean. Not guys to mess with if you get my drift. I'd be watching my back if you see them around."

"Bad boys, huh?" Moore asked.

"The worst on the island. Been busted several times for drugs, menacing and fighting. Involved with a few stabbings, but none fatal." Deere looked over the area. "Looks like everything's back to normal. I'm heading out."

"Thanks, Chief," Moore said as he turned his attention back to the seated trio.

"Would you like to join us?" Yazbek asked.

"Sure," Moore said as he sat at the table.

"I'd buy you a drink, but I don't use alcohol," she said.

"That's no problem," Moore said as he looked at the beautiful woman.

"I owe you," Tang spoke up. "I'll buy you that drink," he said as a server appeared and took orders for the table, although Yazbek opted for green tea.

Moore turned to Tang. "Do you know karate?"

"No. I was just trying to scare them off," Tang responded. "Didn't we see you last night at The Village Restaurant?"

"Yes. I'm here on vacation. My name is Emerson Moore." He decided not to reveal that he was an investigative reporter.

"Wu Tang," Tang responded.

"Greg Orlov," the burly Russian grumbled.

"I'm Hala Yazbek and I want to thank you, Mr. Moore, for intervening on our behalf," she said warmly.

Moore heard a disdainful grunt from Orlov.

"It didn't involve me," Orlov explained.

"You all work at the launch pad at Wallops, right?" Moore asked Yazbek.

"We all do. It's a temporary assignment for us before we each return to our home countries," she replied.

"I met Maya Simon last night at the restaurant and it sounds like you folks have your hands full with the rocket explosions,"

Moore said.

The three exchanged silent looks.

Their facial expressions weren't lost on Moore. "I heard that the explosions started after the three of you began working on Wallops. Any connection?" he pushed. He wasn't wasting any time in focusing on the issue.

"What exactly are you implying?" Orlov asked with indignation.

"Nothing. It probably is coincidental," Moore replied as he noticed the worried look on the faces of Yazbek and Tang. In contrast, Orlov's face appeared to be filled with anger at the implication.

"Let me assure you, Moore, that none of us had anything to do with the explosions," Orlov refuted. "Why would any of us do such a thing?"

"Embarrass the United States?" Moore asked.

"You know nothing, Mr. Moore. We are here to support the International Space Station. We need to send supply payloads there for our astronauts and to ensure the space station's long-term viability," Yazbek explained.

"It's Emerson, Hala. Never Mr. Moore. That's my father," Moore grinned at the woman.

"Emerson, it is," she said warmly as she returned the smile.

"Why are you interested?" Orlov asked.

"Curiosity. I've done some investigating in my past."

Orlov's bushy eyebrows arched. "Are you investigating the explosions?"

"Oh no. Just curious, that's all."

Orlov leaned in. "We're smart enough to know that people are looking at the three of us. People think that one of us had something to do with the explosions, but we didn't," Orlov affirmed.

"That's right," Tang said in agreement as Yazbek nodded her head.

Moore stared at the three foreigners as he thought about their denials. It's what he expected to hear from them.

"Do you have any idea about who might be sabotaging the launches?" Moore asked.

"Maybe somebody on the base," Yazbek suggested.

"Like?" Moore asked.

"Who has the most to gain from the explosions?" Orlov asked. "Think about it."

"I'm not sure," Moore said.

"Maybe Horner," Orlov proposed.

"The head of security?" Moore asked.

"We've been watching him," Tang said as he supported Orlov's comment.

"That's right," Yazbek added.

"But why? I'd think that he's under the microscope now because of the *lack* of security," Moore offered.

"It would give him job security. If he can find a scapegoat to blame this on," Orlov said.

"Especially with the cutbacks coming," Tang said.

"Cutbacks?" Moore asked.

"Yes. NASA wants to slash jobs on Wallops. They've had two accountants reviewing the operation. The employees are worried."

"But we're safe because we're not part of their payroll. We're still paid by our respective governments," Yazbek explained.

Moore noticed that her eyes seemed to linger on him after she spoke. They were soft and alluring, almost inviting.

"I'm hoping to take a tour of Wallops in the next few days. Maybe I'll see something that triggers an idea."

"Let me know if I can help you and I'll see what I can do," Tang said.

"Let all of us know. We want to see this program be successful," Yazbek said.

Tang looked at his watch and stood. "We should be getting back."

The other two and Moore stood.

"Thanks for telling me about your suspicions," Moore said as the four of them walked toward the parking lot.

"Thank you for coming to our rescue," Tang said as they reached their rental car.

"Yes, thank you," Yazbek added.

"You're welcome," Moore said. "Maybe I'll see you folks on Wallops."

"Maybe," Orlov said as he eased his bulky frame into the passenger seat.

"I hope so," Yazbek said with a twinkle in her eyes.

"I do too, Hala," Moore smiled.

As their car pulled out of the parking lot, Moore replayed their conversation. He wasn't sure that he believed any of them. As far as he knew, one of them or all three could be responsible for the explosions. His focus, however, was disrupted by recounting the soft and alluring eyes of the remarkably beautiful Hala Yazbek. What was her story? Moore was thoughtful as he returned to his car and made the drive north to Terry's house.

When he arrived at the house, he saw Terry's car in the driveway and no lights on. He let himself in and headed to his bedroom. It had been quite a day and he was ready to grab some shut-eye.

Even though he was tired, Moore couldn't fall asleep. His impressionable attraction to Hala lingered freshly in his mind, perhaps a little in his heart as well. He was also disturbed that his pal Duncan had taken off. This wasn't the first time that Duncan melted away while the two were together. Moore tried to rationalize the demands on his friend with his involvement in clandestine matters.

Another thing that bugged Moore was the issue with the rockets exploding on Wallops. What a strange crew, he thought as he dwelled upon the evening encounter with Orlov, Tang and Yazbek, along with the Kronsky brothers. He wanted to get to the bottom of the problems at Wallops. With a heavy sigh, he rolled over to block all thoughts from his mind and steadfastly fell asleep.

CHAPTER 9

That Night
Chincoteague Channel

It was after midnight as the boat ran quietly north from Chincoteague Channel to Chincoteague Creek toward the causeway bridge. The boat's running lights had been extinguished to reduce its visibility as much as possible. The lights from the Clam Shells Pub and the street lights didn't aid the boat in its attempt to slip by unseen.

Joe Kronsky was at the helm and wore dark-colored clothes and a black hat to conceal his identity. He had made this run many times and had never been caught. His head swiveled as he looked for any signs of the Coast Guard.

Suddenly, the bright searchlight from a Coast Guard patrol boat knifed through the darkness, lighting up the other boat. A voice boomed from a loudspeaker, "Turn off your engines and prepare to be boarded."

In response, Kronsky shoved the throttle forward and the boat leapt out of the water as it surged ahead. There was no way that Kronsky was going to be caught with his illegal cargo.

In response to Kronsky's action and the quickly accelerating boat, the Coast Guard vessel followed in hot pursuit. With its blue lights flashing, the vessel chased Kronsky's boat. A Coast Guardsman manned the searchlight which sought to keep the smaller boat in its sight.

Kronsky was driven by reckless boldness as he raced toward Chincoteague Bay. He wasn't worried about submerged crab traps or partially hidden pilings. He wasn't worried about sand bars. He was a waterman and knew the bay area as well as any waterman. He also knew that he had an advantage over the Coasties as their boat was slowed by the combined weight of the five-man crew and all their gear. Kronsky could easily outrun them.

He broke into the bay and headed for the marshy island known as The Redeye. He was anxious to put as much distance between himself and the searchlight. Running full out at night was dangerous, as one never knew what kind of debris would be floating on the water.

Kronsky's boat easily expanded the distance between the two craft. As he rounded The Redeye, he headed for Will Hole. It was a tricky area to navigate, especially at night. As he approached it, he slowed and carefully navigated his way through the curves between the marsh islands. A couple of times he looked over his shoulder and smiled. He saw the searchlight probing the darkness, but his pursuers now were more than a mile away.

As Kronsky neared Assateague Island and the service road which ran north and across the state line into Maryland, a truck's headlights switched on and off briefly to signal its location.

He eased back on the throttle as he closed the distance to the shore. He shut off the engine when he was ten feet away and the boat gently came to a halt as it ran aground.

"Sounds like you had some excitement," the man in uniform chuckled.

"How do you know?"

The man held up a radio. "I was listening."

"I outran them."

"Good thing for you," the man said as the two men worked at transferring the bales of marijuana from the boat to shore.

They next loaded the bales in the back of the pickup truck. When they finished, the man reached into a cooler and withdrew a cold beer. "Thirsty?" he asked Kronsky.

"Yeah," he answered as he took the beer, twisted the cap and ingested the cold liquid.

Watching Kronsky, the man leaned against the side of the truck as he struck a match and lit a cigarette.

In the flash of the light, Kronsky noticed the lettering on the side of the vehicle. It read MARYLAND DEPARTMENT OF FISH AND WILDLIFE.

"So which is your real job? Selling drugs or working for the state?" Kronsky asked.

"You've worked with me long enough. You know these late-night meetings make me more money."

"And speaking of money?" Kronsky urged.

"I was waiting for you to ask," the man said as he produced a small briefcase filled with cash. He handed it to Kronsky, who opened it to check the contents.

"It's all there. I've never shorted you," the man assured Kronsky.

"And you better not. Otherwise we wouldn't be having such a friendly-like meeting," Kronsky said in a menacing tone.

The two chatted for a few more minutes and Kronsky finished off another cold beer. The man then pulled a tarp over the bales and Kronsky headed back to his boat. Within a minute, both men departed the lonely meeting spot.

CHAPTER 10

The Next Morning
Roe Terry's House

"Heard you had a run in with the Kronsky brothers," Terry said as he flipped over several pancakes on the griddle.

"News travels fast," Moore replied from his seat at the kitchen table as he savored a cup of freshly brewed coffee and the aroma of bacon cooking.

"It's a small island. News and gossip have a way of getting around," Monnie said as she placed plates and silverware on the table. She turned to her husband and asked, "You finished burning those pancakes yet?"

"Almost," Terry teased.

"I heard that you took on all three of them and beat them up," Terry said without looking at Moore.

"I wouldn't say that I beat them up. I just slowed them down a bit until the police could get there and take over," Moore explained humbly.

"I'm impressed. Those brothers are tough hombres and I didn't think you were the fighting kind."

"I'm not really. I prefer to walk away. Good thing for me that I had some hand-to-hand combat training not so long ago. It came in handy."

Terry turned to face Moore. He pointed the pancake flipper at Moore and spoke in a serious tone. "Emerson, you be careful around the Kronsky brothers. They have a long memory. They love to pay back people, and not in a nice way."

"You have trouble with them?" Moore asked.

"I've known them all of my life and they know not to mess with me."

"That they do," chimed in Monnie. "They know Roe's usually not too far away from his backup buddies—Smith and Wesson."

Her husband chuckled as he flipped the pancakes from the griddle onto a plate.

"Everyone on the island knows that Roe is a crack shot," she added as she set a plate full of bacon on the table.

"But that doesn't work for you if they sneak up on you from behind," Terry warned. "And those boys are sneaks."

"I'll keep an eye out for them," Moore said as Terry and his wife sat at the table and they began their breakfast feast.

"I'd keep both eyes wide open," Terry cautioned. "I also heard you spent some time talking to the three foreigners after the fight."

"I did. That Hala is a beautiful woman," Moore said between bites of the tasty pancakes. "I was asking them about the rocket explosions," he added.

"Learn anything? Everyone thinks one of them is behind the explosions," Terry suggested.

"Not really. They each denied any involvement. They think Hal Horner is linked to the trouble there."

"Dr. Strangelove?" Terry asked.

Chincoteague Calm

"Honey," Monnie said as she placed her hand on her husband's arm.

"Well, he is kind of weird."

"Do you know him well?" Moore asked.

"No, he came in a couple of years before I took my early retirement. Really a strange dude. Kept to himself. Never thought he was wrong. Arrogant jackass to put it mildly."

"Roe!" Monnie said as she pinched the back of her husband's hand.

Moore looked over the rim of his coffee cup. "I'd like to take a tour of Wallops Island. Think you could arrange that for me?"

Terry let an exaggerated moan escape his lips. "You mean that I have to call Horner and see if they'd clear you for a tour?"

"I don't know who you'd have to call, but I would like to tour the place."

"What for? You think a tour is going to allow you to solve the explosion problem?"

"No. I'm curious as to what a NASA facility and its launch pads look like. I've never visited one."

"I guess I can do that for you."

"One more thing, Roe."

"What?"

"When I was at the bar, I met Bullet and Tator Bug."

"Two of the island's leading alcoholics," Terry touted. "And really nice guys."

"When Bullet took me out to meet Floyd …"

Terry interrupted. "Isn't Floyd a hoot? A cigarette-smoking and beer-drinking goat!"

"Yes. I was surprised. But let me explain. I saw Bo White staring at me while I was back there. Then again after the fight, he was on the periphery of the crowd and staring at me again."

"He's a strange duck, that one is," Terry snickered.

"Now that's funny coming from the Duc-Man," Moore also chuckled.

"But he is. Goes to the Clam Shells Pub to buy his beer. Everyone sees him there. I always wonder why he doesn't get his beer at the grocery store," Terry said.

"Maybe you answered the question. Everyone sees him there. Think he wants to be seen?" Moore asked.

"I don't know. Why would he do that?"

"Got me," Moore responded.

"From what I know, the guy is a loner. Doesn't get involved with anything on the island and minds his own business."

"Some people are that way," Moore agreed, although his instincts told him Bo White wasn't all that he was cracked up to be.

"What do you have planned for today, Emerson?" Terry asked.

"I think I'll head downtown. I saw an art gallery there that I want to check out."

"Kevin McBride's gallery?"

"I don't know the name of the place."

"It's probably Kevin's. His gallery is filled with his paintings of the ponies. He's a great talent."

"Good. I'm sure that I'll enjoy it," Moore said as he stood. "Thanks for the fantastic breakfast. I'll do the dishes."

"No you won't," Monnie said as she stood and began clearing the plates from the table. "You're a guest. You enjoy your time while you're here."

Moore smiled at her hospitality. "Thank you. I'll go finish cleaning up and head over to Kevin's gallery."

"And I'm headed to my workshop. I guess I'll give Horner a call and see if I can get you a tour," Terry said as he drained his coffee cup and stood.

"Thanks. I appreciate it."

An hour later, Moore parked his Mustang on Main Street near Kevin McBride's gallery and walked over to the brick building. He looked up at the sign over the door. It read: THE OSPREY NEST.

Moore smiled when he entered the combination gallery and gift shop. The gallery reminded him of the Richmond Gallery in Marblehead, Ohio, near Put-In-Bay. There was, however, one huge difference. Ben Richmond's paintings were ships and familiar sites in Put-in-Bay. McBride's paintings were the wild ponies of Assateague and Chincoteague Islands, and waterfowl of the Eastern Shore region.

Still, Moore felt at home as he wandered through the charming gallery. When he entered the right side of the gallery, he spotted a dark-haired, bearded man sitting on a stool as he painted on an easel.

"Are you Kevin?" Moore asked.

The award-winning artist set down his brush and looked at Moore. "Yes. Can I help you?"

"I'm Emerson Moore. I'm in town for a couple of days as a guest of Roe Terry and his wife Monnie and had to stop in to check out your gallery. I just love your work," Moore said.

"Thank you. I've been at it a while."

"I noticed several of your paintings have blue ribbons."

McBride grinned. "Just a few of the awards they've won."

"I really do like all of the horse and Pony Penning paintings. What a talent you have."

McBride stood and walked Moore around to several of the paintings where he identified several of the horses that he painted, like Riptide and Misty.

Moore then told him of Ben Richmond and his work and the two chatted for several more minutes before Moore excused himself to answer his cell phone. It was Roe Terry calling and he had good news. He had set up a tour of Wallops Island for Moore. Horner had an unexpected cancellation and would be available in an hour.

CHAPTER 11

NASA Launch Facility
Wallops Island, Virginia

Following Chincoteague Road west across the causeway, Moore drove onto Wallops Island. He went past the airport facility and the visitor center to Atlantic Road. Turning left on Atlantic Road, he headed south to the island gate and entrance to the launch facility. After he parked he walked into the badging office to get his visitor's badge and meet the head of Wallops security, Hal Horner.

While he waited, he completed the paperwork to get his badge. Moore's eyes were focused on the paperwork and his head was tilted downward. Out of the corner of his eyes, he noticed a hand reach across the counter and pick up his driver's license.

"Were you sick when they took this photo?" the voice asked.

Moore looked up and saw Horner carefully inspecting his driver's license.

"No," Moore responded as he wondered if Horner got up on the wrong side of the bed.

"You look like you were on your death bed," Horner said as he rubbed his index finger across his thin, black mustache.

Moore sighed as he thought about spending time with the cynical security expert. "You know how those pics go."

"Actually, I don't. My photos always turn out perfect," Horner said in a monotone as his aide handed Moore the visitor's badge and took Moore's completed paperwork.

After quickly scanning the paperwork, the aide turned to Horner and spoke, "Mr. Moore is good to go."

"Follow me," Horner said as he walked around the counter and up a flight of stairs. "Maya wants to greet you."

"Great," Moore said as he followed Horner.

"I don't know why she wants to waste her time on you. She's always complaining how overloaded she is."

As they walked down the second floor hallway, Horner advised Moore, "She will talk a lot, so let her. Her need to talk exceeds her need to listen."

When they reached an open area where Simon's executive secretary sat, Horner walked up to the open door to Simon's office.

"Maya," Horner called.

"Yes?"

"I have our visitor if you still want to let him interrupt your day," Horner said scornfully.

"Oh yes! Bring him in," she said as she stood from her chair and bounced around her desk while the two men entered her inner sanctum.

"Emerson, it is so good to see you again," she said as she leaned forward to grasp his right hand warmly with both of her hands and brushed her full lips against his cheek, giving him a light kiss.

Moore blushed momentarily in surprise at her affectionate greeting. "It's nice seeing you, too. I'm really looking forward to the tour."

"I am so glad that you wanted to take a tour of the launch area," she said as she sat on a green leather sofa. She patted the cushion next to her for Moore to sit while Horner sat on a matching sofa across from them.

Simon crossed her long legs as her short skirt rode up, showing her firm thighs. "Are you doing a story on us? Roe told us you were a reporter."

"Not sure. My primary reason for coming over was to see the facility. It's funny that with all of the time I lived in the D.C. area I wasn't aware of this NASA site being so close."

"Not too many people are. Sort of like a secret between lovers," she said seductively. She liked the handsome reporter seated next to her.

"I saw the airport facility and visitor center when I drove over to Chincoteague the other day. I then asked Roe Terry about your facility and he was a wealth of information."

"That Roe is such a sweetheart. I just love that man," she purred as she waved her ring-filled fingers. "You know that he used to work for NOAA over at the airport complex?"

"Yes, he mentioned it," Moore replied as he noticed Maya's expensive purse next to her desk.

"Your conference call is about to start, Maya," Simon's assistant called in from her desk.

"Thank you, Tracey!" Simon turned to Moore, "It's with the head of NASA. They are always calling me for my advice. It just seems that people can't do anything unless they get my advice," she said pretentiously as she uncrossed her legs and stood.

Moore and Horner rose to their feet.

"Now, if you need to know anything about Wallops and our operations, I want you to call me. I will be your primary contact, especially if you want to write a story," she said firmly. It was obvious that she wanted to control whatever was written, or at least attempt to control it.

"I'll do that," Moore affirmed.

"We can meet here in my office or after hours over a drink on Chincoteague," she offered invitingly as she allowed her eyes to give Moore the once over.

"That would be nice. Thank you again, Maya," Moore said as he turned to follow Horner, who had started walking out of the office.

When they reached the hall, Horner looked sternly at Moore. "I see that she's starting to work on her next ex-boyfriend."

"Oh, I don't know about that," Moore retorted.

"That woman is always me-deep in conversation. When we have dignitaries in or the media, she always crowds me out of the spotlight," Horner grumbled.

Moore was caught off-guard by Horner's sarcastic comments about his superior. Not what he expected at all.

"She has her hands full with all of the problems with the explosions," Moore baited Horner as they walked down the steps and out to Horner's SUV.

"That woman hasn't been right about any of her theories about who caused the explosions," Horner said as he entered the vehicle while Moore did the same.

"Now what?" Horner moaned as his cell phone signaled the receipt of a text message. He scrolled down the lengthy message as he read it and then put the cell phone on the console. He was irritated. "I swear that Maya wears dresses shorter than her text messages."

"Something wrong?"

"Usually Maya," he snickered wickedly, surprising Moore. "No, she wanted to remind me that you're to have a first-class tour as if I would give anything but!" he stormed quietly.

Chincoteague Calm

Moore didn't respond as Horner drove across the causeway that linked the launch pad through the marsh to the launch facility. When they drove onto the island, Horner turned left and started the tour on the north end of the island. He showed Moore the old Coast Guard station and the seawall that had been built to stop erosion along the beach for the northern part of the island.

He also droned on about the various facilities such as the rocket motor storage facility, the dynamic balance facility, the assembly shop, the processing facilities, block houses and launch pads. As they neared the southern end of the island, he pointed out the special projects building and the payload processing and firehouse in Building X-15.

"That's our commercial launch pad 0A," Horner said as he stopped the vehicle close to the water tower that loomed over the island and in front of a fire-scorched area.

"Is that where the last rocket blew up?" Moore asked in disbelief as he looked at the area.

"Yes. Another 200 million dollars up in smoke."

"How many times has this happened?" Moore asked.

"That's the third time. We didn't have any problems until that Russian, Chinaman and Syrian arrived here."

"You really think they're involved?"

"I'm positive."

Looking at the devastated launch area, Moore asked, "Was anyone killed during the explosion?"

"No, and no injuries to the ground personnel either. It was an unmanned flight with about 5,000 pounds of food, scientific experiments and other supplies for the International Space Station. The Antares rocket was climbing off the pad and just clearing the top of the water tower when it exploded in a fireball. Pieces and parts flew everywhere. When the rocket fell back to the launch pad, there was a second explosion and a larger fireball. It set the entire area on fire."

"What caused it?"

"Booster integrity failure? Who knows? NASA has a team investigating."

"I can't imagine what you all went through," Moore said sympathetically. "What about the astronauts on the space station. Are they in danger of running out of supplies since they weren't resupplied?"

"No, they have plenty of supplies. The Russians are scheduled to launch a robotic cargo craft in the next month. It will take them a load of supplies." Horner put the SUV in gear and started to drive back up the island. "I'm real suspicious of that Russian Orlov though," Horner added.

"Why?"

"Our original launch date was postponed two days when a boat wandered into the launch safety area offshore."

"I don't see the connection with Orlov," Moore said.

"It was a Russian trawler. We think it had surveillance equipment on board. The Coast Guard ran them off and the launch was scrubbed for two days."

"I see," Moore said.

"Does Vostochny ring a bell with you?" Horner asked.

"Famous Russian cosmonaut?" Moore guessed.

"No," Horner responded with glee, knowing that he knew more than Moore did and he could lord it over Moore. "Vostochny is Putin's pet project. It's a huge cosmodrome complex in the Russian far east. It's built to surpass anything we have in the United States. It costs more than 13 billion dollars and covers 342 square miles. Besides all of the normal facilities to launch rockets, it has seventeen launch pads and housing for 35,000 people. That's where Russia's greatest rocket experts will work and live with their families."

"I'd guess it's built to do more than supply the International Space Station," Moore suggested.

"Vostochny is designed to put Russia head and shoulders ahead of America. They will beat us in establishing a colony on the moon and stage the first manned missions to Mars. They've been launching their Soyuz-2 rocket from that site for a year."

As they neared Building 15, which housed payload processing, they saw Orlov walk out of the building and light a cigarette. Horner drove the SUV over to where Orlov was smoking.

"Hey Sputnik," Horner called in a sarcastic tone.

"What?" Orlov asked icily when he recognized Horner's voice.

Moore could tell that there was no love lost between the two men. The tone of their exchange was as warm as winter in Siberia.

"Make sure you don't throw that butt on the ground when you're done. Use the container," Horner dictated.

Orlov's response was to blow a ring of smoke toward Horner and turn his bushy head away. He stared blankly to his left as he continued to smoke.

Orlov's reaction irritated Horner and he erupted as he drove away. "I swear that when I prove that he's involved with these explosions, I'll have that cosmonaut's cosmo-nuts!"

"Do you have any evidence yet?" Moore asked.

"Not yet, but I'm watching him, that raghead Hala and chinkerbell Tang. I'm convinced that the three of them are in this together. I'm just waiting for Hala to drive up in a land torpedo one day."

The torpedo comment caught Moore's attention. "Land torpedo?"

"Car bomb. What planet have you been living on?" Horner turned his head briefly to look at Moore as they drove onto the causeway toward the main entrance. "Although Orlov may have a shorter life expectation than any of us."

"Why is that? Is he ill?"

"Lovesick is the only illness General Cosmonaut has."

"I don't get it."

"You should. Think back to the night at the Village Restaurant. You were there with Roe Terry."

"Right."

"You didn't notice that Orlov couldn't keep his hands off Hala?"

Moore thought for a moment about what he had observed at the Village Restaurant and then at the Clam Shells Pub. He recalled seeing Hala slapping away Orlov's hands. "Yes, I did now that you mention it. I put it off to excessive drinking."

Horner snickered at the comment. "You ever not see a Russian who drinks excessively? That's normal in their book."

"I wasn't thinking," Moore responded embarrassed.

"Apparently," Horner commented before continuing. "It goes on all the time. She can't get near him without him trying to grope her or making some salacious comment."

"Why don't you do something about it? You head security."

"Security, yes. Not sexual harassment in the workplace. That's Human Resources' job."

"Hasn't it been reported?"

"Of course it has."

"Why hasn't anything been done?"

"It has. The Russians have been contacted, but they're not inclined to do anything, from what I understand."

"And what does Hala say about all of this?"

Chincoteague Calm

"She gets upset. Orlov better be careful. You get them abba-dabbas mad at you, they'll get even with you," Horner said as he pulled into a parking space and turned to face Moore. "That concludes your tour. I've got a lot of work to do, so it's time for me to ignore you."

What a jerk, Moore thought to himself. "Thanks for the tour. I appreciate the insights you gave me." Moore struggled to be gracious as he exited the vehicle.

"You should," Horner cracked as he exited the vehicle and turned his back on Moore as he walked away.

Moore shook his head in disbelief at the man's rudeness. After he walked to the badge office and returned his visitor's badge, Moore drove his car back to Chincoteague Island and Roe Terry's house.

"How did your tour go?" Terry asked when Moore walked into the workshop where Terry was working on a duck carving.

"That was a trip!"

Chuckling, Terry asked, "So you and your buddy Horner really hit it off?"

"Oh yeah, Roe. Right out of the ball park. Grand slam. That guy certainly likes to slam people. I don't think he had a kind word to say about anyone."

"That self-righteous idiot can give a headache to an aspirin," Terry quipped. "I'm surprised that he gave you the time of day, let alone a tour."

"I have Maya to thank for that. Good thing that she found out about my tour and wanted to see me."

"She sweet on you, Emerson?" Terry asked.

"I don't know. She sure is touchy-feely and flirty."

"That's just the way she is," Terry said. "Probably a good thing that she got involved."

"I'll say. I wouldn't have got anywhere with Horner. How does he keep his job with that attitude?"

"He's connected."

"To the mob?"

No," Terry smiled. "His uncle is a Congressman and sits on one of the congressional space committees. Big-time guy. I think NASA is afraid of any repercussions if they took action on Horner."

Moore shook his head from side to side. "The guy's rectally dysfunctional if you ask me."

"Is that a polite way of calling him an ass?" Terry asked with a grin.

"Interpret it as you like, Roe. He gives me the creeps."

"He should. He's the kind of guy who'd kill his mother for the insurance money. What a bag of wind!"

"I'll say." Moore paused as a thought crossed his mind. "Do you think he's involved with the explosions and is diverting attention to Orlov, Tang and Yazbek?"

"I don't know, although that's an interesting thought," Terry said. "I'm not sure what would drive him to do that?"

"Passed over for promotion. Maybe he wanted the job that Maya was promoted to."

"He's not qualified," Terry said as he focused on his carving. "Sometimes, I think you can totally rely upon his incompetence."

"He sure gave Orlov a hard time when we saw him smoking outside the payload processing building."

"Don't read anything into that. You should realize that he gives everyone a hard time. Was he sarcastic the entire time you were with him?" Terry asked.

"Yes."

"He's always like that, which amazes me."

"What do you mean?" Moore queried.

"I don't know how he comes up with his caustic comments so quickly. I've always thought his brain had four speeds—slow, very slow, incredibly slow and slower."

Moore chuckled.

"What do you have on your agenda for the rest of the day?"

"I want to try that restaurant next door to the Clam Shells Pub. It's called Sweet Mama Mary's."

"The old Shucking House. They've got good food there," Terry said. "Do you like clam chowder?"

"Oh yeah!"

"I'd suggest you go to Chatties."

"I think I drove by it. On Main Street?"

"Right. It's above Don's Seafood House. They're both popular island hangouts, especially for the locals."

"I might start there. Would you and Monnie like to join me?"

"We would, but I've got a guy coming over this evening to buy a dozen of my duck decoys. I better be here. And it could take a while. The guy's a talker," Terry explained.

"I'll be thinking about you while I'm downing that clam chowder," Moore teased as he headed toward the door.

"A word of warning."

"Oh?" Moore asked.

"There's a storm heading this way. Should be here around mid-evening and it could be a bad one."

"I've been in bad weather before."

"I wanted to mention it. If it's a big downpour, you'll see flooding on the road. Just be careful," Terry cautioned.

"No problem, but thanks," Moore said as he walked out of the workshop to his car and drove south to Chatties. He was looking forward to the clam chowder.

A few minutes later, he pulled into the parking lot behind the restaurant and climbed the stairs to Chatties. As he entered, he took in the nautical theme and the amazing view onto Chincoteague Bay. When he asked for a window table, the hostess escorted him to the sole vacant table in the restaurant, as it was packed with locals and island visitors.

When a slender server appeared at his table, Moore noted her name on her badge—Ruby. The woman had striking blue eyes and wore her hair pulled up. Moore glanced down at her hand and saw that she was wearing a wedding ring.

"What can I get you?" Ruby asked warmly.

Too bad she's married, Moore thought to himself. "I'd like a rum and Coke."

"Captain Morgan?"

"Perfect. And I'll try a bowl of your clam chowder."

"You won't be disappointed," Ruby said with a smile and she took the menu that he handed her.

"Roe Terry told me to come down here and try it."

"That doesn't surprise me. He loves our clam chowder."

As she walked away, a voice called over to Moore. "Did I hear you mention Roe Terry?"

Moore turned and saw a bearded man approaching him. He appeared to be in his late forties. "Yes. I'm staying at his house."

"And I suppose Roe sent you over here?"

"He did. He said you had great clam chowder and the food was fantastic here," Moore replied.

"That's my Roe. I need to get some business cards printed for him. He could be a good sales rep for me," the man said. He stuck out his hand. "I'm Tom Clark. This is my place."

Chincoteague Calm

"Emerson Moore, Tom," Moore responded as the two shook hands.

"You on vacation?"

"Trying to enjoy some calm in my life and get some fishing in," Moore replied as he nodded.

"Couldn't have picked a better spot to visit," Clark said. "We've got a storm moving in," Clark said as he looked through the window.

Moore turned his head to look at the bay. He could see the sky to the west darkening on the horizon. The storm could hit earlier than Terry had predicted.

"That's what Roe said too."

"We're probably in for a good storm," Clark said as he stroked his beard and Ruby appeared with Moore's drink and chowder.

"I'll let you enjoy your chowder, Emerson. Again, welcome to Chincoteague," Clark said as he excused himself.

The chowder was delicious and a real treat for Moore because it didn't have onions in it. Most clam chowder was cooked with onions and he was allergic to onions. Finishing his meal, he paid his bill and left. He was anxious to get to Sweet Mama Mary's. He drove the short distance north on Main Street and parked in the shared parking lot with Clam Shells Pub in Landmark Plaza.

As Moore walked to the restaurant entrance, he saw in the far distance the faint flickers of lightning in the approaching storm. It reminded him of watching storms quickly move in from the west and sweep across Lake Erie's western basin to offer a brilliant light show to residents and visitors of South Bass Island. He thought of home, and then entered the aged wooden structure where he was promptly escorted to a bayside table by a statuesque and voluptuous server barely twenty-one years old.

Ordering his favorite, rum and Coke, Moore finally relaxed. He enjoyed listening for an hour to an island entertainer who sang a number of tropical tunes. Moore didn't see anyone he recognized in the bar and decided to leave as he now could hear the thunder of the approaching storm.

The air smelled of rain and the lightning was much more intense. As Moore walked next door to the Clam Shells Pub, a light rain began falling and he wished he had brought his umbrella from the car. He thought about running to the vehicle, but decided to take the shorter route into the dry shelter of the pub as a loud thunder clap exploded nearby.

The pub was crowded as patrons who had been seated on the open patio moved inside to avoid the rain. Not seeing a vacant table, Moore instead walked to the bar where he saw Orlov, Tang and Yazbek huddled at the far end.

"Mind if I join you?" Moore asked the three.

"Always room for one more," Yazbek said cheerily.

"Your drink's on me," Tang offered. "I owe you for the other night," he said as he munched on a chicken wing.

"We do owe you," Yazbek said as her soft, deep eyes subtly locked on Moore's. It was obvious that she found Moore attractive.

"What will it be?" the server asked from behind the bar.

"Captain Morgan and Coke," Moore responded. "Thanks," he added as the server walked away. Moore turned and looked at Tang and Yazbek.

He also noticed that Yazbek pushed away Orlov's hand, which had reached down to playfully squeeze her butt. She had a disturbed look on her face that quickly disappeared when she focused on Moore.

"What are you drinking, General?" Moore asked the very quiet Orlov as he tried to engage him.

"I'll give you one guess," Orlov said with a look of disdain. He

Chincoteague Calm

was irritated that Moore had barged in on their gathering.

"I'd guess vodka."

Orlov didn't answer. He just downed his drink. "I'll be back," he said as he ambled off in the direction of the restrooms.

"Is he always so friendly?" Moore asked.

"Piece of work if you ask me," Tang replied.

"He'd like to be a lot friendlier," Yazbek said in exasperation.

"Has a problem with roaming hands?" Moore asked.

Yazbek nodded her head. "You noticed?"

"Couldn't help but notice. He doesn't try to hide it," Moore answered.

"He thinks I'm his entertainment. Russian pig," she said softly as she sipped her coffee.

As Moore looked down, he was surprised to see that Yazbek was wearing a pair of tan cowgirl boots. "You've got cowgirl boots on!" he exclaimed.

Smiling, Yazbek responded, "I do. There'll actually quite comfortable. I wear them all of the time."

"What made you even think about buying a pair?" Moore asked. He was incredulous about a Syrian wearing cowgirl boots.

"I was at the Houston NASA base and co-workers took me out to dinner at a cowboy-style restaurant. It had a shop that sold western wear. They goaded me into trying on a pair. I loved them, so I bought a pair. They are Lucchese boots, hand-crafted and made in Texas."

"Orlov loves her boots," Tang commented.

Moore looked at Yazbek with a quizzed look. "He does?"

"He teases me about them."

"He's always flirting and teasing her," Tang added.

"He is so crude—saying things like, 'Ride me, cowgirl,'" Yazbek recounted in disgust. "One of these days, I'll quit being so reserved around him. His day is coming," she spoke firmly.

"Hey, don't take away my chicken bones," Tang stopped the server who was attempting to take the plate of discarded bones. "Can you bag them up? I'll give them to my Shih Tzu."

"You're giving your dog chicken bones?" Moore asked in disbelief.

"Yes. She loves them."

"You shouldn't do that."

"Why?"

"Dogs can choke on them. They can get pieces of chicken bone stuck in their digestive track and die. You feed them dog food," Moore explained.

"We feed them chicken bones at home," Tang explained.

"And how long do dogs live in China?" Moore asked.

"Two to three years."

"Here in the States, dogs can live fifteen years," Moore explained.

"Oh, no," Tang said seriously. "Meat much too tough then."

Moore grimaced at the response. Before he could say anything more, Orlov returned and Moore engaged him.

"General, the next round is on me."

Orlov wasn't one to pass up a free drink. He motioned to the server and spoke, "Smirnoff, and make it a double."

While the server scurried away, Orlov turned to Moore. "Thank you." Orlov ran his hands over his thick beard as he stared suspiciously at Moore. "And why did you offer a drink? What do you want to know?"

"Nothing, really. Unless you have insight as to what is causing the explosions on Wallops," Moore answered.

"I wonder the same thing. Maybe a UFO is responsible," he

suggested as the server returned and placed Orlov's drink on the bar.

"A UFO?" Moore asked.

"It's possible. Two years ago, the Russian Space Federation conducted an investigation into a Soyuz rocket crash. At first, they thought it was due to sabotage of a bearing unit in the turbine pump assembly. As they investigated, they ruled out sabotage. They examined video footage of the launch. That's when they saw that a UFO had intercepted the rocket and caused the third stage to malfunction."

Tang added to Orlov's explanation. "I remember that incident. The Chinese government collected debris from the crash site in China."

"There shouldn't have been any debris," Orlov objected in his booming voice. "The rocket would have disintegrated upon impact."

Tang ignored Orlov as he continued. "We also found a strange, spherical object near the crash site. It looked like the remnants of a UFO."

"Was it?" Moore asked intrigued.

"The investigation hasn't been finalized," Tang answered.

"Our video showed the trajectory of the UFO that intercepted the rocket. It was forty seconds before the deployment of one of our sophisticated communications satellites," Orlov explained.

"But don't forget that your Deputy Prime Minister and Roskosmos slapped down the idea that a UFO was involved," Tang pointed out.

"What's Roskosmos?" Moore asked.

"That's the Russian space agency," Orlov said with a touch of arrogance.

It was Yazbek's turn to add to the discussion. "There have been a series of failures in Russia's space program."

"Not failures!" Orlov protested. "There were outside factors causing the incidents."

Yazbek ignored Orlov and continued. "Their Mars-Phobos mission was highly touted in the news media. When they launched it, they couldn't boost it out of the Earth's orbit. The rocket and the space probe exploded and plunged back to Earth. That was a loss of 157 million dollars, right General?" Yazbek seemed to enjoy needling Orlov.

Orlov grumbled and threw down half of his vodka.

Yazbek continued. "The Russians lost a military satellite last February. Then another communications satellite had a disastrous launch. And a Soyuz rocket crashed into Siberia minutes after its launch due to rocket failure."

"When the communications satellite failed, a part of eastern Russia lost internet and cell phone communications for a period of time," Tang added.

"It's the UFOs. They're behind all of these incidents," Orlov said weakly. "Or the United States is causing the problems," he added as he glared at Moore.

"That doesn't make sense," Yazbek countered as she defended the U.S. "Since the space shuttle program ended, NASA now relies on the Russian space program to transport astronauts to the International Space Station. Without Russian rockets, the technicians in the space station are marooned. Not only would they lose their lives, but the $100 billion investment in the space station would be lost."

"I think the Chinese are behind the damage to our program," Orlov proposed.

"We are not," Tang retorted strongly.

"Why do you think that the Chinese are behind the sabotage?" Moore asked Orlov.

Chincoteague Calm

"I think I can help with part of the answer," Yazbek said. "The American space program is in flux and Russia is experiencing questions about the reliability of their rocket launches."

"The Chinese are motivated to slow down Russian and U.S. space programs. They have aggressive plans to catch up to, and pass, Russia's and NASA's space technology. Why do you think Tang is here?" Orlov didn't wait for an answer. "He's a spy!"

"I am not!" Tang said very firmly.

"The Chinese aren't hiding their plans to establish bases on the moon. Ask your intelligence agencies. They'll tell you that those bases are going to be military bases," Orlov said triumphantly.

"Ever since the launch of Dongfanghong 1 in 1970, we've launched hundreds of satellites. Not one was a threat. They were for communications, disaster monitoring, weather and navigation purposes," Tang responded defensively.

"And spying," Orlov added. "We all have spy satellites up there. Who are you trying to fool? Not us Russians."

Tang ignored Orlov's comment. "We've landed on the moon. We launched a robotic lander in 2016 to explore the moonscape," he said proudly.

"The Chinese have had several manned flights," Orlov said all-knowingly. "Their Shenzhou-11 with two taikonauts on board launched in 2016 from the Jiuquan Satellite Launch Center. They're testing space modules so they can build their own space station."

"Another flawless launch," Tang said proudly. "That's why I can help stop the problems here. It takes Chinese know-how."

"Flawless launch, maybe—and unlike the failures NASA has experienced here," Orlov said. Orlov turned to look at Yazbek. "And don't forget about our friends in the Mideast."

"What do you mean?" Yazbek asked.

"The United Arab Emirates has a long-range plan to build a

fully-functioning city for 600,000 people on Mars in the next century. They call it Mars 2117. And with their oil reserves, they can afford it."

"I'm aware of the announcement," Yazbek said coolly, "but I don't work for them."

"Or so she says," Orlov said as he arched one bushy eyebrow. He turned and looked directly at Moore. "Do you know what I've renamed the Wallops Island program?"

"No," Moore answered.

"Red, white and boom!" Orlov snorted at his joke. His snort was followed by a nearby crack of lightning that caused the lights in the bar to dim and brighten.

"I'm ready to go," Orlov said after downing the rest of his drink.

"I guess we have to go," Yazbek said as Tang waved the server over to settle their bill. "The General is the driver."

In more ways than one, Moore thought to himself as he looked at Orlov.

"I am tired and want to go before the storm gets worse," Orlov explained.

"Thanks for the insight, everyone," Moore said as he stood and they exchanged farewells.

The three walked toward the restaurant's exit. Before going out into the driving rain, Moore observed Orlov attempting to pat Yazbek's butt as she passed in front of him. She quickly swatted away his hand and Moore saw her give Orlov a menacing glare.

Orlov had better be careful, Moore thought to himself. Sam Duncan once had told him tales about how deadly Syrian women could be. When Moore turned back to the bar, he noticed that Bullet had magically appeared.

"What a downpour," Bullet said.

Moore looked him over and noticed that he was dry. He must have been in the bar for some time, somewhat ahead of the storm. The strong odor of alcohol in his breath confirmed Moore's thoughts.

"New walker?" Moore asked as he looked at the pink walker that Bullet was pushing.

"Don't even start," Bullet said in an irritated tone. "A lady friend loaned me this one until I can get a new one next week."

"The color becomes you," Moore teased.

Bullet glared at Moore without making a retort.

"You see Floyd tonight?" Moore asked.

"No. I imagine he's under his lean-to," Bullet answered, referring to the small shed that protected the infamous goat from the elements. "I saw you talking to the foreigners," Bullet remarked.

"Interesting group. Do they come in here often?"

"I see them here one or two times a week," Bullet said before taking a sip of his beer.

"Hello," a voice purred behind Moore.

Moore turned to see a slightly built woman in her late twenties with bleached blond hair. Her pale skin seemed untouched by the sun. She had sea-green eyes and too much to drink as she fought to maintain her balance.

She lost the battle and lurched into Moore, who caught her.

"Steady there," Moore said as he tried to help her stand.

"You rescued me!" She kissed him lightly on the cheek, then licked her lips provocatively as she stared at Moore.

Out of the corner of his eye, Moore noticed Bullet shaking his head negatively.

"You need to go back to your boyfriend," Bullet interjected.

"Oh, but I think I like this one better," she said as she draped her arm around Moore's shoulder and leaned against him. Suddenly her demeanor changed when Bullet ran his walker hard over her sandal-clad foot.

"Ouch! What are you doing?" She glowered at Bullet.

"Sorry. My bad," Bullet said feigning concern.

Peeved, the woman pulled away from Moore and started to wobble her way through the crowd. "I know when I'm not wanted."

"What was that all about?" Moore asked.

"That's Kelly O'Brien. I'd advise you to stay away from that one," Bullet warned.

"Why?"

"You remember the Kronsky brothers? You had that fight with them the other night."

"Yes."

"One of them is her boyfriend. Hanging with her is nothing but trouble."

"I believe it. Thanks for extricating me from a potential problem."

"Sure. I figure I owe you."

The sound of thunder overhead and the rain drumming on the roof caught Moore's attention.

"I'd better head out before it gets much worse."

"If you're wanting to see a beautiful sight, drive down to Curtis Merritt Harbor. It's a great view of lightning from there. Sort of like the Fourth of July."

"Thanks, Bullet. I think I'll do that." Moore turned and made his way through the crowd to the exit. He kept an eye out for the Kronsky brothers, but didn't see them. When he walked through the door, he made a beeline through the rain for his car. He was just in time as the sky opened up and the rain turned into a tropical downpour.

Moore turned on his windshield wipers and headlights as he drove slowly through the torrential inundation toward the harbor. There was hardly any traffic and rain was accumulating in low spots on the road.

With the rain beating on his convertible roof, he drove south out of the downtown area and past Captain Bob's Marina. He noticed the door to Bo White's home was open and warm light penetrated the darkness. He continued driving slowly until he reached the harbor, where he parked on the far side and watched the lightning flashes.

After twenty minutes, Moore was ready to drive back to Roe Terry's house and call it a night. He pulled out of the parking lot and made his way north. When he neared Captain Bob's Marina, he acted on a whim and turned into the parking lot. He parked next to White's container home and exited the car, holding his umbrella over his head.

As he walked under the covered porch area, he saw the smoldering coals in the outdoor grill. A steak was burning. Must be dinner time, Moore thought as he looked toward the open door.

"Bo? Bo?" he called.

There was no answer. Figuring that White might have gone to the nearby restroom, Moore leaned against the wall and waited. When five minutes elapsed, Moore decided to help out White with his steak and flipped it onto a plate he found near the grill. He also walked over to the open doorway and peaked in. There was no sign of White.

Holding his umbrella, Moore walked to the corner of the building and looked toward the bay. That's when he saw a strong beam of light penetrating the rain. He watched the light, but it didn't move.

"Bo? Bo?" Moore called again. He thought he heard a faint reply through the rain.

A crack of lightning lit up the sky as he decided to walk down to the edge of the bay. Neither the drenching rain, ominous thunder nor bright flashes of lightning was any deterrent to the prowling Moore. His curiosity was soaring.

As he neared the water, Moore could make out a long wooden pier that jutted at a right angle to the shore, disappearing in the rain. He saw the source of the light he had seen from White's home. It was the powerful beam of a flashlight on the ground. Strange, Moore thought to himself as he picked it up and pointed it at the pier.

Squinting his eyes to pierce the murky darkness, he walked onto the pier as the old and weathered planks creaked below his feet. The pier smelled of mold and seaweed.

Then Moore spotted two planks which had splintered and left a large gap in the decking. He flashed the light's beam toward it and heard a muffled voice.

"Who's up there?"

Moore recognized Bo White's voice. "Bo, it's Emerson Moore," he said as he advanced carefully and directed the beam through the opening. He saw White. He was upside down. His body was contorted and immobilized with his head and upper body on the muddy bottom.

"Good thing for you that the tide was running out. Otherwise, you'd have drowned," Moore said as he knelt carefully on the pier.

"I would have managed all right by myself; but since you're here, I'll let you help out," White retorted pragmatically.

"How do you feel? Are you in any pain?" Moore asked.

"My ankle," White responded as he tried again to reach his ankle to free it. It had become trapped by the broken lumber and seaweed. White groaned when he moved.

Moore closed his umbrella and reached under the pier to break free the broken pieces of lumber that had snared White's leg as he shone the flashlight on the ankle.

"Looks like you've got some nails embedded in your ankle along with it being pinned."

"Use both hands, Emerson. Just pull it all away and don't worry about me."

Moore set the flashlight down, reached through the opening and felt for the splintered wood. Using both hands, he suddenly pulled upward, causing White to shriek in pain as the nails cut a bloody path through his ankle flesh and the ankle came free. White's body tumbled to the mud and he lay for a few moments, gasping for breath.

"You okay?" Moore asked as he picked up the flashlight and directed it at White who was trying to push himself to a sitting position.

"Yeah, I'm fine. Give me a minute and I'll be able to stand."

Moore unbuckled his belt and made it into a loop. He then moved to the edge of the pier and advised White, "When you're ready, you can grab hold of this belt and I can help pull you to your feet. Sorry about the pain I caused you."

"I'm fine, like I said." White paused as thunder and lightning again cracked overhead. "I don't think you should pull me onto that pier. It's too unstable. I should have repaired it weeks ago. No one uses it."

"We'll get you to your feet and you hold onto one end of the belt for support and we both can walk toward the shore. Me on the pier and you in the mud."

"That might work," White said as he reached up to grab the loop.

Moore picked up the folded umbrella and held it in the same hand as the flashlight as the two men cautiously made their way to shore. It was a slow process as White endured the agonizing discomfort from his bleeding ankle.

When they reached the end of the pier and the shore, Moore walked around and helped White step out of the mud onto the firm ground. "Put an arm around my shoulder and I'll walk you the rest of the way home," Moore instructed White.

The deluge was heavy and washed away the mud that covered White. Moore's clothes were soaked as if he had fallen off the causeway bridge. The temperature had dropped and Moore felt a shiver run through his chilled body.

Nearing White's place, Moore smelled the smoke from the burning charcoal grill. The two men walked into the container home, where Moore eased White onto a well-worn recliner.

"I'll get some hot water and we can clean up that ankle," Moore offered.

"I don't have any here," White said. He pointed through the driving rain at the nearby restrooms. "You can get some there. There's a bucket you can use," he said as he pointed to a corner of the room.

"Do you have a first aid kit?"

"No. There's one inside the office, but it's locked up and I don't have a key."

"I've got one in the trunk of my car. I'll grab it while I'm getting the water. I'll be right back." Moore grabbed the bucket and headed back out into the rain. He returned in a few minutes with the bucket of hot water and first aid kit. He set it on the floor in front of White.

Seeing a towel on the back of a chair, Moore grabbed it and knelt down in front of White. Wetting the towel, he raised White's ankle. He saw that White's trouser leg was ripped from the hem upwards for eight inches. Moore rolled up the material and looked at the leg.

"Let's see what we have here," Moore said as he began washing the remaining blood from the ankle.

"It's nothing more than a scratch," White grumbled as he twitched involuntarily when Moore touched one of the punctures. He didn't like anyone making a fuss over him.

"Doesn't look too bad. Bleeding has stopped. Might have a couple of good gouges here," Moore said as he looked at the ankle. "You might need a tetanus shot to be on the safe side."

"I don't need any shots," White countered as Moore applied first aid cream to the ankle and wrapped it with gauze from his first aid kit.

"How about a shot of whiskey?"

"I don't drink."

Moore was stunned by what he heard. "Wait a minute, I saw you buying a twelve-pack at the Clam Shells Pub the other night."

"Doesn't mean I drink it."

"What about all of those beer cans that people find outside this container? I heard that you pile them up."

"Emerson, things aren't always what they seem." White's face had a conspiratorial look. "You want to know what those empty beer cans are all about?"

"Yes."

"You can't tell anyone. Can I count on you keeping it between us?" White felt like he owed Moore some insight since he rescued him.

"Sure," Moore answered, eager to learn more.

"I do it to keep people away from me. Sometimes I sell it to visiting fishermen as long as they give me the empties back. It works. People think I'm a weird drunk and they don't come around here at night to bother me." He eyed Moore carefully. "At least normal people stay away."

"You saying I'm not normal?" Moore asked good-naturedly.

"You're mighty defensive, son. Did I hit a nerve?" White chuckled.

"But Donna told me she smelled beer on you."

White smiled. "Good to know. Sometimes I pop a can and pour some on my clothes so people think I'm drinking it. Glad to know it worked."

Moore shook his head.

"There's an extra towel over there if you want to get out of them clothes and dry off. I can loan you some clothes as long as you bring them back," White offered.

"I am cold," Moore said as he set aside any pretense of modesty and joined White in shucking their clothes, drying off and slipping into dry clothing.

"There's some coffee in that pot. I made it about an hour ago if you'd like a warm-up."

"Sure." Moore stood and walked over to the Mr. Coffee coffeemaker and poured himself a cup. "You want one?"

"That would be nice," White responded. "And thank you for finding me. I could have drowned out there when the tide came in."

"No problem. Glad I could help."

"I'm curious. What made you stop, especially on a night like this?"

"Don't know. Your open door and light beckoned me. Maybe an angel sent me your way," Moore said as he poured the coffee.

"Maybe. Maybe," White repeated himself as he stared at Moore.

Moore poured two cups of coffee. "How do you take yours?"

"Black."

"I should have guessed," Moore chuckled as he returned to White and handed him his coffee.

"Hey, I almost forgot. I pulled your steak off the grill. You want it? Although it's probably cold."

"Don't bother me none. I'll share it with you," White offered.

"Thanks, but I already had dinner. Had clam chowder at Chatties," Moore said as he walked over to get the steak.

"They have good clam chowder there," White said as he watched Moore find him a fork and knife before handing the steak to White.

Moore dropped into another worn chair and said, "There is something that I'd like to ask you about."

"What's that?" White asked as he took his first bite of the steak.

"When we neared the shore, I saw the outline of something pulled up under the dock. It was covered in camouflage netting. What was that?"

A scowl crossed White's face. "What that is, is none of your business."

Moore crinkled his forehead. He wondered why the relaxed White suddenly turned from being affable to going quite cold.

Before Moore could continue, White asked him, "You said you were a reporter, didn't you?"

"Yes. I told you when we first met."

"Tell me about some of the stories you've worked on," White said with a faint groan as he moved his ankle and settled back in his chair.

For the next thirty minutes, Moore ran through some of the

adventures he had written about, including human trafficking, breaking a secret code, a murder trial in Detroit, a Wall Street takeover attempt, German U-boats and terrorist plots.

"You're lucky to be alive," White observed.

"Yes. I've had some close calls."

"You married? Got kids?"

Moore briefly related the tragic death of his wife and son on the bridge between D.C. and Alexandria some years ago. He also told White about his struggle with alcoholism and how he now manages his liquor intake. The heart-rending death of his wife and son seemed to strike home with White, who became somewhat melancholy.

With downcast eyes, White spoke. "I lost my wife years ago due to a divorce."

"I'm sorry."

"I guess it was for the best. But I lost my only son six months ago."

"That had to be tough, Bo," Moore sympathized.

"Words can't describe what a loss it was for me." White looked over the rim of his coffee cup as he tried to decide how much he trusted Moore. He was getting very comfortable with the reporter and his level of respect for him was growing. He decided to open up.

"My son was only twenty-five-years-old. Tomorrow would have been his twenty-sixth birthday." The remorse was etched into White's face. "He was murdered at the Food Lion on Wallops. Bullet to the back of the skull," White blurted out.

"I am so sorry," Moore commiserated with White. "Did they catch the murderer?"

"No, that's why I'm here. I'm going to find out who did it," White said with a firm look of determination in his eyes.

Chincoteague Calm

"Are you working with the police?"

"No. And I don't want you to tell anyone what I'm telling you or you won't be seeing any more tomorrows."

"I don't get it. Why are you telling me anything?" Moore asked, bewildered.

"I liked what I heard from you. You sound like you have a lot of integrity. You're the kind of person that people can trust."

"I've heard that before," Moore agreed.

"Plus, I liked your story about training with a guy from Army Special Forces. I'm a vet and served in Special Forces," White said proudly.

Moore nodded in understanding. "Why aren't you working with the police here? I've met Chief Deere and he seems like a good guy."

"They had their chance. Now it's my turn. No one knows that Jason was my son. I can snoop around and do things that the police can't."

"Did your son work at Food Lion?"

"No, he worked at the NASA site on Wallops Island in the payload processing building."

"What?" Moore was stunned by the revelation.

"Yes. He was so excited. He was onto what was causing the rocket explosions on the island and wanted to be the one who revealed it to the authorities."

"Did he tell you?"

"No. I got some bits and pieces. I know it had something to do with a foreigner. And I know that he was focused on a foreign woman older than himself. I believe it was that Yazbek woman."

"Why her?"

"Do you know of any other foreign woman over there?"

"No, but I don't know all of the foreigners over there."

"She's the only one I know of."

"You know that the Russian general is after her?"

"Yes. I've seen her push him away."

"At the Clam Shells Pub?" Moore asked.

"No. On Wallops."

Moore was surprised by the answer. "On Wallops? You go to Wallops?"

White didn't respond right away. He eyed Moore carefully as he decided if he was going to share his clandestine secret. He decided to go ahead. "I do."

"They let you in so you can conduct the investigation into your son's death?" Moore asked incredulously.

"No. I let myself in," White smiled.

"Bo, I don't get it. What are you telling me?" Moore pushed for an explanation.

"That so-called thing that you saw under the dock."

"Yes?"

"That's my way in. It's a layout boat. The kind duck hunters use. It's a low- profile boat which is exactly what I need."

"A low-profile boat. Why don't you use a bigger boat?"

"The Wallops security team would spot me. They run radar and I'd get picked up."

"I see. Like that Russian trawler that crossed into the launch zone."

"Exactly. I don't want to alert anyone that I'm poking around in their backyard."

"That's a long way to go if you're paddling."

"I have a motor on the boat."

"Won't they hear it?"

"It's electric. Quietest motor you would never hear." White grinned proudly. "Besides, I use the tide to help me."

"How's that?"

"I go through the bay as the tide runs out and come back when the tide runs back in."

"That works," Moore said as he acknowledged White's efficiency.

"I go through the marsh to Bogues Bay."

"Do you go to the old Coast Guard station there?"

"No, it's too far away from the payload processing building. I go down Cat Creek. There's a small channel that runs right up to Bypass Road. I hide my boat in the marsh and sneak across the road. You come right up on the payload processing building."

"Do you go in the building?" Moore asked.

"No. I conduct surveillance on the building. You'd be surprised what you see."

"What's that?"

"I see Yazbek and Orlov sneaking over at night. They go into that building."

"Romantic rendezvous?" Moore asked half-jokingly.

"Orlov would like that, if he had his way. They don't go together to the building, so I doubt it. Sometimes I wonder if he isn't spying on her."

"What makes you think that?"

"From what I've seen, it looks like he follows her at a discreet distance. I'm not sure that she knows he's doing that," White said before draining the remainder of his coffee in his cup. He set the cup on the floor and looked at Moore for a few seconds as he made a decision. "How would you like to come with me one night?"

Moore thought for a moment before answering. "I'd be interested. You never know what another pair of eyes can pick up."

White smiled. "That's true. Maybe tomorrow night. We'll see what the weather is like and the conditions in the bay. If it's rough, I don't go. Too much of a chance of the layout boat getting swamped."

"Sure."

"Sounds like the rain is letting up."

Moore had become so engrossed in their conversation that he hadn't paid attention to the waning storm. He could hear that the thunder had moved eastward over the ocean.

"I should go," Moore said as he stood. Seeing a small notebook, Moore walked over and picked up a nearby pen. He jotted his cell number on a page. "Now you've got my number. Just give me a call when you want to go. I'm staying at Roe Terry's place. You know Roe?"

"No, but I heard Donna talk about him. Sounds like he's good people."

"He is. One of the most interesting characters I've encountered in my career, but he's the real deal," Moore confirmed.

"How many days are you staying on the island?"

"I don't know. I don't have a set schedule. Maybe three or four days more. I'd really like to get to the bottom of what's causing the explosions," Moore said as he stood and picked up his wet clothes and first aid kit. "I'll return these clothes," he said.

"No hurry."

Moore walked to the doorway and looked at the rain, which had changed to a light shower.

"Emerson," White called.

Moore turned and looked back at White, "Yes, Bo?"

"Thank you. I'm glad you came along and even more glad that we got a chance to talk man-to-man," White said in a serious tone.

"I am too, Bo," Moore said before turning and walking through the rain to his car. He was very satisfied with what he had learned from White. He actually liked the guy even more as a result of their conversation. At the same time, he was disappointed to learn that Yazbek might be involved in the rocket explosions. Not what he wanted to hear about the attractive woman.

He started his car and slowly drove north to Roe Terry's house. He was startled by the amount of standing water in the road, but then realized how low the island's elevation was. It would take a while for the water to drain.

When he reached Terry's house, the lights were out except for one in the kitchen. Moore let himself in and walked to his room. He was bushed.

CHAPTER 12

The Next Morning
Roe Terry's House

"Coffee?" Monnie asked Moore as he wandered into the kitchen.

"I'd love a cup," Moore said as he dropped into a chair and Monnie poured a cup for him and placed it on the table.

"You slept in this morning," she said as she settled in a chair across the table from Moore.

"I'll say," her husband said as he walked into the kitchen. "I've been up for two hours, carving up a storm."

"Long night," Moore said.

"Emerson, do you want to tell us more or keep it a secret?" Terry asked with a grin.

"Hush, Roe. Maybe he met a lady last night," Monnie suggested.

"Was she a keeper or did you throw her back in?" Terry asked good-humoredly.

"No. No," Moore protested. "I wish it was something as simple as that." Moore weighed what he should tell them about the previous evening's adventure before he continued. "I ran into Orlov, Tang and Yazbek last night."

"Now she's a keeper, that Yazbek," Terry teased.

"Roe! Let the man talk," Monnie mildly admonished her husband.

"Actually, it was an interesting conversation. I learned a little about each of their respective space programs."

"They're all three spies if you ask me," Terry interrupted.

Moore continued with his story and related the rescue of Bo White, but left out any reference to the murder of White's son or White's night trips to Wallops. Moore was discreet and didn't want to break the confidence that he had built with White.

"They should have torn down that pier or rebuilt it. He was lucky you came along when you did," Terry said.

"Yes. He was in a tough spot. I bet he'll be out there today repairing it."

"What do you have planned for today?" Terry asked noticing that Moore was dressed in a t-shirt and running shorts. "Going for a run?"

"Yes. I thought I'd head out to the beach on Assateague and run there. I need to clear my mind and there's something magnetic about that beach that attracts me."

"One of the most pristine beaches on the East Coast," Terry said proudly.

"I agree. I love the lack of commercialization. And early in the morning, there's hardly anyone there."

Terry glanced at his watch. "I wouldn't call this early. It's a little after nine A.M."

"Roe used to jog on that beach almost every morning," Monnie interjected with a sly look on her face.

"You did?" Moore was surprised.

Terry nodded his head. He knew what was coming next.

"What made you quit?" Moore asked.

Terry looked at his wife. He knew that she wanted to provide the answer, and she did.

"The police got wind of a local woman who liked to run nude on the beach early in the morning and busted her. It seems that a lot of the local guys knew about her before the police did and started running there. A lot of the wives on the island were wondering why their husbands got such an exercise bug. They were up early and running on the beach after her. They all stopped after she was fined and quit running. Right, Roe?"

"I don't know anything about that," Terry countered with a sly grin.

"That's the answer all of the wives got from their husbands!" Monnie snickered.

Moore stood and walked to the sink where he placed his empty coffee cup. "I'll keep my eye out for any nude runners."

"I'm sure you will. Just don't tell Roe when you get back."

"That might be a bit difficult, too," Terry added.

"How's that?" Moore asked.

"Monnie and I are headed over to a duck decoy show in Baltimore later this morning. We'll be gone for a couple of days, but feel free to make yourself at home."

"I can grab a hotel room," Moore offered.

"No. No. You stay here and we'll see you when we get back," Terry insisted.

"Just don't bring any nude runners over here," Monnie teased.

"Right. Wait until I get back from Baltimore, then bring them over," Terry laughed before adding. "As long as they're female."

Moore shook his head and headed out the door for his car. He drove out to Assateague Beach, avoiding the remaining large puddles of rain on the roadway. He parked his car at the far end of the beach parking lot and walked through the thick sand to the water's edge. He began to jog as he headed south in the cloudless morning. Much to his disappointment, he didn't see any nude female runners that morning.

An hour later, Moore was back in the Mustang. He had grabbed a towel and toweled off the drops of sweat. He sat in the car and lowered the convertible's top so that he could enjoy the fresh ocean air as he drove off Assateague Island. He crossed the causeway onto Chincoteague Island and drove along Maddox Boulevard.

He spotted a sign in front of the locally popular Maria's Family Restaurant which advertised their breakfast buffet. Realizing he hadn't eaten, he pulled into the restaurant's white limestone parking lot. Exiting his car, he walked into the gray one-story building and asked for a table near the buffet area.

Famished from the prior night's activities and the morning run, Moore loaded up his plate with scrambled eggs, sausage links, pancakes, French toast and slices of pineapple and watermelon. He washed the food down with a glass of orange juice and two cups of coffee.

As Moore drained the last of the coffee, his server approached.

"How did you enjoy your breakfast?" the server asked as he placed the check on the table.

"Tasty. Absolutely tasty," Moore smiled. "I feel like I need to take another run because I ate so much," he added as he looked around the crowded restaurant.

"Glad you enjoyed it," the server said as he turned away to take the order from a nearby table.

Moore picked up his bill and walked over to the cashier. There were two female patrons in line and Moore overheard them talking.

"Sabotage! Are they sure?" one asked.

"That's what my brother told me when he came home from his night shift," the other replied.

"I hope they find whoever is responsible and throw away the key," the first one said as she paid her bill.

"I bet Horner is all over this," the second woman said as the two walked out of the restaurant.

Moore quickly paid his bill and walked outside where he pulled out his cell phone and called Maya Simon. She answered the phone on the third ring.

"Maya Simon," her voice said in a very professional tone.

"Maya, it's Emerson Moore."

Simon's tone changed immediately. It sounded sultry. "Emerson, it's nice to hear your voice," she purred. "How have you been?"

Ignoring her tone, Moore said, "I heard that there's been a problem with sabotage at the facility."

"My, word gets around fast. We haven't said anything to the press," she replied as her tone became more businesslike.

"I heard a couple of people at breakfast talking about it," Moore explained.

"I see. They need to be more careful talking about our issues," she said thinking that the two were employees.

"What happened?"

"Hal Horner's team discovered it during a check of the pre-launch systems. They called Hal over and he confirmed their suspicions. It was sabotage."

"What exactly happened?" Moore pushed for a better explanation.

"The angular velocity sensors were installed incorrectly. They were installed upside down and it looked like someone took a hammer to them to smash them into position."

"You're talking in a foreign language to me. What are angular velocity sensors?" Moore asked.

"They are sensors in the guidance system which transmit data to the flight control system about the position of the rocket. When incorrect data is transmitted, the rocket can swing wildly as it tries to make the correction and crashes," Simon explained.

"I would have thought something like this would have been caught by quality control."

"They would have been unless someone took action after the quality control inspection. Horner checked the paper trail and it shows that all inspections were conducted properly and by two people each time."

"Sounds like someone went in there and reinstalled those sensors."

"That's what Hal and I think," Simon said.

"Don't you have surveillance cameras set up inside your facilities?" Moore asked.

"No, but we are thinking about it. I'm just glad that Hal's team found the sabotage before launch time." Simon paused before adding, "It was my idea that he expand his security team's scrutiny of our operations. I made sure the head honchos at NASA knew that it was my idea."

Moore shook his head as he thought about how full of herself she was. He was also beginning to wonder about Horner. Was Horner more involved with the sabotage than he let on?

"Maya, I have a favor to ask," Moore started.

"Ask away, my dear," she responded.

"Could I come over and interview Horner?"

"Well, I'm not sure," Simon replied. "We haven't released anything to the press."

"I'd really like to get the jump on this if I could. Especially since I'm the first one to call you. Right? No one else from the media has contacted you?"

"That's right."

Moore played to her ego. "I could interview you and Horner and put a positive spin on how proactive the security team has become under your leadership."

Simon thought for a moment. She was being offered a unique opportunity and one where she thought she could exert control. "Okay. When can you be here?"

"About an hour?"

"Make it two hours. I'll let Horner know you're coming."

"Great. I'll see you then."

"Make it my office. You do remember how to get to my office, right Emerson?" Her tone had shifted again back to sultry.

"How could I forget, Maya?" Moore asked as they ended the call. He entered his car and drove to Terry's house to shower and change.

Two hours later, Moore parked his car on Wallops Island and entered the badge room where he was badged and escorted to Simon's office.

"Emerson, how nice to see you again," Simon said as she walked around her desk and hugged Moore tightly while giving him a brief kiss on the cheek.

"Thanks for letting me come over," Moore said as she released him and walked back to her desk. As she sat, she motioned to Moore to sit in one of the two visitor chairs in front of her desk.

"Any time. I want to do everything I can to help you with your story," she said as she pushed a file across her desk toward Moore. "Here's some background info on the angular velocity sensors."

"Thank you. That will save me time," Moore said appreciatively as he picked up the file and glanced through it.

"I also crafted several quotes from me that you can feel free to use," she added as she smiled demurely from behind her desk.

"Any quotes here from Horner?" Moore asked as he looked closer at the file's contents.

"Oh, you don't need any from him. Just use mine," she said with a wave of her ring-filled hand.

"But I thought his team found the sabotage," Moore said, wanting a quote from Horner.

"They did, but no need to put them in the limelight," Simon explained selfishly.

"I can always get a quote from Horner when I talk to him," Moore suggested.

The niceties disappeared as Simon leaned forward with a clouded look on her face. "I do not want you using any quotes from Horner. Is that clear?"

Realizing that he had pushed the wrong button, Moore backpedaled. "That is clear, Maya," he said quickly.

"Good," Simon said as she settled back in her chair and her appearance returned to normal.

"I saw a comment in the file that you are having employees take lie detector tests."

"That's correct. Anyone involved in the launch or having access to that building will be tested."

"How about your international visitors?"

"They will be tested too, although we are having some problems with Orlov who is trying to declare diplomatic immunity. What a joke!" she said as she wrinkled her brow.

"Interesting. You think he doesn't want to submit because he had a hand in the sabotage?"

"Who knows. That man is just difficult."

"How about Horner and his team?"

"Whatever for?"

"They have access, right?"

"Yes."

"It just seems that you'd want to test them, too."

"That's not necessary. I am confident that they wouldn't be involved." She leaned forward again. "Why do you ask?"

"I thought you'd rather be safe and leave no stone unturned," Moore suggested.

A contemplative look crossed Simon's face. "Emerson, that's not a bad idea. Let's see what the initial results show and then I can decide on the next steps."

"Sounds good to me."

"Emerson, I don't want the mention of lie detector testing to appear in any story," she warned.

"I understand."

"And one more thing, Emerson."

"Yes?"

"I'd like to see the story before you run it."

"I can't do that."

"Why?" she asked.

"We have a policy. No pre-approvals of stories."

"What if you get your story wrong?"

"We're very careful," Moore answered.

A knock at the door interrupted them. They looked toward the doorway and saw Horner standing there.

"Hal, perfect timing. Would you mind taking Emerson over to the pre-launch building and showing him the sensors that were installed upside down?"

"Yes," Horner replied with a cold stare. He didn't like the nosy reporter intruding in his backyard.

Horner's lack of hospitality was not lost on Moore. Moore realized that Horner didn't like him poking around Wallops Island and wondered why.

"Emerson, you'll have to excuse Hal. He's up to his balls in alligators right now." Turning to Horner, she said, "Hal, you don't have to give Emerson an interview or any quotes. I've taken care of all that. Just take him out and show him the sensors and bring him back so he can file his story."

As Simon stood and walked around her desk, Moore also stood. Simon leaned forward and gave Moore a parting kiss on the cheek. "If you have any questions while you are writing your story, please give me a call. I can make myself very available," she said with a husky voice.

The innuendo was not lost on Moore. "Thank you, Maya. I'll do that," Moore said as he walked to the doorway to join Horner.

"You know I live on Chincoteague if you need to meet me after work for more questions," she added.

"I'll keep that in mind," Moore said as he followed Horner into the hallway and to his vehicle.

As they settled into Horner's SUV, Horner, who had been uncharacteristically silent, spoke. "How many times do I have to flush you before you go away?"

Moore was caught off guard, but reacted quickly. "I'm sorry you feel that way."

"You're validating my inherent mistrust of strangers," Horner said coldly.

The two rode in silence to their destination. When they arrived, Horner parked the SUV and the two walked into the building. Moore followed Horner to a small room where a security guard blocked the entrance.

"Unfortunately, he's okay," Horner said to the guard who stepped aside, allowing Horner and Moore to enter.

Horner led Moore to a worktable which contained various parts for the missile. Pointing inside an open compartment on one section, Horner said, "You can see the angular velocity sensors here. They're inserted upside down."

Moore moved closer and pulled his cell phone from his pocket. He wanted to snap a photo.

"No pictures!" Horner bellowed when he saw Moore point the cell phone camera at the sensors. Suddenly, Horner shoved Moore toward the exit door. "We're done here," he grumbled.

"I'm sorry. I didn't know," Moore's words tumbled out of his mouth.

"Didn't you notice the signs on the entrance? No photos. No cameras. What's so difficult to understand about those instructions, brainless?" Horner stormed as he walked out of the building with Moore.

"I didn't notice them," Moore explained meekly.

"Just get in my vehicle. Your tour is finished," Horner said as the two entered his SUV and they drove in silence to the main gate. Moore turned in his visitor badge and drove off Wallops.

While Moore drove, his mind raced. He thought about Horner's rude reaction, the new developments on Wallops and the possible identity of the saboteur. He reached for his cell phone to make two calls. One call was to his editor, John Sedler, to update him. The other call was to Bo White. He asked White if he could accompany him that night to Wallops and White agreed.

When Moore arrived at the Terry house, he sat at his laptop and began writing about the sabotage at Wallops. He referred to the information that Simon had provided him and was surprised to find that she had included a flash drive with additional information as well as several photos of herself to use when he submitted the story. Simon was a very self-serving woman and Moore knew that she had a romantic interest in him. He wasn't interested. She wasn't his type.

CHAPTER 13

Later That Night
Captain Bob's Marina

"You sure you want to go?" White asked Moore after Moore parked his Mustang close to White's dwelling.

"Definitely. I'd like to find out who's causing the sabotage on Wallops," Moore answered.

"I'm confident that there's a link to my son's death. I just haven't caught them yet, but I will," White said firmly.

"If you're ready, follow me. Tide's running out in about fifteen minutes." White looked overhead. "And we should have good cloud cover tonight. You never want to do this on a clear night when the moon can light you up."

"I bet," Moore agreed.

The two men, dressed in black, walked behind White's home and down to the dock at the water's edge.

"I see you fixed the dock," Moore said as he peered through the night.

"The next day," White confirmed as he carefully reached for the ten-foot layout boat and began to pull her out from underneath the dock.

"Looks pretty low to me. You sure she'll hold both of us?"

"No problem. This is a Bankes layout. It's built for two duck hunters to use. They're low-profile and the color blends right in with the water. You can kill a ton of ducks from one of these."

"Is she stable?"

"No worry there. She's designed to be a stable shooting platform," White assured Moore. "But she doesn't do well in rough water," he added. "The waves could swamp her."

Noticing the electric motor, Moore said, "You mentioned that you installed that motor. What kind of motors do these boats typically use?"

"They don't."

"They don't?" Moore asked.

"That's right. There's a stainless bow eye bolted at each end that you can use for anchoring. Usually you use the bow eye for towing the boat near the area you want to hunt. But we can't get a big boat close to Wallops. They'd pick it up on their radar."

"What about heat-sensing radar? You'd think they might have those around the island," Moore suggested.

"They do. But I have a tarp that's been coated on both sides with a reflective paint. It doesn't allow your body heat or any heat from the motor to escape."

"Good planning."

"You got to think things through, Emerson. That's what I learned from my training."

"I can see it's paid off for you," Moore agreed.

As the two men pushed the boat into the water, White instructed Moore, "Jump in."

Moore slid into the fiberglass boat and felt the molded backrest behind him. "What are these nylon cleats for?"

"If you want to tie off, you can use those cleats. There're shelves along the sides for storage. A couple of flashlights should be there," White said as he swung aboard and settled in next to Moore. "Comfy?"

"Yes. Under the circumstances," Moore replied as the two settled in their close quarters.

"Don't worry about this boat's ability to float. She's got foam in the bow, stern and down both sides," White said as he lowered the electric motor into the water and started the engine.

"That sure is quiet."

"That's the idea," White said as he aimed the boat into Chincoteague Bay and started their journey down the bay.

"What about the tarp? Should we pull that over us?" Moore asked anxiously.

"Not yet. We're still out of range," White replied. "We'll be skirting the marsh after we cross the channel."

"What's the water depth?" Moore asked as they moved slowly across the channel.

"Anywhere from nine inches to seven feet. Bogucs Bay is about one foot deep."

White stared straight ahead as he made his next comment. "On our left is Gunboat Point on Wallops and slightly behind us is Fishing Point on Assateague. The last thing you want to do is head out between those two points."

"Why is that?"

"That opens up into the Atlantic Ocean and this craft is not built to withstand the waves. We'd swamp it in no time," White cautioned.

"Where will we go ashore?" Moore asked. "I know you told me the other night."

"On the western side of the island. We'll go across Bogues Bay and down Crane Creek to that side channel I told you about. We'll leave the layout boat there and head inland."

"What about the heat sensors? Won't they pick us up then?"

"No. They're focused farther out."

"Bo, how do you know that?"

White allowed a small smile to cross his face. "I took readings. I'm very careful. That's why they've never caught me."

"What about on the island? I'd think they'd have surveillance cameras."

"There's a few and they're easy to spot. Mostly aimed at doors and the launch pads. That Horner is confident he's got everything he needs in place. Plus, he doesn't have a big budget with all of the cutbacks NASA has pushed through."

As they neared Wallops, White lowered himself in the boat. "Hand me that tarp. It's time to use it," White said as he pointed to a shelf next to Moore.

Moore reached for the folded tarp and passed it to White, who unfolded it and covered the open cockpit and top part of the electric outboard. He pulled the ends together so that he could peer through a small opening to guide the craft to their destination.

As they rode in relative silence, they could hear the sounds of the evening. The swirls and splashes of fish in the water amid the random hooting and cawing of birds added to the mystique of the bay.

They slowly made their way down Cat Creek and turned left into the channel that ended at the island. After a short distance, White cut the motor and they coasted up to the shore.

"Don't need this anymore," White said as he pulled the tarp off of them.

"What about the heat sensors?" Moore asked again with concern.

"Not to worry. We're past them. Out you go," White said as he crouched and stepped over the side into the water. "It's not deep here."

Moore followed suit and stepped out of the craft on the other side.

"Give me a hand," White ordered as he pulled the boat onto shore.

Moore quickly assisted White and then helped him cover it with the tarp.

"That should do for now. Nobody comes off the road to check out anything. Horner's security team is too lazy."

"That's not good," Moore observed.

"Not good for them, but very good for us," White countered. "Follow me."

The two moved cautiously up a slight slope where they knelt behind a tangle of brush near a patch of scrub pine trees.

White glanced at his watch. "We'll wait here until the patrol drives by. Then we can walk over to the payload processing building."

"Why there?"

"That's where my son told me a lot of the problems originated. We'll just have to keep an eye out for the roving patrol."

"No set time schedule?" Moore asked.

"No. But you'll hear them coming. Their SUV has a bad muffler. Great advance warning for us."

White's comment couldn't have been timed better as the

rumbling from an aging muffler signaled the approach of the patrol. The two men ducked low while the vehicle passed them and a spotlight cast a beacon aimlessly at the marsh.

Standing, White spoke. "Let's go."

The two men walked briskly across the road toward a number of structures.

"That's the payload processing building," White whispered as he pointed to one building. He led Moore toward two large tarp-covered piles of material.

"I take a position here and watch the front door to see who goes in and out."

"That's all you do? You've been coming here for how many nights and that's all you do?" Moore asked incredulously.

"I'm an observer."

"Well, have you observed anything interesting?" Moore asked as he began to wonder if he was wasting his time on this misadventure.

"My son was going to meet his contact here late one night. He was onto something that happens in this building. That's what he told me."

"You didn't answer my question," Moore said with a touch of irritation.

"Rarely do any employees work this late at night. I have seen Orlov and Yazbek go into the building on three occasions."

"Together?"

"No. She goes in and Orlov follows within a few minutes. It looked like he was sneaking around by the way he acted."

"And you don't think they were just having a late evening rendezvous?" Moore asked.

"No way. She can't stand the man. You've been with them.

Didn't you get that feeling?" White asked with indignation.

"Yeah. I did." Moore agreed.

Suddenly White's body tensed. "There's Yazbek."

Moore peered around White. "What's she doing?"

"Just watch," White said softly.

The two men watched as Yazbek placed a ladder against the building on the other side of the security camera's lens. She climbed the ladder and slipped a metal frame over the camera. If Moore and White could have seen what the frame contained, they would have seen a lighted picture of the door. Yazbek quickly descended the ladder and set it on the ground. Next, she produced a key from her pocket and entered the building.

"Let's go," White said.

"Where?"

"Inside. After we check what she's done to the camera. I've seen her do this before. We'll see what she's up to."

"Oh, now that I'm here, you're willing to go inside?" Moore asked.

White ignored him as he ran at a crouch toward the building and the back side of the camera where he produced a flashlight. The lens had been covered with black electrical tape and allowed a small beam of light to shine. He flicked it on and aimed it at the camera.

"It's a picture of the door. She puts that up so no one in security realizes that she's gone inside."

"Smart girl," Moore commented as White switched off the light. The intrepid reporter became even more intrigued by the mystery behind Hala Yazbek.

"Follow me," White said as he walked to the door and reached for its knob. Turning it slowly, he was pleased to find that it was unlocked. He carefully opened the door and the two men entered the partially-lighted building.

The building interior was crowded with parts and pieces in boxes and shrink-wrapped. Some of the stacked boxes towered twelve feet high.

"We'll work ourselves along the wall and stay concealed behind these boxes," White whispered. "There's a light on in the back. I bet that's where she is."

The two men had barely crept forward twenty feet when Moore heard a noise from behind. He turned in time to see the entrance door open and Orlov furtively enter the building.

"We've got company," Moore whispered as he tapped White on the shoulder.

"Who?" White asked as he froze in his tracks.

"Orlov."

"Quick. Over here." White pulled Moore between four pallets stacked high with boxes as Orlov closed the door behind him and began to walk down the same row that White and Moore had walked.

Hearing his approaching footsteps, Moore whispered urgently, "He's coming this way."

"Between these two pallets," White instructed Moore as the two men squeezed between two pallets where they waited nervously for Orlov to pass.

Once they heard Orlov walk by, they secretively stepped out from their hiding place. White returned to the walkway and peered around the corner in time to see Orlov walk around another set of pallets and close in on Yazbek.

"It's too dangerous with both of them here. We're out of here," White advised as he motioned for Moore to follow him.

"Don't you want to see what they're doing? Isn't that what we came down here to see?" Moore asked exasperated.

"I'd say yes, but I got a bad feeling in my bones. We need to git!" White said firmly.

The two scurried down the narrow walkway along the inside of the building to the entrance door like a pair of alley cats. White paused, cautiously opened the door and peered outside. Seeing no one, he motioned for Moore to follow him and the two men exited the building, sprinting to their original hiding spot.

Ten minutes later, they saw the building door open and Orlov walking briskly away. He rounded a corner and hid behind the firehouse.

Two minutes later, Yazbek walked through the same door and closed it behind her. She looked around for any witnesses, then turned and locked the door. She leaned the ladder against the building and climbed up where she removed the metal frame that covered the camera lens. After descending the ladder, she replaced it next to the building and started to walk away.

The nearby sound of a sneeze caused Yazbek to suddenly stop. Believing her presence was detected, she turned in the direction of the noise near the firehouse and ran toward it. In a brief moment, she disappeared from view as she rounded the corner.

White and Moore could hear angry voices in the near distance, which they identified as Yazbek and Orlov. Soon, the voices went silent. A moment later, Yazbek reappeared into their view displaying a determined, almost cold look upon her face, before walking away into the night.

"What was that all about?" Moore asked White.

"Orlov caught her apparently and then she caught him," White said as he stared at the corner of the building. "Let's see what Orlov does."

The two men waited for twenty minutes and didn't see Orlov appear.

White turned to Moore. "You stay here. I'm going to go see if Orlov is still there."

"I'll come with you."

"No. It will be bad enough if he sees me and reports me. I'll get arrested for trespassing. There's no need for you to get caught up in all of this." White grinned as he looked at Moore. "Besides, I might need you to bail me out!"

"Yeah. Yeah," Moore lamented. He wanted to accompany White, but understood his reasoning.

"I'll be right back," White said before sprinting to the building.

Moore watched White disappear around the corner. Five minutes later, White returned. He seemed agitated as he wiped his hands on his slacks.

"What happened to your hands?" Moore asked as he looked at White's hands. They were covered in red blood.

"It's Orlov. He's dead. I was too late to help him," White uttered.

"What happened?"

"I'd guess that Yazbek slashed his trachea with a sharp blade."

"We'd better report it," Moore said.

"No, we're not. We're trespassing. We'll see how it plays out and if we need to, come forward with what we saw."

It was obvious to Moore that White was very anxious. "We better head back and not get caught here," Moore suggested.

"That's right, but we'll have to wait for the tide to change so we can ride back up the bay with its help."

"Okay."

"I just hope no one discovers the body before we can get out of here," White said as the two men crossed the road and made their way to the edge of the marsh.

When they arrived at the water's edge, Moore began to push

the layout boat into the channel.

"Whoa, whoa," White cautioned. "What are you doing?"

"We've got to get out of here," Moore spoke anxiously.

"Not unless you want to be swept out into the Atlantic and drown," White said. "The tide is against us. It's still running out."

"What if someone catches us?" Moore asked warily.

"Slow down, son. No one has caught me yet. Think about it."

Moore tried to calm himself. "I guess you're right."

"Of course I am. We weren't on camera."

"Yeah and no one saw us."

"Correct. Orlov's body is near the side of the building. I doubt that the roving patrol will see it. Odds are his body won't be discovered until morning."

Moore looked at White. "I'm sorry about panicking. I don't usually do something like that."

"It didn't strike me that you were the kind of guy who would." White looked toward the slope. "If it makes you feel better, we can ease ourselves up to the top of the slope and make sure that no one is coming after us."

"I think that's a great idea," Moore agreed.

The two men returned to the slope and lay behind some brush. They had a good view of any approaching traffic. For the next two hours, they watched and spoke in low voices, waiting for the tide to change.

"What are we going to do about Orlov's murder?" Moore asked.

"What do you suggest we do?"

"Report it," Moore suggested again.

"And reveal that we were snooping around on the island?" White probed.

"That's a good point."

"We'll see how this plays out. If we don't have to come forward, we won't. If the investigation doesn't lead them to Yazbek, we'll make sure they know."

"How?" Moore asked.

"I'm not quite sure. Let's cross that bridge if we need to. We should be good now," White said after taking another look at his watch.

The two men returned to the marsh's edge and pushed the layout boat into the channel. Within a matter of minutes, they were covered with the tarp and quietly motoring their way up the channel to Cat Creek and across Bogues Bay toward Captain Bob's Marina.

When they arrived at the dock behind White's home, the men quickly stowed the boat and covered it under the dock.

As they walked back to White's place, White spoke. "You certainly picked the right night to join me."

"I'll say."

"Nothing like this happened before."

"I guess death follows me," Moore quipped as he privately remembered Asha's death in New Orleans.

White looked suddenly over his shoulder.

Moore saw White's glance over his shoulder and asked, "Something wrong?"

"I just wanted to make sure that death wasn't sneaking up on me," he said semi-seriously.

"Funny," Moore responded as they arrived at the entrance to the White House. "I'm surprised that Yazbek murdered Orlov. She didn't strike me as that kind of person." Moore's feelings toward her were jolted.

"You never know. And it might have been in self-defense if

Orlov attacked her."

"True," Moore agreed.

"We'll see what is reported," White said again as they neared his place. "You want to come in?"

"No. I'm beat. I'm going to go back to Roe's place and crash for a few hours."

To the east, the first rays of the morning sun were beginning to emerge. It was going to be a cloudless day.

"Lie low like I said and see what breaks on Orlov."

"I will."

With a very menacing tone, White said, "I don't want you saying anything about last night to anyone. You understand?"

Moore was taken aback by the threatening tone in White's voice. It raised his curiosity, but he let it pass. "I'm not saying anything to anybody."

"You call me if you hear anything and I'll do the same."

"Got it," Moore said as he walked to his parked Mustang, started it and drove to Terry's house.

CHAPTER 14

Early Afternoon
Maria's Restaurant

After a few hours of sleep, Moore shaved, showered and drove to Maria's Restaurant. He remembered from his earlier visit that some of the Wallops Island workers dined there. He hoped to pick up the local scuttlebutt about Orlov's death.

As luck would have it, Moore spotted Chincoteague's police chief finishing up a late lunch. The chief's face looked strained.

"Hello, Ebe," Moore said as he approached the chief's table. "Mind if I join you?"

"No, go right ahead. Sit down." Deere took a drink from his coffee cup and looked at Moore. "Been doing any more fishing?"

Moore wanted to respond yes, but not to the kind of fishing that the chief was asking about. He smiled as he answered, "No. I've been learning more about this island paradise of yours."

"That's good," the chief said as he sipped his coffee.

Moore decided to bait the chief. "I did get a chance to tour the NASA facility on Wallops Island."

The chief angled his head as he stared intently at Moore. "You did?"

"Yes. Maya and Horner arranged it for me."

"That's good. You writing anything about Wallops?"

"As a matter of fact, I am. I'm doing a story on the rocket explosions."

The chief hesitated a moment before speaking again. "Did you hear about what happened last night?"

"No," Moore responded.

"One of their international visitors was murdered."

"Which one?" Moore asked as if he didn't know the answer.

"Orlov."

"The Russian?"

"Yes."

"What happened?" Moore asked.

"Somebody slit his throat."

"In his apartment?"

"No. Behind the firehouse next to the payload processing building."

A server appeared next to their table and Moore placed his order for a submarine sandwich and coffee. He then turned his attention back to Deere.

"Do you have any suspects?"

"We do."

"The Syrian woman?" Moore asked without thinking. As soon as the words escaped his mouth, he knew that he had made a grave error.

Deere eyed Moore carefully. "Just why would you suggest her?"

"I saw how Orlov hit on her on several occasions at the Village

Restaurant and Clam Shells Pub. She didn't like it," Moore said as he tried to recover from his slip.

"Good guess," Deere said as he took another sip of his coffee. "Yes, she's a suspect. I had her over to the station today for questioning, but we released her."

"Is Horner leading the investigation?"

"He'd like to, but I'm leading it. I wouldn't be involved except our jurisdiction was changed last year to include Wallops Island. I've got the state police over on Wallops now for forensic work. They've been there since early this morning with one of their mobile crime lab units."

"How long will it take them to get an update to you?" Moore asked as he began to eat his meal.

"I should have their initial findings late this afternoon."

"I bet Maya and Horner are beside themselves," Moore guessed.

"Horner is running around like a chicken with his head cut off. He's pointing fingers at everyone but himself. He has a tendency to blame others for anything that goes wrong, even if it's due to a lack of security by his team."

"That doesn't surprise me," Moore said.

"You spent time with him on your tour. I'm sure you know as well as anyone else who has dealt with Horner that he's a real presumptuous jackass."

"I've got to agree with you on that one, Chief," Moore concurred.

"Maya is flustered. This is her big chance to show that she should be the permanent head of that operation. This doesn't bode well for her either."

"Are you holding a press briefing?" Moore asked.

"We held one earlier on Wallops. That should have made the news." Deere looked closely at Moore. "I was surprised that you didn't get wind of this and attend the briefing."

"I was catching some sleep at Roe's. Slept real late. I haven't checked my email or the internet yet today," Moore said sheepishly.

"We will be doing another briefing later. Got a business card on you? I'll make sure you're invited."

Moore reached into his pocket and pulled a card out of his wallet. "My email address is on there."

"My staff will send you an email or text when we set up the press briefing." Deere stood and threw some cash on the table to pay his bill. "One more thing, Emerson."

"Yes."

"Everything that I just told you about the suspect stays under wraps. I did you a favor by giving you advance insight because I know you. I'll be talking about it at the briefing. So, nothing goes out from you until after the briefing, understand?"

"Got it. Thanks for the update."

"No problem. Talk later," the chief said as he began to walk away. Suddenly he stopped and turned back to Moore.

"Emerson."

"Yes."

"Other than the problems with the rocket explosions, Wallops Island and Chincoteague are relatively quiet and safe. The last time that we had a murder here was about ten years ago and we found the culprit right away. We'll get to the bottom of this."

"I understand," Moore said as he watched the chief turn around and walk out of the building.

Moore gobbled down his meal, paid his check and walked outside to his car. Leaning against his car in the bright sun, he called White.

"Yes?" White answered.

"Bo, it's Emerson."

"Yes?"

"I just talked with the police chief," Moore began.

Anger crept into White's voice. "I told you not to talk to anybody! I shouldn't have got involved with you," he lamented.

"Wait! That's not the way it was. I bumped into the chief at Maria's and he told me about Orlov's death."

"You didn't bring it up?"

"No, he did. And Yazbek is their prime suspect. She's already been interviewed."

"They lock her up?"

"Not yet. They have a forensic team on Wallops gathering evidence."

"They do?"

Moore sensed a certain change in White's tone. He seemed nervous. Moore continued, "There's going to be a press briefing later today and I'll be attending."

"You be sure to call me and let me know what they say."

"I can do that. Are you okay, Bo?" Moore asked.

"Fine. I'm just plain fine," White responded.

Moore sensed trepidation in White's voice. Something didn't make sense, but Moore couldn't put his finger on it. The men ended their call and Moore drove to Assateague Island's beach. He parked his car at the southernmost point and walked through the thick sand to the water's edge. He then began to walk south to the most deserted area. He needed to clear his mind and think about White and what was bothering him. Moore had an uneasy feeling and it was growing.

Two hours later, Moore was on Wallops Island for the press briefing in a conference room in the administration building.

Three TV news teams had set up cameras at the rear of the room and their microphones were placed on the podium.

Maya Simon opened the briefing by lamenting the loss of Orlov and the impact his loss would have on the Wallops Island team. She also mentioned how shocked everyone was by the brutality of the murder and expressed her resolve to support law enforcement's efforts to identify, capture and successfully prosecute the murderer.

Moore could tell how much Simon relished being in the spotlight and admitted to himself that she did an excellent job at the podium. She was the pretty face among the three men standing at the front of the room.

Horner was up next and conveyed an attitude of disbelief that such an atrocity could occur on the island during his watch. He was confident that a rogue employee was the murderer.

Following Horner was Chief Deere, who gave an update of the investigation and revealed that one suspect was interviewed and released. Deere stepped away from the podium after introducing the lead investigator from the forensic team. The forensic investigator gave a very shallow overview of their findings resulting from the preliminary stages of their investigation.

When he finished, Deere returned to the podium and took questions from the eight reporters who were in attendance. Moore didn't ask anything, as he didn't want to give his thoughts away to the other reporters. He hoped instead to corner Deere afterwards.

After five minutes, Deere ended the press briefing and the room began to empty. While Moore waited for Deere to finish talking with the forensic lead, he saw another man in a lab coat enter the room and speak to the two men.

Moore decided to catch Simon before she departed.

"Maya," he called as she wrapped up a discussion with a reporter.

"Emerson," she gushed as she walked over to him and gave him a quick peck on the cheek. "Honey, I wish I was seeing you on better circumstances."

"I do too. I'm so sorry about what has happened here today," Moore said as she hugged him. As she released him from her hug, Moore noticed Horner was glaring at him as Horner walked stiffly out of the room.

"Thank you, Emerson. This has been a tragedy for every employee here. We all are dismayed about the murder," Maya said.

"I'm sure Chief Deere and the forensic team will move quickly to resolve it and you and your team can refocus on the cause of the explosions," Moore advised.

"Oh, you are such a sweetie. It's just so amazing how you can read my mind," Simon responded warmly. "This has been a very stressful day." Suddenly her face lit up. "Emerson, I need to unwind a little tonight. How would you like to meet me for drinks around seven?"

"That sounds good," Moore said as he thought he might be able to learn more about the murder and the explosions in a more casual setting. "Where would you like to meet?"

"Steamers."

"On Maddox?"

"Right," she said.

"I know where it is."

"I'll see you at seven," Simon said as she flashed her eyes at Moore and left the room. She had a slight wiggle in her hips which Moore couldn't help but notice.

When she reached the door, she stopped abruptly and turned to look Moore in the eyes. She saw that he had been watching her hips and smiled at him before disappearing through the doorway.

She was coming on too strong for Moore's liking, but he was

interested in learning more. He smiled to himself as he thought how, at times, his job required him to spend time with beautiful women whether he wanted to or not.

"How did you like the briefing, Emerson? I noticed you didn't ask any questions."

Moore turned and saw Chief Deere standing next to him.

"It was good," Moore replied.

Deere looked around to be sure that no one was near to hear his next comment. "There's been an interesting development."

"What's that?"

"Forensics just told me that Orlov's throat was slashed horizontally."

"Okay," Moore responded, not quite sure about the point the chief was making.

"Think about it."

"I don't know what point you're trying to make," Moore responded.

"How tall is Yazbek?"

"About five-two."

"And how tall was Orlov?" the chief asked.

"Six-foot plus," Moore guessed.

"So how does someone that short slice Orlov's throat horizontally? It looks like it was done by someone taller."

Moore instantly felt an uneasiness in his stomach. Bo White was over six feet tall. Did White murder Orlov? And if he did, why? A number of thoughts instantly raced through Moore's mind as he realized that he didn't see who actually killed Orlov. It could have been either Yazbek or White.

"Earth to Planet Moore. Are you with me?" the chief pushed at Moore.

"Sorry, I was just deluged by a number of ideas," Moore explained.

"Well if you have any that would help us, I'd appreciate you letting me know. We've just expanded the suspect pool."

"I bet you have," Moore said unconvincingly.

"You know who I have my eye on now?"

"No."

"Come on Emerson. Put on that thinking cap that you are supposed to have. Who would benefit from a problem on the Wallops base?"

"Maya Simon?"

"No. Problems hurt her in her role as head of operations. Guess again?"

A light bulb went off in Moore's head. "Horner?"

"Good guess. He's over six feet tall. Doesn't like anyone. Feels that he's been passed over. Stirring things up could work well for him, especially if he can find a scapegoat to frame the murder on. He's got the motive. We'll be watching him closely."

"I'd guess so," Moore responded, although he was still torn inside about the possibility that White had committed the murder. He resolved to go to White's when he left Wallops and confront him.

"There's Wu Tang, too," Deere added.

"Too short," Moore countered.

"We'll see. We're interviewing anyone that Orlov would have worked with. You never know what will surface during an investigation. Maybe he ticked off a co-worker."

"Good luck with your interviews," Moore said. He was anxious to talk to White.

"Our hands are full right now," Deere said as he turned to speak with a reporter who had appeared at his side.

Moore left the building and drove over to White's house on Chincoteague Island. When he arrived, he parked his car and walked up to the door.

"Bo? Bo, are you around?"

"I'm right here," White said as he walked around the corner of the building. "You learn anything new?"

"Yes, I did," Moore said firmly as he looked at White's eyes. "Did you kill Orlov?"

Startled by the question, White asked, "What? What in the world are you talking about?"

"I want to know if you killed Orlov," Moore demanded.

"You should know better than that. You were with me," White retorted aghast.

"I wasn't with you when you went around the building to check on Orlov. Remember you came back with blood on your hands," Moore said seriously.

"I told you that I tried to save him," White said.

Moore was skeptical. "Or so you said."

"I did. Why would I kill Orlov?"

"Because he killed your son?"

"I don't know that for a fact. My son was meeting with a woman, not Orlov," White countered.

Moore was becoming disillusioned about everything White had told him. He was uncertain if White had been telling the truth and had a growing suspicion that White had been doing a convincing con job on him.

"Emerson, you've got to believe me. The only horse I have in this race is to find my son's killer. That's all."

"And what are you going to do when you find him? Kill him?"

White's eyes narrowed. Peering through slitted eyelids, White spoke quietly and coldly as he answered. "I will."

Moore could tell how serious White was. There was no mistaking his intention. "I'm just not sure that I can trust you anymore, Bo."

"I'm not asking you to," White retorted. "Just remember that you were the one who came knocking on my door and intruding in my space. I wish I had never met you. Just get out of here and leave me alone!" White stormed past Moore and entered his metal home, slamming the door shut behind him.

Moore returned to his car and sat in it quietly for a few minutes. He was conflicted by a deep sense of skepticism and replayed the conversation he had just concluded with Bo White. What's the next move, Moore pondered as he started the car and pulled out on Main Street. He could tell Chief Deere about the secret visit to Wallops, or remain silent.

Moore parked in Terry's drive and entered the house where he plopped down in one of the plush chairs in the family room. He allowed himself to fall asleep as he sought to escape the emotional stress he was under.

CHAPTER 15

Two Hours Later
Steamers Restaurant

Their timing couldn't have been more perfect as Maya Simon and Emerson Moore each pulled into the parking lot at the same time. Being the gentleman that he was, Moore quickly parked and ran over to Simon's car to open her door for her.

"How nice of you," Simon purred as she swung her long legs around to exit her car. She pretended she didn't notice that her skirt had edged up, revealing more of her long legs.

The same wasn't true for Moore. He couldn't help but notice as he took her extended hand and helped her out of the car. "My pleasure," he said despite himself.

"What a day this has been!" she said as the two started for the entrance.

Moore reached for the door and pulled it open. Before they could enter, Vice Mayor Bowden walked out.

"Hi, Denise," Moore greeted his friend.

"Hi, Emerson," Bowden replied cordially. Her tone cooled as she greeted Simon. "Hello, Maya. I hope things have quieted down for you."

"Nothing that someone with my capabilities can't handle," Simon replied with aloofness.

Bowden leaned in to Moore as Simon walked through the doorway. "Be careful around her. She's a barracuda," she whispered quietly.

"Thanks, Denise," Moore said as he took in her advice. Moore then recalled Horner's comment that Simon was looking for her next ex-boyfriend. He would be wary that evening. He hurried inside and followed Simon. She turned right and walked into the bar.

"Mind sitting at the bar?" she asked as she continued walking. It didn't matter to her where Moore wanted to sit. She was going to control that evening.

"Wherever you want," Moore replied as Simon spotted a number of unoccupied stools at the end of the bar.

"We'll go there," she said as she waved her ring-covered hand. As they sat on the stools, she set her gaudy purse on the bar top.

"Hi, Maya," the server greeted her as she wiped the countertop with a towel. "The usual?"

"Sure, and I'll take a double shot of Patron, Mary," Simon replied. "What are you drinking, Emerson?" she asked as her cell phone rang. She retrieved it from her purse and looked at the display, then returned it to her purse. "I'll call him back later. What do you want to drink?"

"I don't need a shot of anything. I'll take a Captain Morgan and Seven Up," he replied.

"Oh Emerson," Simon cooed as she reached over and nestled her ample chest against Moore's right arm. "Have a double shot with me," she pleaded.

Moore looked at her as the server waited. Simon's eyes had an inviting look. It was irresistible. It was the kind of look that men struggle to ignore when women gave it to them and Moore was not immune to an attractive woman's magic. He decided to give in and hoped he wouldn't regret it later. "Okay. Give me a double of Patron. That's tequila, right?"

"Oh yeah," Simon's voice hummed provocatively. "You'll like it. Trust me," she meowed.

"Really good stuff," the server said before walking away.

"Really tough day, huh?" Moore asked.

"Yes, but I can handle it."

"Mine was tough, too," Moore said as he thought about White's possible involvement in Orlov's murder.

"It was? Tell me all about it," Simon said as she pulled Moore's arm tighter against her chest.

Moore didn't like her move as he realized that he might be lured into compromising his position while researching another potential blockbuster story. He wasn't very fond of sexually aggressive women, but he also did not pull away from her. He decided to play along with the enticing Ms. Simon.

"It's really nothing compared to what you've gone through today," Moore responded. He was not about to share his thoughts on Bo White, especially any concerns he held. Who knew what she would do with the information. "Let's talk about your day."

Simon relaxed her grip on Moore's arm and straightened her posture. "It was so hectic, Emerson. I had so many phone calls today. Important people needed my attention all day. I had calls from NASA, law enforcement and a flood of calls from the media. I had to have my assistant make more copies of my photos for the media packets. You boys in the media all want my picture," she droned.

Moore thought how self-centered she was, but said nothing as he listened.

"Then I had two calls from the Russian embassy in Washington. They needed to talk to me about Orlov's body and shipping it back to Russia once it's released. So many demands put on me today," she said narcissistically.

"Did Orlov have a family?"

"Yes. I've sent a condolence note and flowers to them. I did that right away. I'm always thinking ahead."

Why did such a beautiful woman have to have such a self-aggrandizing ego about her, Moore wondered before asking, "What about the investigation? Any more news come out this afternoon?"

Before Simon could answer, the server returned with their drinks. Simon reached for the shot glass. As Moore reached for his, she looked at him demurely. She shook a few grains of salt on the back of her hand and said, "Bottoms up!" as she licked the salt, threw down her shot and sucked on the lime slice. Moore did likewise.

"That feels good," she said as she set her shot glass back on the bar top and reached for her drink. "Would you like a sip of my Long Island iced tea, Emerson?"

"Oh no. Those are way too strong for me," Moore said as he reached for his drink and sipped it.

"Two or three of these can turn me into a real wildcat, if you know what I mean," she said seductively before taking a large swallow of her strong drink.

"I'm sure it can," Moore replied as she leaned in closer.

"Now, what did you ask me before the drinks arrived?"

"The investigation. Any news late this afternoon?"

"Other than Hala being the prime suspect, not really. We all know how Orlov flirted with her and chased her. She admitted to being in the Payload Processing Building last night and having an argument with him afterwards near where his body was found. But she said that he was alive when she left him."

Moore's body tensed as he thought about White again and his face clouded over briefly.

"There's one funny thing that I noticed. You know how perceptive we women can be, don't you?" she asked as she leaned closer.

"Yes, I do." Moore wanted to hear more. "What did you notice?"

"She stopped wearing her cowgirl boots. She wore those things all of the time."

Moore recalled the conversation with Yazbek about her love for her cowgirl boots at the Clam Shells Pub. "Maybe they started to bother her feet," he suggested.

"I asked her why she stopped wearing them." Simon pulled back from Moore and took a long draught of her drink as she baited Moore to ask for the answer. She loved playing cat and mouse as long as she was the cat. She also enjoyed playing with her food before devouring it.

Moore took the bait and asked. "What did she say?"

"She said that they disappeared from her closet and she couldn't find them. I bet she can't find them. They're probably soaked with Orlov's blood," Simon said as she crossed her leg, allowing the hem of her skirt to ride up. She looked down at her thigh and then, with a large smile, directly at Moore. "I bet she disposed of them so she wouldn't easily be tied to Orlov's murder."

"Did the police search her apartment?"

"Yes. So did Horner. He searched it before the police arrived."

"Can he do that? I wouldn't think he'd have a search warrant," Moore said with a touch of confusion in his voice.

"Her apartment is on Wallops Island and is part of our housing units. We reserve the right to enter any renter's apartment for inspection. That's how Horner did it. Horner actually surprised me."

"How's that?"

"He took the initiative to search her apartment."

"Why do you think he did that?"

"Well. I'd like to take the credit for sending him over there, but he thought she was the prime suspect after Orlov's body was found in the morning. She was already at work, so he went in."

"When I saw her that morning and noticed that she wasn't wearing her boots, I asked him to go back and look for her boots. He couldn't find them."

Moore nodded his head. "What about the murder weapon? Has it been found?"

"The knife?"

Moore nodded his head.

"No. My guess is that it's long gone."

Suddenly Moore recoiled on his barstool as he remembered that White carried a knife in a sheath on his belt.

"Your drink too strong?" Simon asked as she observed Moore's sudden movement.

"No, Maya. Just had a chill run through me," Moore said as he hid the real reason for his reaction. He wondered momentarily how many times White had lied to him. He was angry at himself for being gullible.

Simon grabbed Moore's arm again and pulled it against her bosom. "Emerson, I can help take that chill off and anything else you'd like off," she slurred.

The strong liquor was having an impact on her, especially on her empty stomach. Moore was glad that his drink wasn't as strong as hers. Someone had to be the adult; besides, he wanted to be able to coherently ask her questions.

"Maya, Maya, Maya. Methinks you've had too much to drink,"

Moore countered as he ignored the tantalizing offer.

"Oh, but I can be so much fun when I drink, Emerson. Don't you like to have fun?" she asked as she again pushed her breasts firmly against Moore's arm.

Not with a man-eater like you, Moore wanted to answer. He wasn't into one-night stands and this one was not someone with whom he'd like to have a long-term relationship. "Yes, I do."

"What do you say, then?"

Moore watched her take another long drink of her beverage as she stared at him.

"What do I say to what?"

"You know," she said coyly and with a seductive wink. She was like a cat on the prowl.

"Maya, you're a beautiful woman and you've had way too much to drink. I don't take advantage of women in that or any other manner."

"Aren't you the gentleman?" she purred.

Moore called to the server. "Could you get us your appetizer plate, Mary? I've got to get some food into my friend, here."

"Party pooper," Simon said as she pulled away and sat up. She wasn't used to being spurned by men.

"Maya, you're a beautiful woman and very tempting, I might add," Moore said softly as he tried to smooth her ruffled feathers. He was going to need her cooperation if he was going to get more information and access to Wallops Island for his story.

Simon finished the rest of her drink. "You have no idea what you're missing," she said as her pouty gaze moved from her empty glass to Moore's face. "No idea whatsoever!"

Moore returned her gaze with a smile. "You're probably right, Maya. But you never know what the next week could hold," Moore said in an effort to give her hope and keep her engaged with him.

"Or if a second offer will be made," Simon smoldered quietly.

"Here are the appetizers," the server said as she placed the plate on the bar in front of the two.

"Let's dig in and get some food in you," Moore suggested as he slid the plate toward Simon.

Reluctantly, Simon reached for an oyster and started to eat.

They discussed Wallops Island for the next hour as the effects of the drinks wore off Simon. After eating, they each returned to their cars and headed to their respective homes.

CHAPTER 16

The Next Morning
Chincoteague Island

After tossing and turning for most of the night, Moore awoke early and made coffee before heading to Assateague Island beach for a morning run. The pristine nature of the beach and early morning solitude provided Moore with the perfect venue for clearing his mind.

As he jogged at the southern end of the beach, he thought about his tormented night. He wanted to approach Chief Deere with his concerns about Bo White and have the forensic team check White's knife blade for Orlov's DNA.

When he completed his run, Moore grabbed a towel out of his car and wiped the sweat from his face and body before putting on his t-shirt. Next, he jumped into his Mustang and returned to Chincoteague Island. He was in a much better frame of mind after breathing in the fresh ocean air and running the stress out of his system. He decided to tell Deere about Bo White.

When he arrived at the police station, Moore parked on the east side and walked to the receptionist window.

Chincoteague Calm

"May I help you?" the receptionist asked.

"Yes, I'd like to see Chief Deere."

"And your name is?"

"Emerson Moore."

Within a few minutes, Moore was seated in front of Deere in his office.

"What brings you in here so early?" Deere asked.

"I've been up most of the night. I didn't sleep well," Moore started.

"I know what you mean. A lot of us haven't been sleeping well," Deere admitted.

"Are you here because of the breaking news?"

Moore sat upright in his chair. "What news?"

"There's been a break in the Orlov murder case."

"How's that?"

"Hal Horner dropped off a pair of cowgirl boots."

"He did?"

"They belong to Yazbek and are blood-splattered."

"What?"

"We obtained a search warrant to analyze the blood splatter. The mobile forensic unit will be over this morning to conduct an analysis of the blood and collect DNA. If the DNA matches Orlov's, we'll be making an arrest this afternoon."

Moore sat back with relief. He was pleased that the murderer didn't appear to be Bo White.

"How did you get wind of this?" Deere asked.

"I didn't. I was here on another matter," Moore answered.

"And that is?" Deere asked.

"It's not important. I had an idea, but this certainly takes precedence."

"I want you to keep this close to the vest, Emerson. Nothing about this until we do a formal press briefing later today to announce our findings and the arrest of a suspect. Can I trust you to keep this quiet?"

"You most certainly can." Moore took a deep breath. It seemed like a huge weight had been lifted off his shoulders. "Listen, I better let you get back to your work," Moore said as he stood.

"I'll make sure you get a text when we schedule the briefing." The chief placed his forefinger in front of his lips. "Not a word about this to anyone, Emerson," he cautioned.

"I wouldn't," Moore said. "I appreciate the trust you have in me to not share anything in advance. I wouldn't violate that trust."

"I wouldn't think you would. I'm pretty good at evaluating people. Comes with the turf, you know."

Moore smiled as the chief ushered him out of his office and to the lobby. When he returned to his car, he drove back to Terry's house. Several hours later, Moore was back at the Chincoteague Island administration building for the briefing which was set up in the parking lot.

Deere conducted the briefing from a small podium to the gathered media. He was flanked by the mayor, Maya Simon, Hal Horner and two of the forensic team members.

After discussing the forensic work that was undertaken and the discovery of a pair of cowgirl boots covered in Orlov's blood, Deere announced that Hala Yazbek had been arrested thirty minutes earlier for Orlov's murder. He also said that her passport had been confiscated and that he expected that she would post bail with the restriction that she could not leave the Wallops Island and Chincoteague Island area. The reporters drilled Deere with questions until he cut them off after ten minutes.

As the briefing ended, Moore began walking to his car.

"Emerson. Oh, Emerson," a voice called.

Moore turned and saw Simon hurrying toward him. Horner was closely following on her heels.

"Hello, Maya. Hello, Hal."

Horner didn't return the greeting and instead stared coldly at Moore. Simon, on the other hand, ran up to Moore and embraced him.

"Emerson. We did it. We caught the murderer," she said merrily.

"That was good work by Deere and his team," Moore said.

"They had nothing to do with finding the evidence that identified the killer. I did that," Horner said scornfully. "Deere is the kind of man you'd use as a blueprint to build an idiot. I'm the one who had to bail him out with the evidence."

"Thanks to my suggestion," Simon added, wanting to be sure that she also was in the spotlight.

"I'd like to ask you a question if I could, Hal," Moore began.

"Try to make it intelligent," Horner responded. "Go ahead."

"How did you find her boots? I thought she always wore them."

"Not all of the time," Horner's eyes narrowed in triumph, knowing that he was in the driver's seat.

"How's that?"

"Yazbek works out early every morning in the employee workout room in the apartment complex. She wears her Nikes to exercise. I searched her apartment while she was not home and didn't find them. I knew that she wouldn't have them on at the workout room."

Horner paused for dramatic effect. He was enjoying showing off how smart he was. "I next checked the dumpster behind her apartment and that's where I found her bloody boots," he concluded with a beaming face. He was so proud of himself.

Moore was instinctively skeptical. "Why would someone who is as smart as Hala trash her boots behind her apartment? I'm really having a hard time buying into that," Moore said.

"Probably panicked. She wasn't thinking. She did something stupid," Horner replied before commenting acrimoniously to Moore. "I'd think you'd understand doing stupid things!" Horner had a derisive look on his face.

Moore ignored the biting remark as Simon changed the topic. "Emerson, it's getting past dinner time. Would you like to join me?"

Moore glanced at his watch. As he did, he thought that dinner could be an opportunity to probe Simon more about the murder investigation. He also realized that she could be trying to make another run at him after failing the previous night. He needed information and it was worth taking the risk. "Sure. I'm available."

Simon turned to Horner. "I won't need a ride back to the office. Please be a dear and lock up my office for me," she said as she flashed her eyes at Horner.

Horner's facial expression showed his disdain for being treated like an underling. Fuming quietly, he nodded his head and walked to his vehicle.

"Where would you like to go, Maya?" Moore asked as he watched Horner pull out of the parking lot.

"Let's go to the Clam Shells Pub," she said as Moore began walking toward his Mustang.

"Oh! A convertible! How fun!" Simon said as Moore opened the passenger door for her, allowing her to slide in

"It is a lot of fun. I enjoy it, especially the feeling of freedom it gives," Moore said as he closed the car door and walked around to his side of the car. Within five minutes, they had parked at the Clam Shells Pub and were escorted to an outside table overlooking the bay. The sky was clear and they had a perfect view for the sunset.

After they each reviewed their menus and placed their orders with the server, Moore started the dinner conversation by asking, "How are you holding up, Maya?"

Simon took a hair brush out of her fancy purse and ran it through her hair a few times before replacing it and answering. She liked to make men wait on her. "Overall, I'm doing well. Life happens and it's leaders like me who know how best to weather the storms," she said a bit pompously.

"You've certainly had your hands full."

"That's an understatement Emerson, but I'm up to the task. That's why I'm in charge of Wallops," she responded arrogantly.

"What a shock! Orlov murdered and Hala arrested. The makings of an international incident," Moore suggested as the server reappeared with their drinks.

Simon sipped her Appletini as Moore tasted his rum and Seven Up. She crinkled her nose at Moore. "I can handle it."

"I'd like to interview Hala," Moore said.

"That's out of my hands. You're going to have to find where she is after she posts bail."

Nodding, Moore agreed. "I just don't understand why she would have thrown bloody cowgirl boots in the dumpster."

"You know she denied it?"

"No, I didn't."

"Chief Deere didn't mention it during the briefing, but he told me beforehand."

"Did she have an explanation as to why her boots were covered in blood and why they were in the dumpster?"

"She did. It was pretty weak."

"What did she say?"

"She said that someone broke into her apartment and stole her boots while she was at her morning workout."

"Was anything else stolen?"

"No."

"Were there any signs of forcible entry?"

"None. Hal used his passkey and searched her place. He didn't see anything amiss."

Moore sat back and thought for a moment. "It sounds to me like Hala could have been set up for this." Moore's brain was working rapidly as he replayed the events of that night. He remembered seeing Yazbek go behind the building where Orlov's body was found.

He also recalled that it had been about twenty minutes or so before White went to see what happened to Orlov. He believed there was no way that White could have been involved with stealing Yazbek's boots, but White had Orlov's blood on his hands. The dots just weren't connecting for Moore. Something was amiss.

"Emerson," Simon spoke, breaking Moore out of his thoughts.

"Sorry. I forgot myself. I was in deep thought about Yazbek and Orlov," Moore said as he apologized.

"You most certainly were," Simon concurred.

"What about Wu Tang?"

"What about him?"

"He seems to be flying under the radar. I haven't heard his name surface during this investigation," Moore said with curiosity.

"No need for his name to surface. He wasn't involved."

"Was he interviewed?"

"Emerson, most of the employees on Wallops were interviewed. Of course he was."

"And nothing came out of those interviews?"

"Nothing. What are you trying to get at?"

The server appeared with Simon's crab dinner and Moore's flounder. They halted their conversation while she set their meals on the table. When she left, Moore resumed his questioning.

"Occasionally, you've got to look at the quiet ones."

"Emerson, really? You're over the top on this. Yazbek's been identified as the killer and it's over. You're chasing clouds in the sky. It's taking you nowhere," Simon said, exasperated. Her objective in having dinner with the handsome reporter was being sidetracked. Moore was focused on questioning her, not on drinking her in.

"I'm going to see Chief Deere in the morning and see if he'll connect me with Hala for an interview. Maybe he can help me out. I'm just suspicious."

"Maybe you should. I'm sure the chief will help you out, but I do have one big favor to ask you."

"Sure. What is it?"

"If you find out anything that I should know, so I can be prepared, would you tell me after you talk to Hala?"

Moore smiled all-knowingly. He respected Simon's fixation on being prepared for the media. She was a planner and probably did an exceptional job. Her preparedness and appearance of being in control would play well in front of the media and her superiors at NASA. She was working hard to be the permanent director of Wallops Island.

"I'll do that for you, Maya," Moore smiled.

"Enough talk about the murder. Let's enjoy another classic Chincoteague sunset," she said as she ordered another Appletini and the two turned their heads to enjoy the spectacular view.

Watching the sun, Simon quickly downed the Appletini

and ordered a third one. Before turning back to the sunset, she commented on Moore's soft yellow shirt. "That shirt looks good on you, Emerson."

"Thank you, Maya," Moore responded graciously.

"Do you know what would look better on you?"

Without thinking, Moore responded, "No."

"Me," she purred.

Moore shook his head at the open invitation and turned back to the sunset.

Shortly after the sun disappeared on the horizon and Simon finished her third Appletini, Simon's cell phone buzzed. She glanced down and recognized the caller. Picking up her cell phone and standing, Simon slurred as she spoke. "Emerson honey, I'll just have to excuse myself for a moment to take this call. It's Hal."

Moore waved her away. "Go ahead." He grinned, although he was becoming more concerned about her alcohol consumption and progressive flirtatiousness. Her suggestive comments were an open compass as to how she wanted to end their evening together.

He watched as she walked toward the entrance, wiggling her hips provocatively. Within two minutes, she returned to the table, pulling her chair next to Moore's before sitting.

"Everything okay?" Moore asked.

"Nothing major. I swear that man can't do anything without my advice," Simon started. "I just don't know what he would do without me. In fact, I don't know what most men would do without me in their lives." Focusing her eyes on Moore she asked, "Emerson, did you know that your body is sixty-five percent comprised of water?"

"No."

"And I'm getting real thirsty. I need a drink of water," she said as her tongue ran provocatively across her lips and she moved closer.

"Emerson, do you have a driver's license?"

Wrinkling his brow in surprise at the question, Moore responded, "Of course I do. Why do you ask?"

"I thought it was suspended because of the way you drive women crazy," she said before placing her cheek against his.

Moore had enough. He knew that she'd had too much to drink again. "Maya, we better call it a night," he said as he stood, looked at the bill and tossed cash on the table to cover it and a tip.

"That's music to my ears," she said as she stood wobbly and grabbed her purse. "My place isn't too far from here," she sloshed her words as she leaned closely against Moore's body.

The two of them made their way through the crowded pub and to the parking lot. When they reached Moore's car, Simon caught Moore off guard as she suddenly spun around in front of him and planted a wet kiss on his lips.

Surprised by her move, Moore pulled away. "Maya, please. You've had too much to drink."

Reaching her hand up to Moore's face, she ran one finger across his lips. "But Emerson, I can be so much fun when I've had too much to drink."

Moore pushed her away and opened the convertible's door. "I'm sure you can be, but now is not the time or the place," he cautioned her softly, but firmly as he helped her into the car.

Walking around the vehicle, he entered it and started the engine. Simon was staring straight ahead, frustrated by Moore's rejection. She was not used to being rejected.

"We need to get you home," Moore said as he drove the Mustang out of the parking lot. He was so concentrated on following her directions to her house that he didn't notice a pickup truck had pulled out of the parking lot and was following them at a discreet distance.

CHAPTER 17

**Police Department
Chincoteague Island**

"That's him! That's the man who assaulted me!" the blonde woman shrieked hysterically as she pointed to her alleged perpetrator. "Arrest him! He was wearing that brown cat's-eye ring when he grabbed me from behind. I saw it when his hand went around my waist and he assaulted me!" she screamed.

The police detective, who had been taking the woman's report inside the Chincoteague Island police station, stood and walked over to the counter. "Mind if I borrow your ring?" she firmly asked the man.

"It's not my ring. I found it on the roof of my car this morning. It looks valuable so I thought I should bring it over here for your safekeeping," the man said as he handed the detective the ring.

Taking the ring, the detective walked over to the woman and showed it to her. "Ma'am, are you absolutely certain that this is the ring?"

The woman, who by then had just barely calmed down, examined the ring and answered without hesitation. "Yes, it is."

"Interesting. Only one person on this island had a ring like this," the detective said as she turned back to the man. "Her name is Maya Simon."

"I know her," the man declared. "I'll give it back to her."

"Not quite," the detective responded. "Miss Simon's torched body was found in a dumpster on the island this morning. We're waiting for positive identification through her dental records. Whoever did that to her was sloppy. Her purse was found on the ground behind the dumpster," the detective said as she carefully eyed the man who appeared to be shocked by the revelation.

Recovering slightly, the man stuttered, "It can't be Maya. I was with her last night at the Clam Shells Pub and drove her home. She was fine and quite alive when I left her."

"She's not fine now," the detective confirmed as she stared suspiciously at the man.

"I didn't have anything to do with her murder," the man pleaded nervously.

"You better follow me back to one of the interview rooms," the detective firmly directed.

"Am I being charged?" the man asked.

"Not unless we have a reason. Are you saying you don't want to be interviewed?" the detective asked as she raised an eyebrow in distrust.

"No. I don't have anything to hide."

"Good," the detective said as she started walking toward the interview room. "What did you say your name was?"

"I didn't, but it's Emerson Moore," the man replied softly. His island vacation getaway was taking an ugly turn.

"I'm Detective Barbara Huffman," responded the woman with short brown hair and brown eyes. She was about five-foot-seven-inches tall and Moore sensed that she could be the life of the party under less serious circumstances.

"Hello, Emerson," a familiar voice greeted Moore from behind the counter.

Moore saw that Chief Deere had walked over.

"Hi, Chief," Moore replied as the detective opened the door for Moore to enter.

"What's he here for, Barbara?" Deere asked the detective.

"The Simon murder."

"The body hasn't been positively identified," Deere noted.

"I realize that, but Mr. Moore just dropped into our lap and became suspect number one," Hoffman responded. She gave the chief a brief rundown as to what had transpired in the lobby.

"I know Emerson," Deere said to Huffman. "Mind if I join you in the interview room?"

"Come along if you like," Huffman said as the three walked down the hallway into a small interview room where she grilled Moore for an hour.

During the interview, Moore learned that the blonde in the lobby was Joe Kronsky's girlfriend. Deere was suspicious of her allegation about Moore assaulting her, especially when Moore was asked to slip on Simon's ring. His finger was too big for the ring. While it was questionable about Moore assaulting the woman in the lobby, Detective Huffman was confident that Moore somehow was involved with Simon's death. Deere was undecided.

When they finished, a somewhat relieved Emerson Moore walked out of the administration building to his parked Mustang. He was accompanied by Huffman, who searched his car for anything that would tie Moore to Simon's death. Moore was fully cooperating with the police and didn't have anything to hide.

Once Huffman finished searching Moore's car, she and a

fellow officer followed him in their respective vehicles to Terry's house where they looked for anything that would connect Moore to the murder. After checking the house, the workshop and the outbuildings, they appeared to be somewhat satisfied.

"I'd like you to stay in the area while we conclude our investigation," Huffman said as she left the Terry house.

"Oh, you don't have to worry about that, detective. I'm not going anywhere until I get this all figured out," Moore said as he watched the two officers climb into their vehicles and leave.

Moore walked back into the house and sat in a recliner. He was exhausted, but wanted to recount the events of the last few days, especially Maya Simon's death. Something again just wasn't adding up for him, but he could not draw any specific conclusions.

He replayed his conversation with Simon from the previous night, trying to see if there was anything that could help. Nothing seemed amiss at Simon's home when he left her. Even though she seemed man-hungry, he had to admit that he was going to miss her and her assistance.

As he sat thinking, he eventually fell asleep. When Moore later awoke, he realized he was hungry and decided to drive over to Chatties for lunch where he ordered a sweet tea and clam chowder. As he sipped his drink and stared at Chincoteague Bay, Moore startled when someone sat in one of the chairs at his table.

"You doing okay, Emerson?"

Moore turned his head and saw Bo White sitting across from him. A twelve-pack of beer was on the table top.

"Making your beer run, Bo?" Moore asked.

"Yep. Got to keep up my reputation. I told you that it helps keep people away from me," White replied in his usual slow speak. "You didn't answer my initial question."

Moore allowed a small smile to momentarily cross his face.

"You are persistent."

"Always."

"I'm doing okay," Moore said as he swung his body around to face White.

"I heard you're a suspect in Maya Simon's murder."

"How did you hear that?"

"This is a small island and word spreads quickly here through our island grapevine."

Nodding his head, Moore commented, "Just like Put-in-Bay—home, back in Ohio."

The server appeared with Moore's clam chowder and set it in front of him.

"Do you want anything, Bo?" Moore asked before the server walked away.

"No, I'm fine," White answered as the server left. White leaned in and spoke softly, "I also know you didn't assault that blonde woman like she claimed."

"How do you know that," Moore asked stunned.

"I was there last night and saw you leave with Maya."

Moore's eyes popped. "Are you following me?"

"No. I was here buying more beer and saw you both leave. That blonde woman is the girlfriend of one of the Kronsky brothers."

Moore now remembered that he had seen her with the three Kronsky brothers the night he had the fight with them. "I bet they put her up to framing me," Moore suggested as his mind raced.

"Nothing like a little payback," White agreed.

"And I bet that one of the Kronskys put Maya's ring on my car, thinking that I would return it to the police department and get blamed for her murder."

"You didn't know that the ring belonged to Maya?" White

asked.

Shaking his head negatively, Moore replied, "I'm not a jewelry guy. I don't notice what kinds of rings people wear. I may notice a ring on their hand, but it doesn't really register with me."

"I know you didn't kill Maya."

Shocked, Moore asked, "How do you know that, Bo?"

"She's at my place," White answered smugly.

"What?" a shocked Moore asked.

"Shhh. Don't tell anyone," White said as he quickly looked around to make sure that no one was within hearing distance. "She's under my personal protection."

"Why? What's going on?" Moore was dumbfounded by White's revelation.

"I wanted to ask her some questions."

"Wait. Wait," Moore said as he repeated himself. "Tell me what's going on. How did Maya end up with you?"

White scooted his chair closer to Moore. "I followed you two to her place last night. After you left her, she came outside and got into her car."

"Wait. Why did you follow us?"

"I've been following a lot of people who work on Wallops Island. I told you that I wanted to find out who was responsible for my son's death."

Moore shook his head. "You can waste a lot of time following everyone who works on that island."

"You're not giving me much credit, Emerson. I have my reasons for doing what I do."

Exasperated, Moore urged White to continue. "Go on."

"I followed her back to town where she parked on a side street near Main. She got out of her car and walked over to the large parking lot by the grocery store where she met the other woman."

"Yazbek?"

White's brow furrowed as he asked, "How did you know that?"

"Just a lucky guess," Moore answered. "What happened?"

"The two of them seemed to argue, but then out of the night Joe Kronsky walked up to them. When he got close to Maya, he had words with her. He grabbed her purse and it looked like he took some rings off her hand."

"Maya let him take her rings?"

"Reluctantly. She didn't resist. Remember, he's a big guy. Real intimidating."

"And you just stood by and did nothing?"

"I couldn't. Remember that I can't do anything that draws any attention to me."

"What happened next?"

"Maya ran to her car and I followed her."

"What about Kronsky and Yazbek?"

"I took a quick look at them and they were talking away like they were old friends."

"I don't get it."

"I'm telling you that this whole thing is complicated." White paused before continuing. "I followed Maya to her home and I abducted her when she got out of her car. I gagged her and tied her up. I threw her in the back of my pickup and covered her with some canvas, then drove back to my place."

"That's kidnapping, my friend," Moore warned.

"I know that," White responded.

"What are you going to do with her?"

"Question her."

"About?"

"My son's murder."

"Why her?"

"I have my reasons. Like I told you once before, that's my business."

Moore shook his head from side to side again.

"And do you want to guess whose body that is in the dumpster?" White asked.

"I'd say Yazbek."

"So would I."

"But why?" Moore asked.

"I don't know," White said. "Yet!"

The server appeared with Moore's check. After paying, he walked out of the restaurant with White. Pausing in the parking lot, White asked, "You want to come to my place and help interrogate Maya?"

"No way. I don't want to be involved. She could press charges against you and I don't need that on top of everything I've got going."

"Suit yourself."

Moore walked to his car and returned to Terry's house. He spent the afternoon thinking about Simon's abduction and what White was really up to. His suspicions about White were growing as he wondered about White's truthfulness.

After sunset, he decided that he needed to go to Captain Bob's Marina and talk White into releasing Simon. He got into his car and headed for the marina.

CHAPTER 18

Captain Bob's Marina
Chincoteague Island

As Moore approached the parking lot, he saw the flashing lights from two police cars and an ambulance. They were parked by White's home. Moore feared the worst as he pulled in and parked.

Moore saw Chief Deere and walked over to him. As he approached, he spotted a gurney parked next to the container home's doorway. It was empty.

"What happened?"

Deere eyed Moore carefully as he decided what he was going to say to Moore, then he spoke. "We're still investigating," he answered carefully.

"Is Maya okay?" Moore asked without thinking.

"Maya? What do you mean, Maya?" Deere asked in response, then added, "She was torched in the dumpster, remember?" Deere scrutinized Moore's face for a reaction.

Realizing what he had blurted, Moore tried to cover his mistake. "Sorry. I meant Bo White. I just got tongue tied," he explained lamely.

Before Deere could comment further, Detective Huffman walked up.

"Chief, White didn't make it. We lost him."

Deere nodded his head. "I'm sorry to hear that. Find anything interesting?"

Moore's heart sank upon hearing that White had died and he wondered who killed White. And why? And what happened to Simon? Did someone abduct her from White? The questions swirled like a tornado in Moore's mind.

"Nothing yet. We're still investigating," Huffman said as she glanced at Moore. "The forensic team is on its way over," she added.

A noise from the open doorway of White's home caused them to look as three paramedics carried a body bag from inside and carefully laid it on the gurney. They wheeled it over to the ambulance, placed it inside and drove away.

"I'm going to go back in," Detective Huffman said as she returned to the residence.

"Who called this in?" Moore asked.

"It was a fisherman going night fishing. He apparently stopped by to ask White a question and found the door open. He peeked in and saw all of the blood around White, then called us."

"Any suspects?"

"You."

"What?" Moore asked incredulously.

"Emerson, we've got a nice and quiet island here. No big problems. All I know is that bodies have started dropping like hail in a hailstorm since you arrived on Chincoteague. Bodies are just piling up. Maybe I should be focusing on you," Deere said suspiciously. "Why did you come over here tonight? To cover your tracks?"

Moore thought quickly and decided to hold back the truth. "I was out for a drive and saw the lights, so I stopped."

"Sure you were." Deere's tone didn't hide his doubt.

Moore decided to shift the conversation. "Did you identify the body from the dumpster?"

"Yes. About an hour ago."

"Who was it?"

"Interesting that you didn't ask if it was Maya Simon," Deere commented as he looked suspiciously at Moore.

"Chief, I've been under a lot of stress here. I'm just not thinking clearly," Moore tried to explain away his question. "Who was it?"

"I'd rather not say."

Moore was torn as he wrestled what to reveal, especially since White was dead. The confidence that White had held him to should be okay to share openly with the Chief, but he wasn't ready.

"Can you tell me if it was Maya?" Moore pushed even though he knew otherwise.

"I can tell you that Maya is home. We've been in touch with her and she reported that she had been robbed of several rings and her purse. She's coming in tomorrow to file a police report."

"I see," Moore said. As he turned, he added, "I guess I'll be heading out and leave you to your investigation."

"That would be a good thing," Deere said as he watched Moore walk toward his car.

Once he reached his car, Moore dropped into the seat. Maybe White had lied to him about having abducted Simon, he thought as he sat. Moore's mind reeled with confusion. He wasn't sure who was telling the truth.

Before starting his car, he reached for his cell phone and called Simon.

"Hello?"

"Maya, it's Emerson."

"Hello, Emerson," she responded warmly.

"Can I come over? I need to see you," Moore said with a sense of urgency in his voice.

"You need to see me?" she asked surprised.

"Yes."

"I have company now. My cousin is here for the night," she explained.

"Do you think you could get away for thirty minutes?"

"I can do that. Where would you like to meet?"

"Assateague Beach. At the southernmost part of the parking lot."

"That works. I can be there in fifteen minutes."

"Good. I'll see you then."

Twenty minutes later, Moore was leaning against his Mustang at the Assateague Beach parking lot. A gentle breeze was blowing in from the ocean. It was a cloudless night and the moonlight shimmered on the waves as they broke on the beach.

Moore glanced at his watch for the fifth time in five minutes. Simon was late and Moore wondered if she was going to show up.

A sound from the road signaled an approaching car. Moore turned his head and saw a vehicle's headlights as the car pulled into the parking lot and drove toward him. As it neared, Moore recognized the vehicle as belonging to Simon. It pulled in next to Moore's and parked. Simon exited the car.

"Meet me on the beach! How romantic!" Simon said as she walked around the car and surprised Moore by embracing him tightly and kissing him on the lips.

Moore pulled back. "That's not what I had in mind," he spoke slowly and seriously.

"Oh, pooh! You're no fun, Emerson Moore," Simon responded with feigned indignation. "What did you have in mind?"

"I heard you were kidnapped last night," he said as he watched her face in the moonlight for a reaction.

"What do you mean?" she asked with surprise.

"I heard that Bo White kidnapped you and held you in his container home."

"I don't know what you're talking about," she stormed quietly.

As Simon's demeanor changed to a cool one, Moore stared at her as he decided what to say next. "Come on, Maya. Be truthful with me."

"I am."

"Then tell me what went on at Bo White's place."

"I told you that I don't know what you're talking about," she protested.

"Don't play games with me, Maya," Moore warned. "What would you say if I told you that Bo White told me that he kidnapped you?"

Simon didn't respond right away. She turned her head and stared at the waves breaking on the beach. After a minute, she spoke.

"Can I trust you?" she asked.

"I think I'm the most trustworthy one here. Of course you can."

Simon started to make a sarcastic comment, but stopped before uttering the words. Instead, she offered an explanation. "Yes, he did kidnap me. I didn't say anything because I didn't want to get Bo in trouble. He has gone through a lot with his son's death."

"You knew?" Moore asked stunned.

"Yes. He told me. How tragic!" she said with genuine remorse.

"Did you kill Bo?"

It was Simon's turn to register a look of shock. "No! What are you talking about?" she asked as her legs gave out and she dropped to the ground in a sitting position. Maya began to cry softly as she lowered her head and looked downward.

Moore sat next to her and explained. "I just came from his place and the police were there. Chief Deere told me that he had been murdered."

"He was alive when I last saw him."

"When was that?"

"About three hours ago. He left to run an errand or meet someone. I'm not sure which. I was able to work myself free and left. I walked home. It wasn't far. Nothing's far on this island," she answered. "Did Deere say how he was murdered or who did it?"

"No, he didn't."

"I don't know why anyone would murder someone like him. He didn't cause anyone any trouble," she reminisced through receding tears.

Moore decided not to tell her about White's night trips to Wallops. He wanted to keep that confidential.

"Are you missing a purse and rings?" Moore asked.

"Why yes, I am. How did you know about that?"

"Before I answer, can you tell me what happened to them?"

"Sure. I was robbed."

"Who robbed you?"

"I didn't recognize him."

"It was a guy?"

"Yes. He came up behind me when I left the grocery store and snatched them. Then he disappeared behind a fence."

"Did you report it to the police?"

"No. I was afraid. This is a small island. I don't need to be causing anyone any trouble and have it come back on me. I can always get another purse."

"But you're getting your purse and rings back, right?"

"My, but you are well-informed," she said as she looked at Moore's face.

"I heard that they turned up at the police station and they're being returned to you tomorrow."

In the moonlight Simon's moist eyes focused on Moore's eyes. "For some reason, I sense that you're suspicious about me."

"Should I be?"

Simon frowned and let out a little distraught whimper.

"No, why would you, Emerson?" she asked.

"I think you're holding back on me, Maya. Bo told me that he saw you and Hala meet up with one of the Kronsky brothers late the other night. I believe he said it was Joe Kronsky, the older one."

"He told you that?" she asked in surprise.

"Yes."

"I didn't know he was stalking me."

Moore was pleased with her response and quasi-acknowledgement. "Can you explain what was going on?"

Simon paused again before answering. "Yes, but you must keep what I'm going to tell you very confidential. Agreed?"

"Agreed."

"Hala and I are special agents. We were working to unmask whoever was causing the explosions of the rockets. They were causing setbacks to our efforts to resupply the International Space Station."

"Hala was working with you?" It was Moore's turn to be surprised.

"Yes. We work for NASA's in-house security department. They

developed cover stories for us and we had the right backgrounds to understand the technology although Hala was more technically trained than me."

"Why were you two meeting Kronsky?"

"We wanted to confront him."

"About what?"

"His involvement with the explosions on Wallops."

"What? Kronsky?" Moore was shocked by her news.

"Yes. Hala and I reviewed surveillance video that showed him appear outside the main entrance gate. He used to work for Horner and quit."

"Why did he quit?"

"I don't know. He didn't give a reason."

"Did Horner help you with your video review?"

"No. We didn't want to alert anyone that we were looking at the video."

"Who did Kronsky meet with?" Moore asked.

"We don't know. Whoever it was stayed in the shadows and we couldn't see the person."

"Do you have any suspicions?"

"Yes. Horner," she answered with confidence.

"What? Your head of security?"

"Yes. It makes perfect sense. He knows where all of the surveillance cameras are and he has access to the digital recordings. He can go in and manipulate the videos to erase any scenes that he's in. He also has master key access to every building on Wallops."

"I know the guy is a smart mouth and difficult for anyone to be around, but why would he do something like this?"

"Money. He's gone through two bankruptcies."

"I had no idea." Moore thought for a moment and then asked, "And who is giving him the money and why?"

"I'd guess Wu Tang and the Chinese government," Simon said confidently.

"Wu Tang?"

"Yeah. Quiet little guy. Smart, brilliant mind. He maintains such a low profile. Keeps below the radar."

"I would never have thought that he was involved. He seemed so low key. Why are the Chinese trying to blow up our rockets?"

"Space war. If they can slow down anything NASA does, it gives them time to work on their programs. I'm sure you've heard about their plans to establish a military base on the moon and explore Mars before we do. They're in the distraction business."

"Keep NASA off balance while they progress," Moore guessed.

"Exactly. And Tang is the money man, arranging wire transfers into Horner's account."

"How do you know that?"

"We've been able to track the deposits by working with some of the other agencies."

Moore looked at a piece of driftwood that had washed ashore. The waves continued to beat it just like Simon's insights were beating Moore's mind. Moore decided to drop a bombshell of his own on Simon.

"So, let's get back to Kronsky."

"Yes?"

"What happened during your parking lot encounter?" Moore asked.

"Of course he denied any involvement with Horner. We told him that we had him on surveillance video. That's when he exploded."

Chincoteague Calm

"What happened?"

"He said that we had nothing on him and he ran off behind the building. Hala and I stayed a little longer and then we both left," she answered.

"Were you ready to go to the police about Kronsky?"

"No, we were still gathering evidence on him, Tang and Horner. But we were close, Emerson."

"What about your purse and rings? When did they go missing?"

"They were gone when I returned home after escaping from White's place."

"Have you seen or talked to Hala since the other night?"

"No."

"You haven't had any contact with her since that night?"

"No."

"What would you say if I told you that it was Hala's burned body that was found in the trash container?" Moore watched Simon's face closely to monitor her reaction.

Simon turned pale. "What?"

"It's logical to me. I wouldn't doubt that Kronsky circled back and caught her by the dumpster, killed her and then burned the body. He probably broke into your home to kill you. But Bo saved your life by kidnapping you. When Kronsky couldn't find you, he stole your purse and ring, too. He then planted the purse by the dumpster before setting the body on fire." Moore didn't tell her about the incident at the police station with her ring and Kronsky's girlfriend.

"Why would he do that?"

"To throw off the police? Buy time? I don't know," Moore responded.

Simon furrowed her brow as she thought. "Or it could have been Horner."

"Why do you say that?"

"What if he was observing us and killed her after the three of us met in the parking lot?"

It was Moore's turn to hesitate for a moment. "I don't know. We'd better go to Deere and get him involved."

"I don't think we want to do that. I told you I'm conducting an investigation for NASA. If we move too quickly, I won't have concrete proof as to who is behind the rocket explosions. I need that proof so that we can prosecute them."

Moore was leery to wait. "I don't know, Maya," Moore said reluctantly. "I'm disinclined to wait."

"We have to. Look. I'll give you an exclusive to the story. Wouldn't that go well for you?"

Still doubting the wisdom in keeping this quiet, Moore said, "I'm not comfortable with this at all."

"Come on Emerson. Go with me on this," she urged. "I'll tell you what I'll do. We can keep this between us for the next forty-eight hours, then go to the police. Okay?"

Against his better judgment, Moore agreed. "I can work with that."

"Have you told anyone else about what's going on?"

"No."

"Good. Let's keep it that way." Simon looked at her watch. "It's almost ten o'clock. I need to get back to my cousin."

"Sorry about interrupting your evening," Moore said even though he was glad that he did and was able to hear her revelations.

"No problem, Emerson," she said as the two walked back to their cars. "I'll be in touch."

"I'm counting on it," he said as she jumped into her car and drove away. Moore slid into his car seat and sat for a few minutes, staring towards the ocean as he thought. He noticed a change in Simon when she left. The touchy-feely stuff had disappeared as she departed without kissing his cheek. That wasn't a big deal to him, but she seemed different. Moore wasn't sure. He smelled the ocean breeze. It smelled like danger to him.

Starting the engine, he backed out of his parking space and drove back to Terry's house. It had been a long evening.

Moore was so deep in thought that he didn't notice a car parked off the road. The car with its lights off pulled out of its parking spot and followed Moore at a discreet distance. It followed Moore as he drove off Assateague Island across the causeway to Chincoteague Island and home.

CHAPTER 19

Four Hours Later
Roe Terry's House

Half a block down the street, the man in the car had been sitting patiently as he watched the Terry house and imagined Moore settling in for the night. He raised his arm and looked at his watch for the umpteenth time. His patience was running out.

Glancing in his rearview mirror to ensure there were no vehicles out at this late hour, the man quietly opened the driver's door and slid out of the seat. He then carefully closed the car door and walked noiselessly to the Terry house, where he approached the enclosed rear patio.

Cautiously, he wiggled the door and found that it was locked as expected. He reached into his pants pocket and withdrew a thin piece of plastic about the size of two business cards end-to-end. Inserting the card into the doorjamb, he worked it around the strike plate and was able to pop the lock. Smiling, he returned the plastic to his pocket and withdrew a .38 caliber pistol from his waistband.

Holding the weapon in front of him, the intruder slowly opened the patio door and entered. Softly walking across the room, he walked to the family room entrance where he reached for the door knob and slowly turned it. Swinging the door open about twelve inches, he paused and listened for a minute. Hearing nothing to cause him concern, the intruder opened the door and stepped into the family room.

The red glow of a laser beam hit his right eye and caught him by surprise. He suddenly halted and looked down in horror as the laser beam settled on his chest.

"Looking for me?" Moore's voice asked from the other side of the darkened room, where he could see the intruder's figure silhouetted in the doorway. "Go ahead, make my night."

Rather than verbally answering the question, the man responded by quickly firing three shots in Moore's direction.

He was too late as Moore dropped to the floor and sent three deadly accurate shots into the man's chest.

The intruder crumpled in a heap to the floor. Moore waited for a few minutes to see if there was any movement. When there was none, he slowly stood to his feet and flicked on the light switch.

Holding his Smith & Wesson .38-caliber semiautomatic handgun in front of him, Moore walked over to the body. He gently nudged it with his right foot and did not get a response. Bending over the body, he saw the blood draining from the man's chest and covering the floor. He bent closer to peer at the man's face and saw that it was one of the Kronsky twins, Louie or Luke. Moore couldn't tell.

Moore reached for his cell phone and began to call the police. He didn't have to bother. Flashing lights from two arriving police cars bounced through the windows and off the walls. Three officers with weapons drawn ran up to the family room entrance.

Setting his weapon on a nearby end table, Moore walked over

to open the door for the arriving officers and was careful to make sure they could see his hands were empty.

"We had a report of gunshots fired," Chief Deere said as he walked into the room followed by the other officers.

Moore quickly explained what had happened as one of the officers knelt next to Kronsky.

"He's gone, Chief," the officer reported.

"Which one of the Kronskys is that?" Deere asked.

"Luke," the officer responded.

Deere turned to face Moore. "Is Roe or his wife home?"

"No. Not yet."

"Like I told you earlier this evening, things were a lot quieter in these parts before you arrived, Emerson. You're chasing away our Chincoteague calm."

"Sorry about that. I prefer calm, too," Moore commented quietly.

"But that wouldn't work for you, now would it?"

"How's that?" Moore asked as he looked at the chief.

"Being quiet."

"I don't follow you, Chief," Moore said.

"How are you going to write a story if it's too quiet?" Deere asked with a touch of irritation in his voice.

"I guess you have a point there," Moore agreed.

"You're damn right I have a point." Deere looked over at Kronsky's body. "This is the second Kronsky to die tonight."

"What?" Moore asked in shock.

"We fished Joe Kronsky out of the channel an hour ago. Somebody put a bullet through the back of his head." Deere pulled a pencil from his pocket as he walked over to the end table and used it to pick up the Smith & Wesson. "Your gun?"

"It belongs to Roe, but yes, I used it tonight."

"How many times tonight?" the chief probed.

Moore shook his head from side to side. "Chief, I used it once to protect myself. I admit to killing Luke here in self-defense, but I didn't have anything to do with Joe Kronsky's death."

"Were you here all night?"

"For the most part. I did meet with Maya Simon earlier this evening."

"What for?"

"I wanted to talk with her about Bo White."

"What about?"

"Just some suspicions I had."

"Emerson, I want you to follow me back to headquarters for a formal chat. Can you do that?"

"Sure. I don't have anything to hide."

"I hope you don't, at least for your sake," Deere said as he turned to the two officers. "Why don't you secure the scene and wait for the coroner and the forensic team to arrive. I'll be back at the station."

"Will do," one of the officers replied as Deere walked out of the house with Moore following him.

The men entered their vehicles and drove back to the police station where Deere grilled Moore for an hour before releasing him.

CHAPTER 20

Mid-Morning
Roe Terry's House

"Sounds like a real mess over there," Sedler spoke into his cell phone after hearing Moore's update of the recent murders, the attempt on Moore's life and Moore's visit during the early morning hours at Chincoteague's police station.

"It is and I need to get this figured out," Moore replied to his boss at *The Post*.

"What are your next steps, Emerson?"

"I'd like to see if I can get into Bo White's home and snoop around. You never know what you can uncover."

"Sounds good to me."

"I'd also like to see if Maya Simon will allow me to review the personnel files on Hal Horner."

"Their head of security?"

"Yes. He's my primary suspect at this point, but I'm not sure what his motive would be."

"Have you run any background checks on him?"

"Not yet, but I plan to this morning," Moore responded as he sat in the enclosed patio area at the rear of Terry's house. "I also want to check out Wu Tang. I want to see his personnel file."

"Think that Simon woman will let you see those files?" Sedler asked skeptically.

"Don't know, but she seems as eager as me to get to the bottom of these murders; especially how they relate to the rockets exploding."

"Good luck on that."

"It's worth a try."

"You be careful," Sedler cautioned Moore.

"I try to be, boss."

"Sure you do." Sedler knew how Moore liked to push the edge.

The two ended their call and Moore made himself a cup of coffee and spent some time on his laptop googling Hal Horner and Wu Tang. After two hours and a shave and shower, Moore headed out the door as he intended to check out Bo White's place.

Moore enjoyed the drive with the fresh air and late morning sun beating on his face as he neared Captain Bob's Marina. Slowing his convertible to turn into the parking lot, Moore saw Donna Roeske's SUV parked next to Bo White's home. Moore saw her place something into her vehicle and then close the door.

When she noticed Moore, she had a concerned look on her face. As Moore pulled up to the building, Roeske hurried to close the open door to White's home and attach a padlock.

"Good morning, Donna," Moore said as he exited his parked car.

"Hello, Emerson," she began nervously. "I didn't expect you to be out here this morning."

Moore's curiosity was flying. He wondered what Roeske had

been doing in White's home. Could she have been the woman that White's son was going to meet? Was she involved in the murders? That would be hard to comprehend as she seemed like such a nice and charming southern lady.

"I thought I'd take a drive out." Looking over her shoulder at the door to White's container, Moore added, "I was hoping that I could take a look inside."

Roeske looked toward the road and back to Moore. "I guess that would be fine," she said. "I was just in there to get a couple of my cooking pans that I'd loaned Bo."

Moore breathed a sigh of relief. He was glad that was the reason that she was in there and hoped she was telling him the truth, but he wasn't entirely certain.

Unlocking the door, she pulled it open. "You go ahead and look around. I'm going back to the marina office, so you be sure to lock it up when you're done."

"I'll do that," Moore said as he watched her climb into her SUV and drive it the short distance to her reserved parking spot next to the marina office. He saw her exit the vehicle and walk into her office. He then turned and walked over to the open door.

Stepping inside, Moore saw the bloodstains from White's body on the floor. He leaned inside the doorway and tried to imagine what might have occurred that night. After a few minutes, he focused on the room's contents.

It looked like someone had searched the room. The cushions on an old love seat had been slashed open, as was the mattress that White slept on. The contents of various boxes and jars of food had been emptied on the floor. Pockets on clothes were pulled inside out. Someone was looking hard for something, or somethings. Moore wondered to himself if it had been the murderer, Roeske or the police.

Shrugging his shoulders, Moore began to look through the contents to see if he could find anything of interest. He worked his way slowly from one end of the container to the other without finding anything noteworthy other than a copy of the *Koran* and a prayer rug. Moore hadn't realized that White was a Muslim.

Deciding to leave, Moore began walking toward the door and tripped over a throw rug. He smiled to himself at his clumsiness and then his eyes widened as he looked in the corner of the room where an old upright sweeper stood. Why would White have a sweeper when he had a throw rug that could be shaken out, Moore asked himself. What a perfect hiding place, he thought.

He walked over to the vacuum cleaner and opened the bag compartment. When he looked inside, he found several envelopes addressed to Bo. The return address showed that Bo's son had sent them from Wallops Island.

Interesting that White had hidden them, Moore thought as he sat down to read the one with the most recent postmark. It confirmed what Bo had told Moore about his son meeting with a female to solve the mystery surrounding the rocket explosions and sabotage. The female's name was not mentioned.

As Moore looked through the other letters, he found a photo of a young black man who Moore guessed was Bo's son. He was more intrigued by what he saw in the background. It was Captain Bob's Marina.

Moore wondered if Roeske was connected to the son's death and to the explosions. He also realized why Bo had decided to use Captain Bob's Marina as his home. It would have made it easier for him to keep an eye on Roeske. Moore was conflicted. He knew that he'd been wrong about people in the past and was having a hard time thinking that Roeske was involved. She had such a nice personality and seemed so genuine.

Moore sat back and thought for a few minutes before deciding to walk over to the marina office to speak with Roeske.

As he stood up, he noticed that a business card had fallen out of one of the envelopes. Moore stooped and picked up the card, turning it over in his hand to read it. He was stunned. The card had Bo's son's name on it and it showed that he was a special agent for the FBI. The picture was getting clearer. Bo's son was on an undercover mission for the FBI.

Moore returned the business card to the stack of correspondence and placed his findings in the trunk of his Mustang. He then walked across the parking lot and into the marina's office.

"Hi, Donna," Moore said as he walked up to the counter where she was standing.

"You lock it up?" she asked as she smiled at Moore.

Moore liked her smile. "Yes, I did."

"I want to be careful and not cause any problems for Chief Deere," she commented with a touch of hesitancy.

"I understand. He's a good guy," Moore added.

"He is."

Without mentioning the other items he found in the vacuum cleaner bag, Moore showed Roeske the picture that he found. "I found this picture over there. Do you know him?" Moore closely watched Roeske's reaction as she took the picture and examined it.

"I do. He came out a couple of times with a bunch of the folks from Wallops to go fishing. They rented one of my boats."

"Do you know his name?" Moore asked after seeing nothing concerning in her reaction to the picture.

"No. One of the other guys signed the rental agreement."

"Was there a female in the group?"

"No, they were all men," she responded. After pausing, she

added, "There was an Asian with them."

"Really?" Moore said with a raised eyebrow. "Did you hear his name mentioned?"

"Yes, but I don't remember it," she replied before adding, "It did remind me of a breakfast drink".

"Tang?" Moore suggested.

"Yes. That's it."

"Good guess on my part," Moore smiled. "I drank that stuff as a kid."

"Why are you asking so many questions about the picture?" she wondered.

"Just curious. Not sure if there's any significance," Moore explained.

"Do you want me to let you know if any of them come around again?"

"Yes. I'd appreciate that."

"I'll give you a call if they show up."

Moore expected that she wouldn't be calling about Bo White's son showing up since he was dead. "Thanks. I guess I should be heading out."

Roeske gave Moore a warm smile as she looked at him with her pretty aqua blue eyes. "You let me know if I can help you."

"I'll do that," Moore said as he walked to the door and returned to his car.

Late that afternoon, Moore drove over to Wallops Island. He was anxious to see Maya Simon. Parking his car, he climbed the stairs to Simon's office. As he entered the hallway, he saw someone duck down the back stairway. Wonder what that was about? Or am I becoming too suspicious, he thought to himself.

"Hi, Emerson," Simon greeted Moore as he walked into her

office. She walked around her desk and gave Moore a quick hug and peck on the cheek. "It's always so nice to have you around."

Moore noticed that she seemed more like her old self. "It is?" Moore asked hesitantly.

"Yes, it is. There's something calming about your presence," she replied as she returned to her side of the desk and sat. "And I need all the calmness I can get with everything going on. I just had a visitor."

Moore smiled to himself at having seen the fleeing figure. "Oh?"

"As a matter of fact, I've had several visitors. Several employees have been talking to me privately about their suspicions about Hal Horner."

"What kind of concern?"

"They think he may be behind the explosions."

"Why do they think that?"

"They've seen him sneaking around the facility at night. Going into buildings where parts have been found to have been damaged."

"Maybe Horner is just doing his job. Checking on the facilities," Moore suggested.

"I don't know. He can be pretty smart about things."

"Like the fox in the hen house?" Moore surmised.

"Could be."

"But nothing concrete? No one has seen him sabotage anything?"

"No."

"Can't do anything unless there's proof," Moore suggested.

"I know. Here's his personnel file and Wu Tang's file," she said as she handed them across the desk. "You can look through them here, but you can't take them out of the office."

Reaching for the files, Moore asked, "If I see something of interest, is it okay for me to take a photo of it with my cell phone?"

Simon frowned. "I wish I could let you, but I can't. You can jot down notes, but no copies of anything. I'd be in big trouble."

"I guess I'll have to work with that," he said as he opened Horner's file and began to review it. Over the next hour Moore went through both files while Simon stayed busy with other tasks on her desk.

Pushing the files toward Simon, Moore spoke. "Nothing here that stands out to me. I'm not sure that I'd expect anything to stand out."

"Why is that?" Simon asked.

"I'd think that their backgrounds were sanitized so that there was nothing glaring."

"Including Horner?" she asked.

"Maybe, although that would be more difficult to do." Then Moore asked, "Did you know two of the Kronsky brothers were killed last night?"

Simon sat back in her chair. A shocked look filled her face. "No!"

"The police found Joe in the channel and I killed Luke," Moore said as he watched her closely for her reaction.

"What? You killed Luke?"

"After we left Assateague Beach last night, I went home. A few hours later, the sensor outside the house beeped that someone had pulled into the driveway. I wasn't expecting anyone at that hour so I grabbed Mr. Smith and Mr. Wesson, then headed to the rear of the house. I heard someone fiddling with the rear patio door and waited in the family room. When the intruder walked in, he shot at me. I dropped and returned fire. I guess I was a little too accurate with my shot placement."

"I didn't know that you were familiar with weapons," she said.

"From my past," he replied as he found her comment about his weapon skill interesting. He had expected her to focus on Luke's death or the purpose of his intrusion.

"Why do you think he broke in?"

"Don't know," Moore answered.

"Was there anything at Roe Terry's house that would interest Luke?"

"Me."

"What do you mean?" she asked with a puzzled look.

"I wasn't positive, but I thought that a car followed me from Assateague Beach. I wonder if it could have been Kronsky."

"Emerson, are you sure? Why would he want to follow you?"

"I don't know, Maya. I don't have a good answer for that. As a matter of fact, I don't have good answers for a lot of what's been happening here."

"Me neither," Simon agreed.

Simon stared into space for a moment before turning back to Moore. "I just remembered something. One of our employees thought they saw Luke Kronsky on our grounds yesterday. I wonder if he could have been working with Horner."

"If he was, then maybe they were worried that you and I were on to them," Moore offered.

"And they should be. We've got to get to the bottom of this," Simon said firmly. "If we can identify who's behind all of this, you'll get a great story for your newspaper and I'll have a chance to become the permanent head of this facility."

"Win-win."

"Win-win indeed," Simon agreed.

Moore paused for a second, and then asked, "But I thought you

Chincoteague Calm

were an agent investigating the explosions. You want to give up that life to run this site?"

"Actually, I do. I've given it a lot of thought. I've been enjoying this gig and I've been told that I've done a great job. So, why not?"

"Okay then. Let me take a crack at Horner and see what I can get out of him."

"Sure," she said as she reached for a portable radio. "Hal. Come in."

After a few seconds, Horner responded. "Yes, Maya?"

"I've got Emerson with me and he'd like to talk to you. Where are you?"

"I'm at the Payload Processing Building. I can come over."

"No, that won't be necessary. I'll send him to you."

"Unescorted?" Horner asked in disbelief.

"It's okay. I'll authorize it."

"Okay. I'll watch for him."

"Out," Simon said as she ended the transmission and looked at Moore as she handed him a map. Pointing at one of the buildings, she said, "That's where he is. Think you can find it without any trouble?"

"Yes, I can," Moore said as he briefly looked at the map and stood. "I'm not looking forward to talking with him."

"I know what you mean. He's so sarcastic."

"I bet as a kid, he licked the beaters while they were running," Moore quipped.

"Emerson Moore, I'm surprised hearing a comment like that from you," she said with feigned indignation.

"I have my moments, too. I'll let you know if I learn anything," he said with a smirk as he headed to the doorway.

"Emerson," she called before he walked out of her office.

He stopped and turned. "Yes?"

"Thank you. I'm glad we met," she said as she gave him a warm smile.

"I'm glad we met, too," he said quietly as he turned and left her office.

He walked downstairs and outside to his car. He drove across the causeway to the launch area and the payload processing building. Parking his car, he exited it and walked toward the building. The side door opened and out stepped Horner. He was not happy to see his unexpected visitor.

"Hello, Hal," Moore greeted the frowning Horner.

"You validate my inherent distrust of strangers," Horner said as he gave Moore a cold welcome.

Trying to let it run off his back, Moore said, "Oh come on, Hal. I'm not that bad."

"Moore, I will always cherish my initial misconceptions I had about you."

Moore ignored the sharp comments and took the high road. "Hal, I realize that there's a lot of pressure on you. I just want to help you."

"So what are you? Some knight in shining armor who shows up to save the damsel in distress? Well a big 'Hi-yo Silver!' it's the Lone Ranger here to save the day," Horner retorted sarcastically.

"Whoa. You are stressed," Moore observed.

Horner surprised Moore with his next comment. "Really, Moore. I like you."

"You do?" Moore asked incredulously.

"Yes. You remind me of when I was young and stupid," Horner said in a cutting tone.

"If your strategy is to throw insults to make me go away, it won't work. Maya sent me down here to help and that's what I'm going to do," Moore countered.

"Name dropper," Horner said coolly as he realized that all Moore had to do was call his boss to get heat put on him. Horner resigned himself to working with Moore. "What can I do to help you?" he asked reluctantly.

Moore closely watched Horner for his reaction as he spoke. "Joe and Luke Kronsky were each killed last night in separate incidents."

"That doesn't surprise me," Horner said emotionlessly. "Those boys were troublemakers."

"I find it interesting that you didn't ask me how they died," Moore said as he continued to observe Horner's reaction.

"Why do I care?" Horner said flippantly. He then asked, "Drug overdose?"

"No. I said they each were killed. Joe's body was fished out of the channel last night and Luke was shot when he broke into a house." Moore decided not to reveal to Horner that he had killed Luke.

"Good riddance," Horner said nonchalantly. "Now, what can I do for you?"

"Have you made any progress on who's responsible for the rocket explosions?"

An all-knowing grin of superiority appeared on Horner's face. "I have."

Moore waited for Horner to continue. When he didn't, Moore probed. "Are you going to share it with me? Or should I get Maya on the phone?"

"A couple of things. I haven't found any evidence of tampering with any of the rocket components since the deaths of Orlov and Yazbek."

"So you believe one of them was responsible?"

"That's the second thing which is perplexing. Late this morning, Wu Tang was helping me. I noticed that a box appeared to have been opened. So I first checked it for fingerprints and I found three sets."

"Were you able to identify them?"

"Yes. That's where I encountered a conundrum."

"How's that?"

"The system I use is linked to the FBI and I found prints from Orlov, Yazbek and Joe Kronsky."

"Amazing. The three of them must have been working together."

"Or their ghosts," Horner said pridefully.

"I don't get your point," Moore said with a puzzled look.

Horner couldn't help himself as he cracked, "Sometimes I wonder who ties your shoe laces for you."

Moore ignored the comment. "What do you mean? I don't get the ghost thing."

"The delivery we checked was made this morning. You want to explain to me how those three dead people had their fingerprints on the package?"

Moore's mouth dropped open in amazement. "I've got no idea."

"And neither do I."

Seeing Moore roll his eyes, Horner let go with another missile at Moore. "Keep rolling your eyes. Maybe you'll find a brain back there."

This guy doesn't quit, Moore thought to himself as he ignored the comment and spoke. "This just doesn't make sense."

"Amazing. I believe this is the first time we agree on something," Horner remarked snidely. "That's scary."

Moore's mind was racing with possible explanations, none of

which he felt were reasonable. "What about the contents? Were they damaged?"

"Yes. Wu Tang verified that they were. Two key sensors were damaged and would have caused the next rocket to malfunction. We have to reorder the sensors."

"Does Maya know about this?" Moore asked as he wondered why she hadn't mentioned it while he was in her office.

"No. I'll let her know shortly when I stop in her office. You have any other questions?"

"I do, but I'm flabbergasted by your fingerprint revelation." Moore was anxious to pay a visit to Chief Deere. "I'm going to head back to Chincoteague. I'll let you know if I have an opinion on this later."

"Okay, but if I want your opinion, I'll give it to you," Horner said belligerently as Moore ignored the rude comment and walked to his car.

Within twenty minutes, Moore had parked his car at police headquarters and walked into the lobby. The first person Moore encountered was Detective Huffman and she wasn't a happy camper.

"What kind of trouble are you stirring up now?" Huffman asked as she eyed Moore with obvious suspicion.

"I'd like to talk about the murders of Orlov, Yazbek and Joe Kronsky," Moore replied.

"What about them?"

"I have a few questions that I'd like answered."

"Not sure that we want to comment on active investigations, Mr. Moore. I'll check with Chief Deere," she said coldly as she turned suddenly and walked back to Deere's office.

Within minutes, she returned to the lobby and ushered Moore to Deere's office. She and Moore sat in chairs across the desk from Deere.

"Emerson, Barbara tells me you have a few questions," the chief started.

"I do. I was over at Wallops and I met with Hal Horner."

"Yes," the chief said as he listened.

"He mentioned that he found fingerprints belonging to Orlov, Yazbek and Joe Kronsky on a package that was delivered today," Moore said. He watched Deere look quickly at Huffman and back to Moore.

"That's an interesting turn of events," the chief said quietly as Huffman eyed Moore closely.

"That's an understatement." Moore stared directly into Deere's eyes. "Are they actually dead or are they being held in protective custody?"

"Steady there, Emerson. Don't go jumping to conclusions. All three are very dead. Just like Luke," the chief answered.

"Then how could their fingerprints turn up today?"

"I assume the package came from some distance away."

"I'd guess so. Horner didn't say."

"Barbara, would you close my door for me?" Deere asked the detective.

Huffman stood and walked over to the office door. After closing it, she returned to her chair.

"Emerson, I really do like you. I did check you out with some folks and they tell me you're a straight shooter."

"I am," Moore agreed.

"I'm going to tell you something that must remain confidential. You cannot share this with anyone."

"I'm good with that."

"Chief, are you sure?" Huffman had a worried look on her face as she anticipated what the chief was about to reveal.

"I believe we can trust Emerson. In fact, you may be able to help us."

"Sure. Anything I can do to get to the bottom of this," Moore said assuring the chief.

"There's a bit of information that we have not revealed to the public and might explain what Horner found."

"And that is?" Moore pushed.

"When the bodies of Orlov, Yazbek and Joe Kronsky were found, each of them was missing their right hand."

"What?" Moore asked in disbelief.

"That's right. They were sliced off cleanly at the wrist bone by someone who had a very sharp knife," Deere explained.

"That's weird. Why would the murderer do that?" Moore asked as his mind flashbacked to the knife that Bo White had carried.

"Because murderers can be gruesome," Huffman interjected.

"They are," Deere agreed. "We don't know, but this is the first report of the missing hands turning up."

"I don't get it."

"Like we said, serial killers can be psychotic. Who knows what kind of reasons the killer had for cutting off their hands."

"Don't I recall that Muslims cut off a hand for stealing?" Moore asked before answering his own question. "Yeah, they do. I think they do that in Saudi Arabia at noon on Fridays."

Deere nodded, then continued. "For what it's worth, I should tell you that one other body was missing a right hand."

"Whose body?" Moore asked with a worried look. He knew that it wouldn't be Luke Kronsky's.

"Bo White's."

"What?"

"Yes, but we haven't heard about fingerprints from Bo White turning up anywhere," Deere mentioned.

Moore felt a shiver of revulsion run up his back. "Do you have any suspects?" Moore asked.

"That's not something I'm comfortable with sharing with you at this point. I only told you about the hands since Horner mentioned it to you."

"You might want to give Horner a call. Wu Tang was with him and may know about the fingerprints. And Horner was going to see Maya and let her know," Moore cautioned the two officers.

"Barbara, could you track down Horner and tell him to keep this hush-hush and the same with Tang and Maya if they are aware?" Deere asked Huffman.

"Sure. I'll do it right now," she said as she stood and started to leave the office to make her calls.

"And ask Hal if you and I can stop by Wallops within the next thirty minutes to visit with him about the fingerprints," Deere added.

"It's after five," Huffman noted as she glanced at her watch.

"I bet he's working overtime on this. See if he has time for us," Deere urged before he turned back to Moore. "Emerson, unless you have something else pertinent to this investigation, I need to go."

"I guess not," Moore responded as he stood and, escorted by Deere, headed for the lobby. His mind was twisting with questions about the information he had just learned.

Fifteen minutes later, Moore had returned to the Terry house and began mixing up a salad for dinner. As he prepared his meal, he stopped several times to sip on a rum and Coke. When he finished making his salad, he carried it and his drink to the enclosed patio which provided a view of Chincoteague Bay.

Sitting at a table, he held the cold glass to his forehead and allowed it to soothe the headache he had developed on the way back from the police station. His brain felt like it was on overload with the deluge of information it had processed over the last few days.

Moore tried to enjoy the setting sun's soft rays as they streamed between the window blinds. He watched mindlessly as it dropped below the horizon and Chincoteague Bay.

As the evening's shadows began to creep in, Moore switched on a nearby table lamp and picked at his salad. His appetite had waned and disappeared like the sunset. After five minutes, he stood and took his plate to the kitchen and poured himself another rum and Coke.

When he returned to the enclosed patio, he set down his drink and his laptop, which he had carried to the patio. Turning it on, he sipped on his drink while he waited for it to connect with the internet. He needed to do some research.

After researching for thirty minutes, Moore found several interesting articles on right hands being severed at the wrist. It was a form of punishment for theft in Saudi Arabia, Yemen, Sudan, Somalia and Sharia-controlled areas in Nigeria.

Moore sat back for a moment and took a large swallow of his drink as he thought about the murder victims and their severed hands. Was it the work of a Muslim who had been offended and, if it was, how did it tie into the rocket explosions? It just wasn't coming together.

Moore leaned forward and began searching Donna Roeske online. He hoped that he wouldn't find anything tying her to the murders, but he'd been surprised in the past by people he thought weren't involved. Some people were very good at masking their motives and actions.

An hour later, Moore reached for his cell phone and called Steve

Nicholas in Washington. He was formerly the assistant director of the top secret National Intelligence Agency and had worked for a number of intelligence agencies in and around Washington. He knew everyone, including congressmen and presidents and had a wealth of contacts. He was always willing to dig for information for Moore whenever he needed assistance.

"Hello, Emerson," Nicholas greeted him.

"Hi, Steve. I need your help," Moore said. His voice was filled with exasperation.

"Of course you do," Nicholas chuckled. "You always call when you need my help. Where are you?"

"Chincoteague Island."

"I know the area. It's near NASA's Wallops Island facility."

"Right you are."

"What can I do for you?"

Moore quickly told Nicholas about the rocket explosions and murders.

"I've read about some of the explosions. And where do you need my help?" Nicholas asked.

"I have three key suspects and the police are keeping their investigation close to the vest," Moore explained.

"As they should," Nicholas commented. "Who are your suspects?"

"Hal Horner the head of Security on Wallops, Wu Tang the Chinese rocket specialist and Donna Roeske who owns Captain Bob's Marina.

"What do you need from me?"

"I'd love to see if any of your alphabet agency contacts have anything revealing in their records. Or if NSA has anything interesting about conversations for the phone numbers that these three might use."

"Emerson, that might be a little difficult. Besides, I'd think these people are smart enough not to use the phones."

"You've got a point," Moore said dejectedly.

"But, I do have a friend who is very adept at hacking emails. Would you like her to see what she can find in their email trails?"

"That would be great, and maybe sixty days before and after the rocket explosions over the last two years."

"I'll have her do that."

"You might have her check the emails for two of the murder victims—Grigori Orlov the Russian and Hala Yazbek who worked with the French," Moore suggested. "You never know."

"Orlov could take some extra time if he has some emails in Russian," Nicholas cautioned. "We'd have to get those translated."

"I hadn't thought of that, but it shouldn't be a problem."

"Glad to help. You stay safe."

"I'm doing my best," Moore replied. "Thanks for your help, Steve."

"Sure. I'll be back to you as fast as I can."

The two men ended their call and Moore returned to his laptop. Two hours later, he walked into his bedroom. He was drained from his research and three rum and Cokes. He would sleep well that night. He needed a restful sleep.

The next morning, Moore's phone rang, waking him from a deep sleep. "Hello?" he answered groggily.

"Emerson, it's Roe. How are things going? You didn't burn down my house while we've been gone, have you?" Terry teased.

"No," Moore answered. Deciding not to update Terry on the murders until Terry returned home. Moore added, "Things have been relatively quiet here."

"Good. Nothing quite like spending time on peaceful Chincoteague Island."

"Yeah. It's been pretty tranquil," Moore responded as he chuckled quietly to himself. He couldn't wait to tell Terry about how wild the events of the past few days had been. Island life would never be the same.

"Yep. Chincoteague is a great place to go for peace and quiet. Fantastic place to meditate."

"You mean medicate?" Moore asked jokingly. He felt like he was ready for some strong medication.

"No, meditate," Terry responded. "I wanted to let you know that Monnie and I should be home in the next couple of days. We're hanging out with some decoy carving friends of mine a little longer than expected."

"Sounds like fun. Have a great time. I'll look forward to seeing you."

They ended their call and Moore stood. After stretching, he changed into his running clothes and went for a run out to Assateague Island and back. Then he jumped into the shower and changed clothes. He fixed some scrambled eggs and a large cup of coffee and took them to the kitchen table. He had taken four bites of his eggs when his cell phone rang. It was Maya Simon.

"Emerson?"

"Yes."

"I wanted to let you know that some top-level NASA security guys are coming over tomorrow to do a thorough review of Wallops security."

"I bet that will have Horner in a tizzy," Moore offered.

"He'll be beside himself over their arrival."

"You haven't told him yet?"

"No. I'll wait until they get here," she answered.

"Maya, do you know Donna Roeske?"

"Yes. She owns Captain Bob's Marina. Why do you ask?"

"Do you have any idea whether she knows Horner?"

"Now that you mention it, I have seen her on Wallops a couple of times with Hal."

"Do you know why she was with him?"

"Arranging a fishing charter? I don't really know. I've never thought anything about it. Why are you asking?" Simon asked, perplexed.

"I'm suspicious that she might be involved with Horner, but I can't make a connection."

"I think you're wrong on that one, Emerson. I'm more focused on Horner and Tang working together."

"Did Horner update you on the fingerprints?"

Simon hesitated before responding. "Yes, but I can't discuss that."

"I was in Chief Deere's office when he had Detective Huffman called you folks. I know all about the fingerprints from the severed hands of the victims. That's just plain weird!" Moore persisted.

"Murderers are that way, Emerson," she agreed. "What else do you know?" she asked.

Moore quickly updated her on everything he had learned since his visit with her the day before.

When he was finished, she commented, "You've been busy."

"That's for sure."

"Listen Emerson. I have an idea. If we can break this wide open, I will have a good shot at being named the permanent head of operations here."

"What's your idea?"

Moore listened closely and agreed with her plan. She would work quickly to put it in motion.

CHAPTER 21

Clam Shells Pub
Chincoteague Island

After parking his Mustang in the lot, Moore walked into the pub and requested an outside table overlooking the bay. As he followed the hostess to the table, he noticed the sky had a pinkish tint as sunset neared. The clouds overhead reminded him of cotton candy.

Seated facing the entranceway, Moore saw Simon enter the pub and waved to her. Her face broke into a wide smile and she hurried through the outdoor area to him. She planted a wet kiss on Moore's cheek before sitting next to him.

Moore's hand unconsciously reached up and wiped his cheek. "That was a pleasant surprise," he said to her as he smiled.

"I just want you to know how much I appreciate your helping me with all of the trouble that's been going on. You're my knight on a white horse."

"More like a fool on a jackass," Moore cracked. "We're just not making the progress that I expected."

"Stop it, Emerson," she cooed. "You're being too hard on yourself."

"Honestly, all of this mess has me stymied."

"We'll resolve it. We're a good team," she said as she looked around the pub. "Looks like we're the first ones to arrive," she said as she stroked Moore's left arm.

When Horner walked through the entrance, he saw Moore, who waved him over to the table.

"Hello, Moore. I didn't realize that you were joining us," Horner said as he sat. His face looked stern. "I don't know what it is about you, but when I look at you, I hear the theme music from the movie *Jaws* playing in the back of my mind."

"Hal, you're being overly dramatic," Simon said, defending Moore.

"Whatever!" Horner replied before placing a drink order with a server.

"That's a bit uncalled for," Moore said to the rude response.

Horner eyed Moore through slitted eyelids. "Everyone has the right to be stupid, but some people abuse the privilege," Horner said as he drummed his finger on the tabletop and looked toward the bay and the setting sun.

"I can see this meeting is starting off on a positive note," Simon said sarcastically.

"Hello, everyone," Tang said as he walked over to the table and sat on one of the chairs.

Horner looked from Tang to Simon and Moore. "I thought it was just going to be the three of us."

"I guess I forgot to mention the other two in my email," Simon said.

"Other two?" Horner questioned.

"And number three is here now," Moore said as he stood and pulled out a chair for the woman.

"Sorry I'm late, Emerson," a southern-accented voice said as she sat.

"I believe most of you know Donna Roeske from Captain Bob's Marina," Emerson said as he returned to his seat.

Horner looked with disdain at the group. "I was going to call this a gathering of eagles, but maybe it's a gathering of the lost."

"Stop it, Hal. You shouldn't talk to nice people like that. I swear that you'd get road rage just walking behind slow people in the grocery store," Roeske drawled sweetly, dishing out a reprimand as only a charming southern lady could.

Horner threw Roeske a dangerous look, but didn't speak.

"I didn't realize that you two knew each other so well," Simon said.

"Not as well as he'd like," Roeske replied. "He's always calling me to arrange fishing charters and to hit on me, right Hal?"

Horner didn't comment. He stared across the bay.

"I'll tell you one thing. If you run across him in the grocery store and see him buying lemons, I'd suggest you go the other way. It's not for lemonade," Roeske said.

"What do you mean, Donna?" Moore asked. "I don't follow."

Roeske smiled before answering. "That's because when life gives Hal lemons, he squeezes them in your eyes."

Horner's face reddened as he glared at Roeske. Before he could speak, Tang changed the topic. "Why are we here, Maya? What's this all about?"

"Emerson and I have been working together to solve the mystery of the rocket explosions and the recent murders on the island."

"What?" Horner exploded. "That's my responsibility!"

"Calm down, Hal," Simon said firmly. "We are augmenting

the fine work you are doing," she explained as she tried to soothe Horner's feelings.

"And then why are we here?" Tang asked, as he emphasized the word *"we."*

"That's just what I was going to ask," Roeske added.

Simon glanced briefly at Moore, who nodded his head before she spoke. "Like I said, we wanted to talk to you about the rocket explosions and the murders that have taken place here."

"Wait one second!" Roeske's southern charm disappeared as she snarled. "I had nothing to do with any of that. There's no reason for me to be here!" she said indignantly as she stood. She glared at Moore. "I thought you knew me better than that. Apparently, I was wrong."

Moore allowed a small smile to escape from his lips at her reaction. It confirmed to him that she wasn't involved and he was glad, but he had to see that reaction in front of everyone to be sure.

"I'm sorry, Donna," Moore started, but she was in no mood to talk further. She whirled around and marched out of the restaurant, fuming as she walked.

Moore's eyes swung back to look at Horner and Tang. One down, two to go, Moore thought to himself.

Horner was the first to comment angrily. "Maya, why would you think for one moment that I'd be involved with any of this? Is this miscreant misdirecting you?" Horner stormed as he scowled fiercely at Moore.

"Hal, simmer down. Wait. We want to talk to Wu first," Simon replied.

Tang's narrow eyes widened. "Why would you think I'm involved?" he echoed Horner's inquiry.

"Go ahead, Emerson," Simon spoke calmly.

"If we were to look at a motive, Wu, it would be to take

advantage of delaying the U.S.'s rocket program because of unsafe launch problems like the rockets malfunctioning and exploding."

"Why?" Tang asked.

"I've spent a lot of time researching the Chinese space program and potential Chinese aggression in space. I saw that China now has the ability to destroy any nation's satellites with rocket weaponry. You can neutralize strategic systems for intelligence, navigation, missile warning and communications."

"That doesn't give you a motive. Shouldn't any country develop the best defensive weapons?" Tang countered.

Moore ignored the question as he continued. "China's developed powerful lasers, electromagnetic railguns and other high-powered weapons for space-based attacks on satellites. It's public knowledge that you tested a laser gun with pinpoint accuracy that took out a low-orbiting satellite.

"Last year, China tied the U.S. with twenty-two orbital launches and moved ahead of Russia in the number of launches. Anything that can be done to slow down our efforts to support the International Space Station provides China with additional time to move ahead of us."

"You are wrong," Tang commented quietly.

"I'm not so sure about that. You've launched your first cargo-carrying spacecraft, Tianzhou-1, which carried five tons of supplies to your orbiting Tiangong-2 space lab, which is manned by two taikonauts. That space lab and cargo ship are test platforms for creating a space station in support of your planned moon missions."

Tang shook his head negatively as Moore continued.

"China returned to the moon several times to gather soil samples and set up recording instruments as it moves forward with plans to build a military base there. You have several lunar missions lined up in the future." Moore paused and looked at Tang. "You certainly have the motive for causing problems here and committing murder to cover it up."

"You are wrong. You are absolutely wrong, Mr. Moore. I did not have anything to do with sabotaging any of the launches," Tang protested. "And I had nothing to do with the murders. The thought of hands being sliced off is revolting."

Moore's and Simon's eyes widened at the comment.

"I didn't say anything about hands being cut off," Moore said as his eyes tried to penetrate Tang's mind.

"I told him," Horner butted in.

"Why would you do that, Hal?" Simon asked.

"Wu was helping me conduct an investigation. I told him before the police department said to keep it confidential," Horner explained with an air of distaste. "Now, is the dynamic duo ready to say why I'm a suspect?" he asked contemptuously.

"I'll start, Hal," Simon spoke. "Of all the employees on Wallops, no one has freer access to the facilities than you. You know where all of the surveillance cameras are located and you know where critical components for the rockets are stored."

"Knowing does not constitute a motive, Maya," Horner said in a biting tone.

"No, it doesn't," she acknowledged coolly before continuing. "You have access to the apartments and it may have been you who created the evidence suggesting that Hala was involved in the sabotage."

"Oh, please!" Horner whined haughtily.

"I thought it was a bit too convenient how you found Hala's bloodied boots in the dumpster behind her apartment. She would have been much smarter than that," Moore added.

"That's right," Simon agreed.

"You're going to have to excuse me for a minute. My bladder calls," Horner said scornfully. "I should take a dump while I'm in there with all of the excrement you two are throwing at Wu and me," he commented acerbically as he stood. "Wu, you need to go?"

Tang who had been seething quietly nodded his head. "Yes. I need to step away," he said as he stood and followed Horner into the enclosed portion of the restaurant and to the restrooms in the back next to the kitchen.

"Afraid you'll get lost if you don't have someone with you?" Moore called. He couldn't resist throwing the barb after having to deal with Horner's attitude.

"Do you think this is worthwhile?" Simon asked as she looked intently at Moore.

"I don't know. It could be a mistake because we've alerted them that we're watching them. They could end up being more careful. They're probably corroborating their stories now," Moore suggested.

"Maybe. We have the security team coming down tomorrow. They're trained interviewers and we'll see what they can get out of these two," she said. Suddenly she looked down inside her open purse. "There goes my phone vibrating. Excuse me," she said as she reached into her purse and picked up her phone.

"You must have good ears. I didn't hear anything," Moore said as he watched her look at the phone and tap it twice before placing it back into her purse.

"Nothing important," she said as she took a quick look toward the back where Horner and Tang had gone. "What do you think we should do when they return?"

"Commit hari-kari?" Moore jested.

"No, I'm serious," she pushed.

Before Moore could respond, a huge explosion shook the

restaurant and sent shock waves blowing out the patio windows. Shards of glass and other flying debris showered and injured patrons and servers as they were knocked to the floor.

Flames began to bloom as the fire rapidly spread. The fronds of the palm trees were ablaze and showered patrons with sparks that burned their clothes. Patrons swatted at their clothes and hair as they attempted to put out the fire. Some ran screaming and jumped into Chincoteague Bay.

The inside of the restaurant suffered the most damage from the blast as the fire raged and thick clouds of smoke billowed out.

Bodies littered the floor. Some were injured and had bad burns, but most, including all of the kitchen workers, were burned beyond recognition and had died on the spot.

Those who could started a slow and pain-filled crawl toward the patio. Only a few were successful as the rest were overcome by toxic smoke.

A second explosion caused a fireball to burst through the bar entrance and into the open-air patio where Moore and Simon had been knocked to the ground.

"Are you okay, Maya?" Moore asked as he brushed off soot from her blouse.

"I-I think so," she stammered as she raised her head. "Careful, Emerson. You have a piece of glass sticking out of your arm."

Moore looked down and saw the small shard. He reached down and carefully pulled it out of his arm. It bled only a little. He was lucky.

"No big deal," he said as he surveyed the destruction. "Can you make it out of here by yourself?"

"By myself? What do you mean?"

"I'm going to help get some of these people out of here," Moore said as he looked around the patio area at the injured.

"I'll help too," she responded as the two slowly stood to their feet and felt the heat of the blaze on their faces. "Do you see Tang or Horner?"

"No, and they were inside where the brunt of the destruction happened. I wouldn't be too optimistic that they survived this," Moore said. "Let's get moving."

The two joined several other patrons who were helping the injured and transporting them out of the restaurant and into the parking lot. Patrons from nearby bars and restaurants raced to help carry out the injured.

As they worked, the sound of approaching sirens signaled the arrival of the Chincoteague Volunteer Fire Department. They pulled up on both sides of the burning structure where blue-veined flames towered fifty feet. The fire's intensity was so bright that the downtown street lights paled by comparison.

As the two pumper trucks, ladder truck, two engine trucks, ambulances and command vehicle parked, they saw a number of diners walking aimlessly in the parking lot. Some were talking to loved ones on their cell phones as they wandered. Paramedics raced to aid the victims in the lot and in the burning building.

The firefighters lugged out hoses and connected them to fire hydrants and the pumper trucks. They worked quickly to begin dousing the flames as the fire chief called in mutual aid from the Atlantic Volunteer Fire Company, Wallops Fire Company and New Church Volunteer Fire Company.

A triage area was set up in the far parking lot for the paramedics and others with medical backgrounds to attend the victims. A call went out for more ambulances. A couple of air-ambulance helicopters along with two news media choppers were in-flight to the island.

After Moore and Simon carried one injured woman from the

fire, they bumped into Denise Bowden, who was coordinating the triage area.

"What a disaster!" Moore said to Bowden.

"Worst fire we've had on the island. We don't have enough ambulances to transport the injured to the hospitals. Some of the locals have to drive them there."

Bowden eyed the two with their singed hair and clothes and asked, "Were you in the pub?"

"Yes, but we were sitting on the patio and missed the first blast," Emerson answered.

"You two were lucky," Bowden commented.

"We were. And I have one bad habit that I like," Moore added.

"What's that?" Bowden asked irritated. She had more serious business to attend to.

"I have a knack for breathing," he grinned despite the aura of despair in the air.

"You better be glad that you have that bad habit. We got a lot of people here who don't have any habits anymore," she said seriously.

"It's sad," Moore said more soberly. "You really do a lot for this island," Moore observed as he looked at the shooting flames.

"Vice Mayor, rescue squad, fire department spokesman, tour guide, lawn care business. Yep, I'd say I keep myself busy. Listen, I can't chat now. Too much going on, Emerson," she said hurriedly as a resident backed her SUV up to pick up a couple of injured patrons.

"No. No. I understand," Moore said as he and Simon hustled back to the patio area to help the firefighters in rescuing patrons.

When they neared the entrance, they saw that the firefighters had set aside an area where a number of smoldering bodies were lying. "I wouldn't look if I were you," Moore cautioned Simon.

They each focused on their task as the fire trucks from the neighboring communities arrived.

Twenty minutes later, Moore and Simon had finished their work and made their way to the causeway bridge, where they stood with other spectators as they watched the firefighters working feverishly to extinguish the fire.

Suddenly, Moore spotted a man crawling near the channel. "There's somebody down there," he said as he started to walk briskly down the causeway bridge. Simon followed on his heels.

As they neared the man, they could hear his moans and see that he was badly burned. It was Hal Horner.

Simon dropped to the ground to kneel beside him. "Hal, are you okay?"

"If this is what you call being okay, I guess I am," Horner snapped despite his pain.

"You hang in there. We'll get you help." Moore said as he dropped to one knee. "Where's Tang?"

"I don't think he made it. He was inside when the place just blew up," Horner mumbled with a groan.

"How did you survive, Hal?" Simon asked.

"I went out back for a smoke," Horner answered quietly. It was obvious by his facial features that the pain was intensifying.

"I'll be back with help," Moore said as he stood.

"I'll stay with him," Simon said as she reluctantly stroked the side of Horner's face that was not burned.

Horner recoiled at being touched by her. "I don't need that," he stormed angrily.

Moore then sprinted for help and returned within several minutes with the rescue squad who loaded Horner onto a gurney and rushed him to the hospital.

As the ambulance pulled away, Moore spoke. "Lucky for Horner that he went out back for a smoke."

"Yes, except for one thing."

"What's that?"

"Hal doesn't smoke. He quit years ago," Simon said in a suspicious tone.

Moore wrinkled his brow as he thought. "That is strange."

"Makes you wonder what he was really up to doesn't it?"

"It does. And poor Wu," Moore added. "I liked him, despite our suspicions."

"If he is actually dead," Simon cautioned. "Sometimes, I'm not sure who is being truthful."

"I know what you mean," Moore concurred. He had been feeling that a lot of people were lying. "I'm sure once the bodies have been identified, Tang's will be one of them."

"Maybe. We'll see."

The two wandered over to the front of the restaurant where they could see the firefighters making progress on extinguishing the blaze. After ten minutes, Simon spoke.

"I'm going to head for home, Emerson. We can talk more in the morning after I meet with the FBI."

Moore looked at the parking lot and saw that his Mustang was blocked by the fire trucks in the aisles. "You think you can get out of this lot?"

"The lot was full when I pulled in. I had to park in the street," she said as she walked away. "Talk tomorrow."

"Sounds good," Moore said as he walked the short distance to his car to inspect it for damage. He was relieved to see that the paint hadn't blistered from the heat of the fire, although he did find some burned spots on the convertible top. He was thankful that he had the top up. He leaned against the car and watched the firefighters finish dousing the flames. An hour later, several of the fire trucks pulled out of the lot and Moore was able to head back to the Terry house.

CHAPTER 22

The Next Morning
Roe Terry's House

His buzzing cell phone interrupted Moore's research on the internet. He reached for his phone and answered.

"Hello?"

"Emerson, it's Maya."

"Hello, Maya."

"I've got two things to share with you."

"Yes?"

"First, I did get a call from Chief Deere and he said that one of the bodies identified last night belonged to Wu Tang."

"I'm sorry to hear that," Moore said, genuinely sad.

"Yeah. Me too. The other could involve you."

"How's that?"

"The FBI won't be here until noon, which gives me time to do some sleuthing. I'm heading up to Horner's house. It's across the border in Salisbury, Maryland. Would you like to go with me?"

"What are you going for?"

"Since he's in the hospital, this will give me a chance to search his place for any clues that could tie him to the explosions and the murders," she explained.

"Do you have a key?" Moore asked, concerned about breaking and entering.

"Yes."

Interesting that she had a key to Horner's house, Moore thought quietly to himself. "And you're comfortable with going into his house?"

"Oh, sure. Hal gave me a key some time ago so that I could check on his house when he was out of town at seminars or conferences," she responded. "I still have it."

Moore was a bit reluctant, but agreed. "Let's do it." He was anxious to see if they could tie Horner to the murders and explosions.

They agreed to meet at the Royal Farms gas station on Wallops Island, where Simon would park her car and they would ride together for the forty-minute drive to Horner's Salisbury home.

Grabbing his car keys, Moore jumped into his car and drove down Main Street to the traffic light where he turned right. As he crossed the causeway bridge, he looked to his left and saw the smoldering remains of the Clam Shells Pub. One fire truck was on the premises and two fire inspectors were going through the debris.

When Moore pulled into the Royal Farms gas station, he saw Simon standing next to her parked car. She appeared breathtaking in a tan dress that clung to her curves. A bright blue jacket with deep pockets and bright blue heels complemented her outfit.

"Hi, Emerson," she said as she opened the car door and slid into the passenger seat. "Ready for an adventure?" she asked provocatively.

Moore smiled. "Always," he replied.

"I think we're on to something," she added.

"I hope so," he said as he drove onto the road and started towards Salisbury.

Following Simon's directions, Moore found the charming Cape Cod-style home that sat on a treed lot on the south side of Salisbury. The gray-sided house had scarlet shutters and a large porch. It also had an attached two-car garage.

"Nice-looking place," Moore said as he parked and the two exited the car.

"It's really too big for him," Simon said as she walked to the back door and inserted a key to unlock it. "I don't know why he bought a four-bedroom house."

"Resale value?" Moore guessed as he followed her through the garage and into a large open kitchen whose countertop had several pieces of mail scattered about. Walking through the breakfast area, he could see into a large, rustic family room with a cathedral ceiling and a floor-to-ceiling rock fireplace.

"That fireplace is so huge, you could park a Volkswagen in it," Moore observed before looking through to the screened porch.

Hearing drawers being opened and shut in the kitchen, Moore shouted, "I'll start with the bedrooms," as he headed upstairs to the second story. After he finished checking the three bedrooms and bathroom with no success, he returned to the first floor where he saw Simon exiting the master bedroom.

"Any luck?" he asked.

"Nothing," she responded. "I checked his home office, too, and didn't find anything that bothered me."

"Did he have a computer there?"

"No."

"That's strange. People usually have a work computer and a home computer," Moore noted.

"I don't know. Maybe he had a laptop in his car. It must still be parked at the Clam Shells' parking lot," Simon suggested.

The two turned their attention to finishing their search of the first floor and found nothing. They ended up standing in the kitchen. Simon was leaning against the refrigerator, while Moore leaned against the kitchen cabinet. That's when he spotted the plastic bag.

"What's that?" he asked as he walked to the side of the fridge.

"What do you mean?" Simon asked as she turned to see Moore pull a clear plastic bag from behind the fridge.

"I saw part of this bag sticking out," Moore said as he held up the bag so that they could see it. Inside was a butcher's knife. Its blade appeared to have blood residue on it.

"I knew it—I just knew it!" Simon exclaimed smugly.

"I better put this back," Moore said as he returned the bag to its hiding spot and straightened. He reached for his cell phone.

"What are you doing?" Simon asked suddenly.

"Calling Chief Deere," Moore replied.

"Why? I'll just tell the FBI when I meet with them this afternoon," she said stonily.

Moore guessed that she wanted to be the one to reveal the news and it might be helpful for her in getting that promotion she so desperately wanted. He handed the phone to Simon. "It's still ringing. You can tell him."

"Hello, Emerson," Deere answered.

Hearing Deere's voice, Simon replaced her frown with a growing smile as she spoke. "Hi, Chief. It's Maya."

"You caught me by surprise, Maya. I was expecting Emerson."

Chincoteague Calm

"He's here with me. We're in Salisbury."

"What are you doing in Salisbury?" Deere asked.

"Solving your murder investigation," Simon said proudly.

"You are? Well, what do you have for me, Maya?"

"We're at Hal Horner's house and we found the knife that Horner used in cutting off the hands of the victims," she pronounced pretentiously.

"You did?" Deere was fully attentive and listened closely.

"Yes. It was hidden behind his fridge."

"That's good news. We'll coordinate with the Salisbury police and get forensics in there."

"Good. I have a meeting with the FBI this afternoon and I'll let them know," Simon remarked firmly.

"That's fine with me," Deere agreed. After a pause, he asked, "Maya, what are you doing in Horner's house? Did you break in?"

"Oh, no. Hal had given me a key some time ago so I could check on the house when he was out of town."

"I just wondered," he said.

"With Hal being in the hospital, I thought I better check his mail. Emerson rode along with me to keep me company." Simon didn't want to reveal to the chief her real reason for their intrusion into Horner's house.

The two ended their call.

"Nice job, Maya," Moore said as he complimented the dark-haired beauty.

"Couldn't have done it without my partner," she said as she unexpectedly wrapped her arms around Moore and hugged him close to her. "You've been so encouraging to me throughout this tribulation."

"I'm glad that I could help," Moore assured her as she stepped back and looked at her watch.

"We need to head back. I've got that meeting with the FBI this afternoon. I might just make it on time," she said as she walked toward the garage and back door. "We're going to have to celebrate tonight," she smiled as she looked over her shoulder at Moore who was following closely. "You available?" she asked with a "come hither" look.

The look was not lost on Moore. "Sounds good to me," he replied.

"You come to my house and I'll cook one of my delicious meals for you. We'll make it a real celebration," she said as she locked the garage door after Moore walked through, and then she joined him in his car.

"Nothing like a home-cooked meal," Moore agreed as he started the car and backed out of the drive.

"And I have something special planned for dessert," she said seductively as she reached across the console and warmly patted his hand.

Simon was giddy with the success of their discovery. She flirted with Moore the entire drive back to her car on Wallops Island.

"See you tonight around seven," she said before getting in her car. As she exited his car, she gave Moore a sultry wink.

"See you then," Moore smiled as he guessed what she had in mind. He drove out of the gas station and returned to the Terry house. He was anxious to call Steve Nicholas and let him know about their discovery.

After completing the short drive to the house, Moore parked and went inside. He made himself a rum and Coke and headed to the enclosed patio at the rear of the house. Sitting down, he took a long, celebratory drink from the glass. He allowed the cool liquid to swirl around his mouth before swallowing, then he called

Nicholas on his cell phone.

"Hello?" Nicholas answered.

"Steve, it's Emerson."

"Perfect timing. I was going to give you a call this afternoon."

"Do I ever have news for you," Moore interrupted Nicholas.

"I'm all ears. What do you have?"

Moore quickly updated Nicholas on what had transpired over the prior few days.

"So, it looks like Horner is your suspect?" Nicholas ventured.

"Yes."

"And do you think Tang was involved?"

"Yes."

"Don't ask me how I know this because I'm not at liberty to reveal my sources. Horner and Tang had several large amounts of money wire-transferred into their accounts over the last couple of weeks," Nicholas responded.

"Over the last couple of weeks?"

"Yes."

"Did you check back over the last year?"

"Yes."

"And the large deposits were made only over the last two weeks, right?"

"Yes."

"That's strange."

"Why do you say that?"

"Because the problems with the rocket explosions and sabotaging of parts have been going on for the last year or so. Why would they get paid now?"

"That's a good question, Emerson."

"Can you trace the source of the wire transfers?"

"We're working on that. I can tell you that various banks and shell companies were involved. We're trying to dig through that data to see who is actually behind all of this."

"I'm anxious to know," Moore said, exasperated.

"I'm sure you are. We are too," Nicholas spoke calmly. "I'm going to send you a login to a dropbox account we've set up. You'll be able to read some of the emails that we hacked into as you asked."

"Anything interesting?"

"Not really. Just the usual gibberish."

"I don't get it. Why would whoever is behind all of this go to the trouble of sending an agent, or agents, on-site at Wallops when they could have hacked into the systems remotely and still played havoc with the launch, like what is being done with North Korea?"

"There's a problem with that approach, Emerson."

"What's that?"

"That type of backdoor entry can leave tracks. There's so much technology out there today that no matter how hard you try, it is difficult to mask your intrusion. There's software, and it's highly technical, that can lead you back to the country that is trying to infiltrate your operations. If you create the right covers, it can be easier to send in an agent and then disavow any links and call the agent a rogue if the agent is captured."

"I don't think either approach is safe."

"You're absolutely right. There's no fail-safe route to go. They both have their flaws," Nicholas remarked. "Take a look at what I'm giving you access to. With those eagle eyes of yours, you may find something we missed."

"I'm not so sure about that, but I'll take a look."

After they ended their call, Moore spent two hours reviewing the emails. It was toward the end of his review that he caught a pattern emerging. He didn't like what he was seeing.

Moore's phone rang. When he answered, Nicholas spoke. "Emerson, I found some interesting information on Tang and Horner. You said Horner is in the burn unit at the hospital, right?"

"Right."

"Has he been secured?"

"Not that I know of. Maya told Chief Deere and the FBI about the knife we found."

"You might want to call Deere and make sure that someone is keeping an eye on Horner."

"You think he might escape? I'd say he's too badly burned to walk out of there."

"It's a precautionary measure, Emerson. Here's a couple of other things I turned up." Nicholas continued with his update for the next five minutes. When he ended the call, Moore sat back in his chair. He was stunned by what he heard. After staring into space for several minutes and digesting Nicholas' revelations in his mind, he called Deere and updated him on the conversation, but only with regards to Horner. Deere agreed to have an officer stationed outside of Horner's room.

After thinking through his next steps, Moore next reached for his cell phone and called Simon. "Hi, Maya."

"Hello, Cowboy," she purred. "Can't wait for tonight so you had to call me?"

Moore ignored her comment. He was very focused. Very businesslike and it came across in his tone. "I wondered how the meeting with the FBI went."

Simon was caught off-guard by the lack of warmness in Moore's voice. "It actually went very well. They were very pleased by my discovery of the knife."

Moore noticed that she had referred to it as her discovery and not their discovery of the knife. "That's good," Moore said in a monotone. "I wanted to let you know that I did have a friend do some additional background checking for me."

It was Simon's turn to lose the warmth in her voice. "You did?" she asked perplexed.

"Yes."

"And what did your friend find?"

"There were several large deposits of funds made into the bank accounts of both Tang and Horner."

"I knew it," she said as the warmth returned to her voice.

"I saw a couple of other things that were troubling to me as well," Moore said solemnly.

"Oh? What are they?"

"I'd rather not say over the phone."

"Do you want to tell me at dinner tonight? You can tell me while I'm cooking."

"No. I don't want to wait. Can you break away now?"

Simon glanced at her watch. "It's almost five. Sure, I can leave now. Do you want to come over to my house?"

"No. Why don't we meet at Captain Bob's Marina?"

"Sure. I can be there in about twenty minutes." Simon was curious as to what Moore had learned. He appeared to be very serious.

"Good. I'll see you then."

They ended the call and Moore returned to his computer screen. He became so engrossed by what he was reading that the time got away from him. When he looked at his watch, he saw that twenty minutes had elapsed and realized that Simon was probably at the marina. He sent her a quick text message to let her know that he'd be there in ten minutes.

CHAPTER 23

**Captain Bob's Marina
Chincoteague Island**

As Moore pulled into the marina parking lot, he saw the CLOSED sign on the door of the office. He also noticed that the parking lot was empty except for Simon's car. It was parked at the far end, near the last dock at the edge of Chincoteague Bay. As he drove over, he allowed his eyes to scan the boats at the dock. He didn't see anyone around as he parked next to Simon's car.

"Hi, Maya," he greeted her as he exited the Mustang and walked over to the dock. He saw that she was still wearing the tan dress with the bright blue jacket. She looked gorgeous.

"Hello, Emerson," she purred warmly, even though she was anxious to hear what breaking revelations Moore had to share with her. "Looks like we'll be in for another beautiful sunset," she said as she hugged Moore and stepped back.

"Yes, it does," he agreed as he glanced at the sun as it continued its trajectory toward the horizon. The sky was a deep blue. It matched Simon's jacket color.

Moore turned with his back to the sun and looked at Simon as they stood near the end dock. "Maya, does the name Jason White mean anything to you?"

"Yes. That was the name of a young man that worked for us. He was murdered and his body was found behind a grocery store. Why do you ask?"

"Did you know he was working for the FBI?"

Simon looked away for a moment, then turned back to Moore. "Yes, I did."

"Was it widely known?"

"No. I was aware he had been sent over from Quantico on an undercover assignment and was investigating the rocket explosions."

"Did anyone else know what he was doing?"

"No."

"What about Horner?" Moore asked as he drilled in.

"No."

"Isn't that strange that the head of your security didn't know?"

"Not in this case. You don't have the whole picture, Emerson."

"Maybe I don't."

"I'll give you some insight, but this has to remain between the two of us, okay?"

"Sure," Moore agreed.

"Prior to White joining us, I had a meeting in Quantico with the FBI. I explained my concern about the explosions and asked for their help."

"Did anyone in the upper levels of NASA know?"

"Yes. I made sure I cleared it with them. Emerson, I wanted to lead the charge to find the party or parties responsible for the sabotage. That way I could become the permanent head of operations on Wallops," she explained earnestly.

"And Horner was excluded?"

"Yes, because I suspected him."

"Go on."

"At the meeting, they introduced me to Jason and assigned him to the case."

"Did you know Jason's father?"

Simon wrinkled her brow. "Why on Earth would you ask me a question like that? Why would I know his father?"

"Actually, you did know him."

"Emerson, I don't know what you mean," she stammered.

"You knew him. He lived over there." Moore pointed to the shipping container that had been Bo White's home.

"Bo was his father?" she asked with a stunned look.

"Yes. I spent some time with Bo and he was trying to identify who killed his son. He had some bits and pieces of information and was trying to figure it out."

"Was he FBI, too?" she asked.

"I don't think so," Moore replied.

"Did he figure out who was causing the explosions?"

"No, but I think he was getting close."

"Damn," Simon swore with frustration as her attitude changed. "But we were able to show that Horner was behind the murders and the explosions," she said proudly.

"The discovery of the knife would lead you to believe that Horner was behind the murders."

"They'll find his fingerprints on the knife," she said assuredly.

Ignoring her comment, Moore continued. "But that doesn't prove Horner was behind the explosions."

"It will if there are no more explosions while he's recovering from his burns and we don't find any further evidence of sabotage," she suggested. Simon had a perplexed look on her face. "Emerson, why are you pissing on my parade?"

"I'm not, Maya. I'm just trying to solve this mystery."

"We already have."

"What about Wu Tang?"

"Like I told you earlier, I suspected that he and Horner were working together to cause the explosions."

"And the motive would be?"

"Emerson, we've been through all of this." Simon was getting frustrated.

"Be patient with me. Tell me why," Moore urged.

"Tang had a vested interest in delaying our program since the Chinese were pushing forward with theirs and Horner had an eye on replacing me if he could make me look bad," she stormed quietly.

"Did you know Tang was an undercover FBI agent?"

A look of shock crossed Simon's face. "No!"

"Did you know that Tang and Horner were working together?"

"You know that I do, because they were causing the sabotage!" she said firmly.

"Would you be surprised if I told you that they suspected Hala Yazbek was responsible for the explosions?"

"What? How do you know that?"

"Be patient with me." Moore wasn't ready to reveal everything that Nicholas had found during his research. "I was on Wallops the night that Orlov was murdered."

"You were!"

"Yes, and with Bo White. He had been conducting reconnaissance on the island. We saw Yazbek enter the Payload Processing Building and Orlov follow her."

Chincoteague Calm

"They were working together?" Simon asked.

"Not sure. From what I gather, he had a thing for her."

"He did," Simon agreed. "He was always making comments of a sexual nature to her. You saw her kill Orlov that night?" she asked warily.

"No. We saw them together, but we didn't think she killed Orlov. There was an argument behind the firehouse and she left. Shortly after that, we heard a vehicle drive away."

"Horner," Simon guessed.

"No. The person who drove away would be a person who had free access to Wallops."

"That would be Horner," she said.

"That person also killed Kronsky after he killed Yazbek. That person killed Tang, too."

"What?"

"Be patient. That person meant to kill Tang and Horner, but Horner lucked out by going behind the restaurant."

"Where are you going with all of this, Emerson? You're really confusing me."

"Who are you really, Maya Simon? Who do you work for?" Moore asked directly as he looked seriously at Simon.

"Emerson, what are you saying? You think I'm behind all of this?" Simon asked incredulously.

"It was there all of the time and I just kept missing putting two and two together. It was you," Moore added. "And I saw you detonate the explosion at the Clam Shells Pub."

"What do you mean?"

"I remember seeing you reach inside your purse for your phone and key in a number, then slip your phone back into your purse. I didn't give it much thought at the time, but I do recall it."

When she turned around, she brought her hand out of the jacket pocket and was holding a small 9mm Beretta handgun. It was pointed at Moore.

"Emerson. Emerson," she repeated herself as she looked confidently at Moore. Her entire demeanor had changed. "Who else knows about your conclusion?"

"A friend of mine in Washington knows," Moore said as he gauged the distance between the gun and him.

"You've really made things messy," she lamented.

"I'm not sure that I'm the one doing the making, Maya. If you hadn't gotten involved, none of this would have happened," Moore surmised.

"This is just not the way I planned this evening to turn out," Simon said with a touch of sadness in her voice. "You have no idea what I had planned for you—and you would have enjoyed it!" she said in a husky tone.

"You can put that gun away and we can head over to see Chief Deere," Moore suggested.

"Now Emerson, do you really think I'm that easy?" she said, surprised by his suggestion.

"Yeah, I didn't think you were going to buy in," Moore said, knowing better.

"You give me no choice but to do what I don't want to do," she said stoically.

"You're going to kill me?" Moore guessed.

"Certainly, I have no other option."

"Well then, humor me before you do," Moore suggested. "Who are you really and who do you work for?"

"My real name is of no consequence to you. As far as who I work for, let's just say that I'm part of an organization that doesn't

Chincoteague Calm

like seeing cooperation among the U.S., China and Russia."

"That's all you're going to give me?"

"Yes."

"Tell me about the murders. Did you kill Orlov?"

"Yes. The oaf was assaulting Hala and I had enough of his sexist attitude toward her. Besides, we didn't know what he had seen Hala do."

"We? You mean that Hala was working with you?"

"Silly boy, yes. It was a part of our master plan where she infiltrated the French space program and was able to position herself to be transferred over here. It worked quite well."

"So you two weren't special agents for NASA?" Moore asked.

"No," she laughed quietly. "For a smart guy, you sure can be deceived at times. I've told you so many stories and you swallowed them whole."

"But not all of the time," Moore countered, although he was frustrated with how much he had trusted her. "What about the blood splatters on her cowgirl boots? You said Horner did that. Did he?"

"No. I did. I grabbed a small bottle out of my car and took a sample of Orlov's blood after I killed him. Pretty fast thinking on my part," she bragged. "Since I have keys to all of the facilities, including the housing units, it was easy for me to access Hala's apartment and steal her boots. I splattered them with blood and tossed them in the trash container so that Horner could find them," she boasted.

"Why would you do that to implicate her?"

"It was only a matter of time before she would be exposed as the one behind the sabotage."

"And yet she protected you when she became a suspect in

Orlov's death. She didn't rat you out."

"Hala made a big mistake."

"How's that?" Moore asked.

"She trusted me. When Orlov's body was found, she asked me what to do. I was in the background coaching her. I was her puppet master." Simon had an evil smile on her face. "I was getting ready to take her out anyway."

"Did you kill her that night?"

"No. I had Kronsky kill her. He killed her and burned her in the dumpster."

"I don't get the bit with your purse being found by the dumpster and your ring on my car," Moore said, hoping for an explanation.

"Simply misdirection—to make sure that I threw off any suspicion on me and you all wasted your time chasing false trails."

"Who killed Joe Kronsky?"

"I did. I had to cover my connection. I killed Bo White too," she said matter-of-factly.

"I guessed that you did, but why?" Moore asked.

"He kidnapped me and was going to interrogate me. He was the smartest one of the bunch. He figured that I was behind everything, although I didn't know his son worked for the FBI."

"Did he figure out that you killed his son?"

"Yes. He told me. But Bo wasn't as smart as me. He should have secured me better. I was able to break free, and then I killed him."

Moore shook his head. There was no remorse in her voice. "What was the deal with severing the victims' right hands and then having their fingerprints show up on rocket parts after their death?" Moore pushed.

"You like that?" she smiled. "That was my idea. More confusion. More misdirection. That's all."

"And you tried to blame everything on Horner?"

"Yes. I went to the hospital early this morning and found him sedated. I had the knife with me in my purse and pressed his fingers on the handle. When you were upstairs at Horner's house, I took the plastic bag out of my purse and hid it behind the fridge so that you could find it. The FBI will find his fingerprints on the handle. The DNA will match the victims. Pretty clever of me," she gloated.

"And you might have gotten away with everything if I didn't have this confrontation with you today," Moore stated.

"Oh, Emerson, I'm still getting away with it. You've really screwed up my plans. I was working on moving up the ladder at NASA where I could do some serious harm to the space program. Now that's going to change."

"The FBI will be all over your computer and your files."

"I'm not concerned. If anyone tried to hack in, I have a program loaded that automatically wipes the hard drive—and it's not recoverable. You can trust me about the technology."

"So you'll just leave? Just disappear into thin air?"

"I have to now. I'll stop at the house I rent and set an incendiary device I have. It will wipe out everything there. No trace of poor Maya Simon, who will just disappear."

"Leaving the country?"

"Yes. I have a fake passport that I can use. I can catch a flight out of Norfolk and make a connection in Washington. Then I'm untouchable," she smiled assuredly.

Moore had been standing with his back to the evening sun and saw Simon squint as a passing cloud allowed the sun's rays to momentarily blind her. Moore quickly made his move. He closed the distance between them as he tried to knock the weapon from her hand.

In the wrestling match for control of the gun, it discharged, missing both of them.

Simon shrieked in pain when Moore's hand closed tightly around her wrist and she dropped the gun over the edge of the dock. The gun landed on the water's edge and Moore rolled down to grab the weapon.

As he did, Simon hurriedly stood, picking up a nearby concrete block. She raised the block over her head to dash it into Moore's head before he had time to pick up the gun.

It was then that a rifle cracked in the distance from the open window of the marina office. Its bullet found a home in the side of Simon's skull, knocking her and the concrete block to the side, where she fell to the ground.

Blood poured out of the headshot wound as Maya died.

Moore stood with the Beretta in his hand and walked up from the water's edge. He bent over Simon's body and checked her pulse. He didn't expect to find one and he didn't.

"You okay, Emerson?" a voice called from the direction of the marina office. Moore turned and saw Roeske walking toward him. She was carrying a rifle.

"I am, Donna. Thank you. You saved my life," Moore said appreciatively.

"It looked like you were in trouble," Roeske added with concern.

"I was. Where did you come from? I didn't see your vehicle when I pulled in," Moore asked.

"It's in the shop. I was in the office working on some paperwork. I didn't know that anything was amiss until I heard that pistol shot. When I looked out, I saw you scramble down to the water. When I saw her picking up that concrete block, I just reacted. Grabbed the rifle and shot her. Good thing for you that my office window was open; otherwise she would have clobbered you with that block. You'd have been a goner."

"Thank you, Donna," Moore said as he stepped forward and gave her a big hug.

"Nice hug, Emerson. I like that. You need anyone else shot?" she teased. "I can use hugs like that any time," she smiled.

"I'm just sorry that you had to get involved."

"Don't worry about that. I didn't like that woman. Especially after her accusations at the Clam Shells Pub."

"It was all misdirection."

"No sweat, Emerson," she said. "And one more thing."

"What's that, Donna?" Moore asked.

"I've got your back," she answered firmly.

"Thanks," Moore said. "The worst feeling in the world is to know you were used and lied to by someone you trusted."

"I know what you mean, Emerson," she said. She then added as she tried to cheer him up, "You've come full circle at Captain Bob's Marina. This is where your adventure on Chincoteague Island started and almost ended."

Moore grinned. "You're absolutely right, Donna. Whoever would have guessed that my initial fun-filled fishing trip would have evolved the way it did?"

"That's what I'm saying," she smiled.

Moore reached for his phone. "I better call Chief Deere."

"That would be a good idea," she said as the two of them walked back to the marina office and Moore called Deere.

Twenty minutes later, Chief Deere and Detective Huffman arrived. Moore updated them on his confrontation with Simon and her attempt to kill him, while Roeske explained her part in saving Moore's life.

After the two police officers excused Moore and Roeske and walked over to examine Simon's body, Moore turned to Roeske, "Looks like they're done with us. Do you want me to give you a ride home?"

"No," she said as she glanced at her watch. "One of the guys from the garage should be along with my vehicle. I'll be good."

"Are you sure?"

Roeske pointed to the rifle which she had returned to the corner of her office. "I've got my buddy to keep me company," she smiled.

"I'm not too sure that you'll be keeping it. I'd think that Deere will want to take it along as evidence, even though you have nothing to worry about."

"That's no problem, Emerson," she smiled again as she pulled open her middle desk drawer and withdrew a pistol. "I still have my Glock."

"You are an amazing woman, Donna!" Moore said sincerely.

"Flirting with me will get you somewhere," she teased with her southern charm as she returned the Glock to the drawer.

Moore grinned. "Okay, then. I'm going to drive up and visit Horner. I want him to know what happened and that Maya was behind everything."

"I'm sure that would have him rest easier," she commented. She added, "You're welcome to come back tomorrow if you'd like to relax and get some fishing in."

"I might just do that," Moore said as he headed for the door.

Moore left the building and walked over to his car. As he neared the car, he saw Deere standing by Simon's body while Huffman examined it.

"Good thing for you that Donna was here," Deere said to Moore.

Chincoteague Calm

"I'll say. I owe her big time."

"Even better for you that she's a sharpshooter. She learned that from her father."

"I agree," Moore said.

"I'd like you to stop at the station tomorrow and give us a formal statement. Would ten o'clock work for you?"

"That works. I'll see you then," Moore replied as he sat in his Mustang and started it. Putting it in gear, he drove to the hospital as the sun set on the horizon. While he drove, he placed a call to Nicholas, but the call went directly to voicemail. He'd call later so that he could update him on his encounter with Simon.

When Moore arrived at the hospital, he sat in the parking lot for a couple of minutes. He wasn't looking forward to talking with the obnoxious Horner, but felt that he should know. Moore exited his car and walked into the hospital where he located Horner's room. When he walked in, he saw that Horner was awake and watching TV. Horner's arms and legs were bandaged.

"Hello, Hal," Moore greeted Horner as he entered the room.

Horner turned his head from the TV to look at Moore. "Look what was just flushed into my room," he said. "Better call for cleanup in aisle four."

Moore realized that even while in pain, Horner maintained that same caustic attitude.

Ignoring the greeting, Moore spoke. "I hope you're feeling better."

Horner gave Moore a look of disbelief. "You hope I'm feeling better? Why would you care about me after the hard time I've given you?"

Before Moore could respond, Horner continued, "You feel bad because of what happened to me? Watch me pretend to care about how you feel."

−257−

Not to be deterred, Moore spoke. "I've got some good news to share with you."

"Good news from you is like checking my fridge. There's nothing good," Horner countered.

"Seriously. We've solved the mystery of who's behind the murders and sabotage," Moore said.

"It was Maya," Horner spoke quickly.

"You're right. How did you know?" Moore asked.

"I've suspected her for a long time, Mr. I-can't-figure-it-out."

Moore proceeded to update Horner on what he had uncovered. As he did, Horner continued to interrupt with sarcastic comments.

When Moore wrapped up his explanation, he smiled at Horner. "So, bottom line, you're in the clear."

"So his lordship pronounces that I'm in the clear. I was waiting with bated breath hoping that the omnipotent Emerson Moore would clear my unworthy name of any involvement. Oh, thank you, oh Great One," Horner vocalized acerbically.

What a pompous jerk, Moore thought to himself. Getting a serious look in his eyes, Moore leveled them at Horner. "Listen, Hal. You've been giving me crap since the first day I met you. And from what I understand, that's the way you treat other people. You really need to get a life and treat people less disparagingly. I didn't have to stop here tonight and give you the news, but I did," Moore snarled.

Horner wasn't up to taking advice about interpersonal relationships from Moore or anyone else. Instead of being grateful, he sneered, "I'm going to give you a piece of medical advice, Moore."

"What's that?"

"Go see a doctor so you can become the Cro-Magnon man you think you are."

"I don't think I'm a Cro-Magnon man," Moore replied.

"See if a doctor can write you a prescription for two testicles. I think Maya cut yours off the way she suckered you in. I wasn't fooled one bit."

"I think I've had enough," Moore said as he stood from the chair next to Horner's bed.

"I was hoping for a battle of wits, but you appear to be unarmed." Horner wasn't letting up.

Moore shook his head and walked out of the room. He stopped suddenly. He decided to do something that was a bit out of character for him. Putting aside his gentlemanly ways, Moore walked back into the room and strode defiantly up to Horner's bed.

"You are such a horse's ass, Horner," Moore spoke quietly, but firmly.

Horner was stunned as he watched Moore walk out of the room. He was speechless. He wasn't used to people throwing it in his face.

Moore made his way to the hospital exit doors. He thought about Horner. He was the kind of guy that Moore would have liked to give a high-five in the face with a chair.

Moore truly felt sorry for Horner. The guy was relationally challenged, big time. He felt worse for Horner's co-workers—what they must go through on a daily basis with Horner's crap. Moore walked to the parking lot and entered his car.

On the drive back to Chincoteague, Moore called Nicholas, but the call went to voicemail—making Moore think that Nicholas was tied up in a late dinner meeting. Moore decided to call him in the morning.

When Moore pulled into the driveway, he saw the Terrys' vehicle parked in the driveway and the lights were on in the house. Roe and Monnie were home.

Moore parked his Mustang and put its convertible top up before heading for the door to the family room. When he walked in, he saw that Roe and Monnie were relaxing in their favorite chairs.

"Welcome home," Moore smiled at his two hosts.

"It's good to be home, Emerson," Roe grinned back.

"I'll say. Did you have dinner?" Monnie asked.

It was then that Moore realized that he hadn't eaten and his stomach growled loudly in response.

"Oh my!" Monnie said as she heard Moore's stomach making noises. "You must be hungry!"

"I guess I could do with a bite."

"I'll make you a sandwich," she said as she hurried into the kitchen without waiting for a reply.

"You look drained, Emerson," Roe observed as he eyed Moore.

"You have no idea, Roe," Moore said as he dropped his body on the sofa.

"By the looks of things, I'd say that you're ready for a rum and Coke."

"That would be wonderful!" Moore said as he relaxed for the first time in days.

"I'll get you one, then you can tell Monnie and me what you've been up to," Roe said as he began walking out of the room.

"Roe," Moore called.

"Yes?" Roe responded.

"Could you make that a double shot of rum?"

Roe chuckled. "Sure can."

Roe and his wife soon returned with the beverage and sandwich for Moore. They settled into their chairs and waited until Moore took a long drink and several bites from his sandwich.

"This hits the spot, Monnie. Thank you."

"You're welcome, Emerson," she replied.

"What have you been up to?" Roe asked as he suspiciously eyed Moore.

Moore proceeded to relate the events of what had transpired since they went out of town. Several times, Roe and his wife interrupted him with questions or comments.

At the end of Moore's story, Roe commented, "I always wondered about that Maya, especially after Monnie told me that there was something amiss with her."

Monnie nodded her head. "Call it woman's intuition, Emerson. Something about her didn't sit right with me."

"She fooled a lot of people," Moore agreed.

"And you were lucky that Donna was there to save your butt," Monnie added.

Moore nodded. "I was very lucky."

"You don't want to be the person messing with Donna. She's a crack shot."

"I'll say. I think the biggest surprise for me was finding out that Hal Horner wasn't involved in that mess. I was so suspicious of him," Moore said.

"His persona would make you think that he'd be involved," Roe offered.

"Yeah, that guy has no personality. His caustic comments were over the top. He had no sense of graciousness. I don't think that I've ever met someone who specialized in being so sarcastic."

"Yeah," Roe concurred. "He's the kind of guy who deserves to have his crotch infested with fleas and then have arms too short to scratch it," Roe snickered.

"I kind of wonder if insanity runs in Horner's family," Moore said.

"Oh no. It doesn't run in his family, it gallops, I'm sure," Roe chuckled.

Moore drained the remainder of his beverage. "I'm bushed," Moore said as he stood with his empty glass and plate. "I'm going off to bed."

"You sleep well," Monnie said as Moore returned his dishes to the kitchen and headed for his bedroom.

CHAPTER 24

The Next Morning
Roe Terry's Workshop

Pushing open the door to Roe's workshop, Moore walked in and greeted Roe. "Morning."

Moore enjoyed the workshop and its shelves filled with wooden ducks that Roe had carved. There was something peaceful about its surroundings.

"You slept in!" Roe said as he set his sharp carving knife down and stopped working on the wooden duck he held in his left hand.

"Oh, come on now. It's only 8:30," Moore replied as he took another bite of the energy bar in his hand.

"I've been in here since 6:30," Roe responded. "Going for a run?" Roe asked as he looked at Moore in his running attire.

"Yes. I'm running out to the beach," Moore said. "I need to work some of the stress from the last few days out of my system."

"If it were me, I'd just have another rum and Coke," Roe teased.

"The run, not rum, will do me good at this hour. I'll be back in a bit," Moore said as he turned to leave and Roe picked up his carving knife and focused on his craft.

"Be sure to let me know if you see that naked female runner out there. Might make me take up running again," Roe chortled.

"Will do," Moore laughed.

Moore left the workshop and did a few stretches on the stairs before beginning his run down Main Street. When he reached Maddox, he turned left and jogged out to Assateague Island.

As he ran along Assateague's road to the beach, he saw several of the island's wild ponies near the lighthouse and smiled at the freedom they enjoyed. He continued along the tree-lined road to the far end of the beach's parking lot.

He turned left and walked through the deep sand and between two of the sand dunes to the water's edge where the sand was packed harder. He picked up speed as he ran past two surf fishermen to the southernmost end of the beach. There was just something about the early morning solitude that was invigorating.

When Moore reached the end of the area known as Toms Cove Hook, his cell phone rang. He slowed to a walk and reached into his pocket for the phone. Withdrawing the phone, he saw that it was Steve Nicholas calling.

"Hello, Steve," Moore greeted his friend.

"Hi, Emerson. Sorry I couldn't return your call last night. I was tied up," Nicholas responded. "What's up?"

"We were right about Maya. She was the one behind the murders and sabotage," Moore confirmed.

"I'm glad that we were right on that account. Did the FBI take her into custody?"

"She's dead."

"What? You killed her?" Nicholas asked stunned.

"No, I didn't, but she almost killed me."

"What do you mean?"

Moore quickly brought Nicholas up to speed on the confrontation and Roeske's lifesaving rifle shot.

"Good thing for you that Roeske was still at the marina. You would have been a goner, Emerson."

"Yeah. That one was a little too close for comfort," Moore surmised before telling Nicholas about his subsequent visit with the arrogant Horner.

"I'm sure that you're not going to miss interacting with that character. Sounds like a real S.O.B."

"Not my problem," Moore remarked. "I do appreciate you helping me by digging up that intel you gave me, Steve."

"You know me, Emerson. I'm always glad to help you and, as it turns out, stop that sabotage business over there at Wallops."

"Maya never did tell me who she worked for. I asked her several times, but she wouldn't open up."

"The Mossad," Nicholas revealed.

"What? Israel's Mossad?" It was Moore's turn to be stunned.

"Yes. She and that Hala Yazbek."

"Hala, the partner she murdered?" Moore asked.

"Yes."

"I can't believe that Maya and Hala were working for the Mossad and against the U.S.," Moore said stunned.

"They worked for a rogue splinter group within the Mossad. Thanks to your getting me involved, I contacted one of my senior level friends at the Mossad. As he helped me, he discovered the rogue group and he's made several arrests there and in a couple of offices outside of Israel," Nicholas explained.

"And who do you trust?" Moore asked skeptically.

"You never know. Sometimes you can't trust an ally when they try to provoke you into action."

"How's that?" Moore asked.

"Like when Israel attacked the U.S. in 1967."

"What do you mean? I don't recall reading anything about an attack," Moore asked perplexed by the comment.

"It was downplayed. Israel wanted the U.S. to believe that Egypt was actually the attacker so that the U.S. would join Israel in fighting Egypt. On June 8, 1967, four Israeli fighter jets attacked one of our super-secret spy ships in the Mediterranean. The *USS Liberty* was monitoring communications between the Arabs and their Soviet advisors during the Six-Day War. She was thirteen miles off the Sinai Peninsula."

"A case of mistaken identity?" Moore suggested.

"That's what Israel said at first. They said the pilots confused it with an Egyptian transport that was half its size. The ships' profiles weren't similar at all. Confused? Ha! They knew it was the *Liberty*. They had circled her the previous three days and knew she was there to help.

"On the fourth day of the war, the jets suddenly strafed the deck of the *Liberty*, shooting at the crew who were sunning themselves. Thirty-four of her crew died that day."

"That's terrible," Moore commented.

"That's not all that happened. The fighter attack was followed up by an attack by three Israeli torpedo boats. They machine gunned the decks of the *Liberty* and launched a torpedo that blew a 39-foot hole in its starboard side."

"Didn't the ship radio for help?" Moore asked.

"They did. Two squadrons of Navy fighter-bombers were launched from the American 6th Fleet's aircraft carriers four hundred miles away. They could have been there before the torpedo boats attacked and saved U.S. lives."

"Could have been there? What do you mean?"

"They were recalled," Nicholas stated.

"What?"

"Defense Secretary Robert McNamara ordered the battle group commander to recall the planes. He said that President Lyndon Johnson didn't want to go to war with Israel over a few sailors."

"What a screw up!" Moore said in frustration. "Sounds like a Benghazi to me."

"Israel held a naval court of inquiry. They decided the attack was a tragic accident and officially apologized. They paid reparations of $6.7 million to the injured survivors and the families of those killed in the attack and another $6 million for the loss of the *Liberty*."

"A sham to lure the U.S. into fighting Egypt."

"There are internal White House documents in the Lyndon Johnson Presidential Library that show no one privately believed those attacks were a mistake. Then-Secretary of State Dean Rusk and chief intelligence advisor Clark Clifford were quoted in a National Security Council meeting that it was inconceivable the attacks on the *Liberty* were a case of mistaken identity."

Thinking about Simon and Yazbek, Moore asked, "Did rogue agents have a hand in that one too?"

"I don't think there was anything rogue about that attack. That came from the top. No ifs, ands or buts about it," Nicholas said firmly.

Turning back to the Wallops Island rocket explosions, Moore said, "I'm glad that the murders and sabotage here have been resolved."

"And you're still alive," Nicholas chuckled softly.

The two ended their call and Moore next rang his editor at *The Post* to update him on what had transpired. That was a mistake, as Moore was given a tight deadline to submit his story. There went his afternoon.

Placing his phone in his pocket, Moore took a deep breath of the fresh ocean breeze and turned to run back up the beach. When he entered the parking lot, he spotted Denise Bowden's van and ran over to it.

A number of beefy, young men with beach gear in their hands were exiting the vehicle labeled Teaguer's Tump Tour. Moore ran to the driver's side where the window was lowered.

"Hi, Denise," he said.

"Don't distract me," she said as she looked at him and turned her head to watch the well-built young men walk away. "You're ruining my view," she teased.

"Customers?"

"Oh yeah. Navy guys from Norfolk up for the weekend. Nice eye candy," she grinned as she turned back to Moore. "You out for a morning run?"

"Yeah. Worked off some stress," he answered.

"Based on what I heard last night and this morning, you should have a boatload!"

"You know?"

"Honey, this is a small island. Word gets around."

"Like Put-in-Bay," he grinned.

"You finished with causing a disturbance here?"

"I hope so."

"All I know is that this wonderful touch of paradise has never had so many murders as it has since you arrived," Bowden commented.

"Purely coincidental," Moore offered.

"You need a lift back to Roe's place or are you going to run back?"

"I'll take the ride. Time has eluded me and I have a meeting with Chief Deere," Moore answered. He walked around the vehicle and climbed into the passenger seat and Bowden drove through the beach parking lot.

"Wrapping up a police report?"

"Yep. Then I'll head back and spend the day writing my story."

"You be kind to Chincoteague," she said quietly.

"You can count on it. There's just something about Chincoteague and Assateague that steals your heart like Put-in-Bay. You've got such picturesque sunrises over the Atlantic and sunsets over Chincoteague Bay."

"And the ponies and Assateague lighthouse," Bowden added as they drove by several of the ponies grazing near the lighthouse.

"The beach here is so pristine," she continued. "No homes or hotels towering over it. We call it the Chincoteague calm. That's right. You going to squeeze in some more fishing with Roe?"

"Tomorrow, I hope. I'd like to head down to Captain Bob's Marina with him and take one last fishing trip before I depart. Need to say my good-bye to Donna too."

"You're leaving tomorrow?"

"Late afternoon. I'll drive back to Alexandria, then over to *The Post* the next morning for meetings."

As she pulled into Roe Terry's drive and stopped, Bowden said, "Emerson, I hope you come back and visit us. We'd like you to think of Chincoteague as your second home."

"I'll second that," Roe said as he walked over to the van. "You need to enjoy some of this Chincoteague calm."

Coming Soon

The Next **Emerson Moore** Adventure

Flight